THE DUTY OF WOMEN

THE DUTY OF WOMEN

CAROLINE WILLCOCKS

atmosphere press

"...trusted midwives are saying,
welcome this pain.
It opens the dark passage of Grace."

- Rumi

This book is dedicated to my own mother,
Felicity Harcourt 1929 – 2000

With thanks to all those who have helped me at
Atmosphere, and my nearest and dearest, John, Tom,
Claire, Jimmy and Jenny.

CHAPTER 1

So that was it. My courses had stopped, and my breasts felt swollen and sore. I knew I must be with child. But God in heaven, how did it come to this?

Daughter, I was in a state of deep anxiety when I discovered I was pregnant. And I had no man to protect and provide for me. It was almost like it was when I turned up at the court of Katherine of Aragon, without a family, friends or money. I could not bear the thought that I could go back to having nothing, and no one to love. So how did it happen? Daughter, have patience and I will tell you, and I pray that you will not condemn me for the mistakes I made.

Will and I started our married life living under Thomas Cromwell's roof at Austin Friars. We were saving so that, in time, we could afford a house. Cromwell was the only other living person who knew the secret of my identity. I was the legitimate child of King Henry VIII and Queen Katherine of Aragon, born scarcely breathing and left for dead. I could have been disposed of, with the stained linen, the wet towels and the empty bottles of wine that had been brought out of the birthing chamber. But a midwife noticed me stirring. She was a witch, this woman, and I wonder if she had brought me back to life somehow, as the doctor had said I was stillborn. But there I was, a tiny scrap of a thing, hanging on to life so fiercely, she had to save me. She took me to Tom and Joan, who fostered me, and brought me up with their son, Will. It was only later, after my mother had died, that I made my way to Queen Katherine, and even then, it took me years to put all the pieces together and work out the mystery of my birth. It was Will who helped me to do that, and who persuaded me, at last, to marry.

I worked for Katherine of Aragon until I grew up, and only at the end did I tell her that she was my mother. I'd seen her once since then. She was exiled from court, and more or less imprisoned by the King who had once sworn he adored her. No one who ever loved her was allowed to visit. I grieved for her, but in the first days of my marriage to Will, I was madly in love with him, and nothing else much mattered.

Lady Anne Boleyn was more or less queen by then, and she employed me as a musician. I did not play at the grand royal occasions. I was, by virtue of my sex, able to play in Lady Anne's privy chambers, to lull her to sleep, or to soothe her whenever she erupted in frustration at having to wait ever longer for the King to get his divorce, so that they could get married. Nobody doubted now that they would get married. King Henry was passionately in love with her, and Lady Anne would not come to his bed without a ring on her finger.

"I'm not going to be like my sister," she said as she looked up from writing a letter to the King. I was playing the lute quietly in the background, while she scratched furiously with her quill. She was sitting at her desk, surrounded by piles of books. Lady Anne was an adherent of the new ways of thinking. She wanted to challenge the authority of priests and the Roman Church. She knew, from her reading, that people could have a direct relationship with God, and not be ordered about by old Italian priests. And yes, she was completely sincere in that. I didn't always like her, but I always respected her. She paused for a moment.

"I love the man! That's the problem. Does he think I don't want him to make love to me? I long for it! I have saved myself just for him." I wondered, daughter, about her two past suitors, Harry Percy and Sir Thomas Wyatt. Had she really remained a virgin in the face of their entreaties? Looking at her, I thought she was telling the truth. She was beautiful, no doubt about it, with her glossy dark hair and black eyes. But what burned within her was spirit, not a love of the flesh. She wanted to work for a new church in England. And she knew that she could only do that as the King's wife.

I noticed a small line across her forehead, brought on by screwing up her eyes in the candlelight, and felt sorry for her. She was not like Queen Katherine, she didn't have women who loved her, who would stroke her hair and tell her to rest. Anne's sister, Lady Mary Carey, was in the country now, bringing up the two small children that the King had fathered on her. Her mother, Lady Elizabeth Boleyn, was around. But her ambition was so over-arching that she would never allow her daughter to forget what was expected of her. The Boleyns saw Lady Anne as their pathway to absolute power. The fact she was also their daughter had been forgotten.

"Just tell him, Anne, he can't be waiting for the Pope to give him a divorce. It won't happen. He has to take matters into his own hands and marry you. Don't you go to his bed and give in to him now!" Anne pressed her lips together. It made her look severe, but I could tell that she was trying not to cry. She hunched her slim shoulders over the desk, and I sensed that she sometimes found this burden too much. She was carrying her love for the man, but far heavier than that was her family's ambition, and her urgent desire to change things.

Lady Jane Seymour entered the chamber, bringing a flagon of wine and some goblets on a tray. Her eyes were downcast. She'd told me privately that she missed Queen Katherine and was only serving Lady Anne because her father had told her to do so. She bent over the desk and made to place the flagon beside Lady Anne. She didn't like looking directly at her mistress, so she fumbled, trying to find a space. She leant forward too quickly, and some of the wine spilled out.

"What was that? You clumsy bitch, it's all over my skirt!" Anne's voice was hard and unforgiving. She found Jane irritating and didn't forgive her clumsiness. Jane thumped the tray down on a side table and curtseyed deeply.

"I am so sorry, my lady. I was not looking," she said. I could see there were tears in her eyes.

"Don't just curtsey, go and get a cloth and some water!" Elizabeth Boleyn said. "I pray for your sake, girl, that you haven't ruined that velvet!" Anne's sky-blue velvet gown now had a deep red stain on it. Jane Seymour hurried off and returned with a ewer of water and a linen cloth. She bunched up the cloth and poured a little water on it. Then she bent down and started scrubbing at Lady Anne's skirts.

"This gown was a present from the King," Lady Anne said icily. "Will you tell him that it was your inattention that spoiled it so completely?" The tears suddenly spilled out of Jane's eyes and started dropping like rain down her cheeks and onto the stained blue velvet. Maybe Anne then felt a little pity for the girl, because she brushed her off gently.

"It is only a gown, Lady Jane," she said. "Don't worry about it. I shall get my laundress to have a look at it. It would always do for my sister, or for you Kat." She turned to me and smiled that dazzling smile. Jane scrubbed at her face with her hands and said shakily,

"Thank you, my lady. I promise I won't do it again." She backed away, nearly bumping into a chest beside the door, corrected herself, and finally left.

"She better not do it again!" said Lady Boleyn. "Why you have to put up with her stupidity, I will never know!" Lady Anne shrugged her shoulders and turned to me.

"Would you like this gown, Kat? My maid will do her best

with it tonight. Let me give it to you tomorrow." I stopped playing, and spoke eagerly,

"It is the colour of the sky, my lady. Yes, I would like it, if it pleases you."

"Then you shall have it," Lady Anne pronounced. "Now, get back to your husband. I do not need you to stay tonight. Come in tomorrow morning after mass. I shall need some sweet music to calm me down!" She laughed ironically and waved me away.

I was happy to go. My dismissal meant that I would be able to spend the evening with Will, back in our room at Thomas Cromwell's house. I felt a shiver inside me at the thought of him, and what we might do together. We were married but three months, and the wonder of exploring each other's bodies was still fresh and delightful. I hurried through the antechamber, heading for Thomas Cromwell's office in the palace. I was sure that Will would still be there. He was a hard worker and devoted to his master.

I took my lute and put it in its case. Then I fetched my cloak, tied it at my chin, and made to leave Lady Anne's apartments. A forlorn figure was standing to one side of the guard, her head buried in her hands. I put down my lute and hurried over to her.

"Lady Jane! Don't cry. She is sharp, but her bark is worse than her bite," I assured her, remembering how much I had disliked Lady Boleyn when I was a child.

"It's, it's no good Kat! Everything I do is wrong," Lady Jane was crying again. Much as I had sympathy for her, she was not a woman like me. Yes, I had felt tears well up in my eyes, but I had often had to push them down. Being a strange child at court, I had not the luxury of tears. But I had always spoken my mind, even when it got me into trouble. And I had loved Queen Katherine, who, despite many troubles, had only cried when her heart was breaking.

"I wish I could go and serve Queen Katherine." Jane sniffed, wiping her eyes with a handkerchief. "She was so kind; she never said a cruel word to anyone." I patted her on the arm.

"I know my lady. Queen Katherine was the best mistress we could ever have had. But she is banished now, and you know we are not allowed to be with her. I was close to her, you know that. I think of her at night, on her own. But what can we do? We are only ordinary women." Jane stiffened a little, and I remembered my place, "Of course, my lady, you are gentry, and I am not. But as women, we are not mistresses of our fates." Lady Jane smiled tearfully at me.

"You are more a mistress of your fate than I am," she said. "You married for love. My father will marry me to whoever he decides. I will have no say in the matter." I took her hand in mine and kissed it.

"My lady, I shall make a prayer tonight, that whoever you marry will be the love of your life!"

"You will pray to the blessed Virgin Mary?" Jane asked, brightening a little. Now I didn't believe in all of this praying to saints and our Lady. I believed then, and I believe now that I can pray to God directly. But I wasn't going to upset Lady Jane.

"Yes, my lady, I will indeed. Now, please excuse me, I have to find my husband. I must drag him away from his office!"

"Of course, Kat, and thank you," she fluttered her hand towards me. "He is a lucky man to have you."

"Yes, and I tell him so every day. He has married above him." With that joke, I curtseyed to Lady Jane, picked up my lute, and hurried away. What Lady Jane didn't know was that I was telling the truth. Will knew that I was the child of King Henry and Queen Katherine, and he often feared that I would consider myself too good for him. But I loved him, and I wanted no other. And only Will, Cromwell and Queen Katherine knew the secret of my birth. It was impossible for me to tell the court. With Lady Anne Boleyn in the ascendant, another child of Katherine of Aragon would not be welcomed. Indeed, Thomas Cromwell believed that I might well be in danger, both from Anne Boleyn's faction, and from supporters of Princess Mary. Either side would see me as a threat. Therefore, a secret it remained.

I walked through the dark chambers of the palace. The winter sunlight was fading, and the candles were being lit. Every now and then I passed a servant bringing refreshments from the kitchen, or a courtier hurrying to meet friends. But I didn't slacken my step.

In another, more workman-like, part of the palace, I found Will still at his desk. He was writing out a document, slowly and carefully, concentrating intently. I loved him so much. For a moment he wasn't aware of me, and then he heard the rustle of my skirts as I carefully placed my lute on the floor. He looked up, and his face brightened with a warm smile of recognition.

"Well met, Mistress Kat," he stood up and embraced me. I still couldn't get used to the feeling of being in his arms, so strong and hard. I looked up at his handsome face and realised that I was indeed lucky. Standing on tiptoes, I gave him a long kiss on his lips, and he pulled me even closer to him. I was very aware of the rise and fall of his chest, and of the erection beneath his hose that he was pressing against me. At last, he pulled back, cleared some papers off a seat and motioned for me to sit down.

"Wait five minutes wife, and we shall go home together," he said, his eyes examining every inch of me. I felt warm, and silly, and girlish all at once. I had once vowed never to get married, but I was glad I had renounced that vow. Will had always been a friend, a soulmate and an ally. But now, we were linked by the pull of our bodies, the rolling tides of desire. I wondered whether Queen Katherine had ever felt that for the King. Maybe at first, when they were both young. I hoped so, for her sake.

We walked down to the river and took a skiff to Austin Friars. The tide was against us, so the boatman had to work hard. It was dark, and I could barely see Will's face. But he held my hand tightly, and we whispered to each other as the boat dipped and rose against the waves. When we disembarked it was only a short walk to Austin Friars. We were still living with Thomas Cromwell until we could afford to buy a house. With Will's wages and my small pension from Katherine of Aragon, it might be soon. I couldn't wait. Thomas Cromwell had made us both welcome, but I wanted some independence, a house of my own, maybe even a maidservant.

"So, what are you working on at the moment, Will? You are always busy." I matched my stride to his. That was us, two partners.

"I am kept busy drafting arguments and amendments, Kat. There is going to be a change soon, and Cromwell is preparing all the points for and against. We are consulting with scholars, and we want to have a solid case to present to Parliament."

"Case for what? I thought the divorce was being handled by Rome now. And it has all gone very quiet. Lady Anne is very anxious about it all. It doesn't put her in the best of moods. She made Jane Seymour cry today."

We reached the house and went up the stairs to our room. Will sat down heavily on the bed.

"Did she now? Master Cromwell doesn't like that about her. We may have been enemies, but Queen Katherine was more considerate."

"So, tell me, what case are you preparing, Will? Are you saying that it will break the deadlock?"

Will nodded grimly. "Yes, it will. And in a way that no one could have predicted."

"So tell me Will? What is going to happen?" I had served Queen Katherine of Aragon for twelve years, and I had experienced the pain and frustration she had felt over the last four. Surely anything was better than this agonising waiting?

"Kat, I will tell you. We hide nothing from each other. But you must not tell anyone else. Not Lady Anne, not her mother, not even your confessor."

"You know I don't go to confession anymore," I reminded him. "It makes me feel uncomfortable. I don't like some old man listening to all my private life."

"Kat, you and me the same. And most of London, if you ask me. We have misgivings about the church. We want an end to the dictatorship of the priests, and we hate the corruption." I nodded impatiently.

"But the King likes the old Church, even if he doesn't always agree with its decisions." Will started to whisper.

"Not even Master Cromwell must know that I have told you this. Now, for years, the King has been working to force, persuade, or even bribe the Pope to grant his divorce. Where has that got him? Nowhere! Four years, and nothing to show for it! And all the time, there was a solution waiting, if he could only accept it. We become a Protestant nation, as so many of us wish."

"The King would never accept that. He hates Protestants," I objected.

"Not as much as he has a passion for Anne Boleyn. Cromwell is talking with him all the time. If we were to have a church that was separate from Rome, the King would be at its head. And as for granting himself a divorce, he could do it in a morning!" My mouth dropped open. Will corrected himself,

"Not literally in a morning, but don't you see, he would have the power to free himself from Katherine?"

"But who will support him in this?" Will looked at me and grinned widely.

"All of us Kat. All the people who are tired of the Roman Church. He may not like Protestants, but if he wants to split from Rome, he needs our support. His lust for Anne Boleyn will bring us a new settlement, a new church, which we can form ourselves." He chuckled.

"Cromwell is a reformer; this is what he wants. But we cannot speak too loudly of it yet. It will be accomplished in

the next year, Kat, and the world will become very different."
I sat on the bed, considering this.

"I agree with you Will, that reform is needed. But what about poor Queen Katherine? It will kill her to see the King break away from the Holy Roman Church." Will shrugged his shoulders.

"Kat, she is a wonderful woman, Queen Katherine. Cromwell has great respect for her. But her obstinacy has brought nothing but harm to her faith, and to her daughter. If she had agreed to a divorce years ago, everyone, including the Church, would have been very relieved. She would have been given estates, money, and paid great honour at court. Who knows, some way might have been found to keep Princess Mary as an heir, after any sons Anne Boleyn may have."

As I listened, I felt immensely sad. Everything Will said was right, but that was what Queen Katherine was like. She had taken a vow to be Henry's wife, and nothing would make her change it.

"You must respect her though, the way she has stuck to her principles. There are not many like her." I would always defend her, even to my own husband.

"No, I don't respect her, not anymore. She says she is fighting for her faith, and yet I tell you, her actions will mean England will leave the Church she so loves. She says she loves her daughter, but her actions mean that Princess Mary isn't allowed to see her and is left alone to suffer! Are those the actions of a woman of principle?"

"You are talking about my mother, Will! You are attacking the only person who cared for me once I was on my own." Will looked coldly at me.

"So, I never cared for you?" His voice was cold.

"If you had, you wouldn't say these things. You see things as a man. Don't you understand Will? The King has disdained her and disrespected her! Of course, they were married in the eyes of the church! And now he gets to push her aside and look as if he's being very pious about it. I hate him Will, I really do." Will put his hand on my shoulder.

"Don't get angry sweetheart. You can't blame the King for this."

"Yes, I can, and I do! I like Lady Anne, but she is not Queen! All of this is because he wants to have her." Will shook his head.

"Yes, he lusts for her. But think for a moment, Kat. If Lady Anne were not on the scene, do not suppose that the King would not wish to divorce Queen Katherine. He has a duty to provide an heir for England."

"He has an heir, or had you forgotten?" I snapped.

"A male heir, Kat, he needs a male heir." Will sat back, as if the argument was won.

"So, you don't believe I am your equal? You are saying that a man is better than a woman?"

"Kat, you are my superior in every way. But to rule England you need a man." I turned away from him and went to wash my face.

"Come sweetheart, let's not fight. I haven't seen you for three days, and I'm aching for you." I dried my face with a cloth and walked to the bed.

"Will, how can I lie with you when you have just disrespected me and all my sex?" I sat on the side of the bed and took my shoes off. Then I lay stiffly on top of the covers, fully clothed. Sighing, Will lay beside me. We were silent for about half an hour, until I felt the merest flutter of a touch on my folded hands. Will was lying on his side, gazing at me.

"Kat, I'm sorry. I must not forget you are a Tudor woman, daughter of the King and Queen Katherine, and you will always fight your corner. I love your fiery spirit; I love your courage and your intelligence! I will never disrespect you; I promise." I turned on my side towards him. My anger had subsided, and I was grateful to him for giving me a way out.

"So, you respect me?" I asked softly.

"I respect every part of you, from your thin white feet to your beautiful face. You know that Kat." I sat up on the bed and started to peel off my hose. He leant over and helped me, pulling gently on the toes.

"See? I love your feet, and I love your toes. I will kiss them one by one." I wriggled my toes as he kissed them and licked them with his warm tongue. "And I love your ankles, very fine ankles, and your calves, and your beautiful sturdy thighs." As he spoke, his mouth was moving up my legs, kissing every inch delicately, and yet with an iron purpose. I felt the sensations moving from my feet upwards towards the nerves that centred in my vagina. I was breathing faster now and feeling less and less in control.

But I didn't let him take over. I rolled over and pulled his hose down. His legs were well muscled, with black hairs brushing across his white flesh. I loved him. I kissed those hairs and felt his muscles tauten as I worked up to his groin.

Then we were both pulling at each other's clothes, frantically unlacing each other, impatient for the moment when we would both be naked. At last, we fell together in the bed, and I felt his body lying on mine. He was heavy, but I welcomed it. I welcomed his tight furry belly, his hard muscles, and his swelling cock. I had never meant to marry, but I loved this man to distraction, and had loved him all my life.

We moved together, him plunging into me, me bucking up against him, making him groan with pleasure. But he held himself back and continued to move inside me, letting his weight excite and awake me. At last, I felt an explosion of pleasure, and then wave after wave of delight. As I shook, he cried out and finished inside me. I praised God, who had created us to have such pleasure, giving and taking, ecstasy and, in the end, fulfilment.

That was it, the coupling. It always made things right between us. Our bodies would not allow us to be enemies for long, they had their own longings, which we couldn't resist.

Afterwards we lay there, in each other's arms, murmuring sweet endearments, sleeping, and then drowsily kissing. We may not have slept for long, but those nights together gave us all the refreshment we needed.

Quickly, next morning, we washed and ate some stale bread left out in the kitchen. It was still early, but we had to be back at Greenwich. We rushed down to the river and got into a skiff, which brought us down river faster than we would have liked. We disembarked, and kissed hurriedly, before rushing off to our work. I turned as I reached the door to the private apartments and saw Will disappearing into the work rooms of the palace. I felt a little pang and wished for a moment I could be with him all day. But no! I was a person in my own right, and I was not going to hang around his neck, waiting for him to be nice to me. I took my lute and made my way up to Lady Anne's apartments.

The chambers were familiar to me. They had once been the Queen's, although all signs of her had been erased. The tapestries she had loved were gone, replaced by newer designs. Her symbol, the pomegranate, had been removed from every ceiling boss and mantelpiece. We were in Anne's privy chamber, but her coat of arms had yet to go up, and so there were bare patches every few feet, waiting to be filled in.

Lady Anne was sitting with her mother, Lady Boleyn, both listlessly playing cards. She looked up as I came in and curt-seyed to them both.

"Ah, Kat. You are late."

"I am sorry my lady, the boatman was not speedy." She nodded impatiently. She didn't know where I lived, only that I was now married and living with my husband.

"Play me something cheerful Kat!" I started on 'Pastime with Good Company', only for her to snap,

"Not that one! I don't even want to think about the King this morning!" It turned out that she had not received a let-ter from the King, although she had been expecting one. He was away for a few days, and she always got anxious when she hadn't heard from him. I strummed heartily at the lute, and she hummed along for a while. Then she held up her hand for me to finish.

"Kat, I have been meaning to ask you something," she said. "Something puzzles me about you."

"Of course, my lady. But there is nothing puzzling about me," I asserted, my voice a little trembly. What is she about to ask? Does she know about my birth? But how could she? Had anyone at Cromwell's house overheard Will and me talking? But they wouldn't betray us, surely?

"You say you were a foundling, and I have heard that you were indeed taken in as an orphan by Katherine." I noticed that Lady Anne was no longer using Queen Katherine's title. "But you act like a lady. You are better educated than most ladies at court. You are a musician. You did not learn that on the street? You even have the look of a Plantagenet, the white skin and red hair. I wonder Kat, if you are a bye blow from an earlier time."

"No, no, indeed my lady," I said. "I was no Plantagenet's bastard, just a foundling, as you were told. I was fortunate that I was given an education by..." and here I paused. "By the old Queen."

Anne sniffed, not best pleased.

"Do you still think of her as the Queen?" she demanded.

"Oh no, indeed not. It was just a slip of the tongue." I wondered where all of this was going. Anne smiled, but her eyes were cool. She thought for a moment, and then nodded.

"Yes, Kat, we all have our way to make in court, don't we? But just be careful. You cannot afford to lose this post, because of past mistakes."

"My lady, I know that you are the future, and I respect you deeply. You will not find me disloyal." I put down my lute and curtseyed deeply to her. The kind of curtsey one would do for a Queen. I hoped that she would be pacified. She came over to me and raised me up.

"Look me in the eyes." Her intelligence burned within them, and maybe a touch of amusement. "There's just one question I have Kat. There is something about you which you have not told me. Why do you hide the truth from me?"

CHAPTER 2

My stomach lurched and my mouth went dry. Had Lady Anne found out the truth about my birth? If she had, that was the end of my career at court, maybe even of my freedom. The last person she would want around her was another legitimate child of Katherine of Aragon. Anne was staring at me intently, her black eyes piercing through me. I decided that I would lie and brazen it out. Stammering a reply, I ventured,

"My lady, what truth do you speak of? I hide nothing from you."

Suddenly, Anne's face relaxed, and she started to laugh.

"Oh Kat, I heard today that you are lodging with Master Thomas Cromwell. You did not tell me!"

"My lady, when I am not at court, I am living with my husband, who works for Master Cromwell. There is nothing to hide." To my surprise, Anne's laughter became louder and she gave me a hug. Purkoy, her little dog, sensed the mood and danced around our feet. I remembered the time when I had first met her and her sister. They were girls not much older than me, and outsiders at court. We were close then and spent many afternoons together. But now Anne was approaching the crown, she was not usually so familiar. She let me go and smiled conspiratorially at me.

"I know, dear Kat. But it will be helpful for me to have a pair of eyes in the Cromwell household. He tells the King he has found a way out of our problem. But I don't know if we can trust him." I replied quickly,

"I think you can madam. He is a kind man." Anne shrugged her shoulders.

"We shall see Kat, we shall see. Meanwhile, tell me anything you overhear while you are there. I will have to give you more nights off!" I did not intend to spy for Anne, but I would not disagree.

"I will, my lady, but I don't overhear much." Anne twinkled at me.

"You may hear something; you merge so much into the background, Kat. However, dear girl, I worried you just then, did I not? Your face went white. It makes me wonder if you really have secrets that you are hiding from me." If only she knew. But she didn't know, and she would never know. I smiled agreeably.

"I am too dull to have any secrets my lady. As you say, I just merge." Anne wrinkled her nose, as if to acknowledge that she had not been fair.

"Come Kat. I have a secret to tell you!" Lady Boleyn looked at her daughter dubiously.

"Do you think you should, Anne?" Lady Anne waved her mother's objection away.

"Of course, Mother, it was decided last week! Will you go and tell them in the presence chamber that I shall be coming through now?" Lady Boleyn sniffed and made her way out of the chamber. Anne bent forward to me and whispered,

"Do you know what the King told me last week? He said that near the end of the year, we are going to France on a state visit. I will be accorded all honours as a queen. I will sit beside him, and the French King, lead the English ladies, and wear the Queen's jewels! That gives me hope Kat. He is determined to make me his wife. He would not take me to the French court as his consort, if he did not intend to marry me. A few months Kat, and then I will be crowned."

"That is good news, my lady," I agreed. Quietly, I wondered what Queen Katharine would say to the request for her to relinquish her jewels for her rival. But that was not my problem.

Would Anne claim that those who thronged to her presence chamber were friends? So many of them, men and women, were people who had known which way the wind was blowing and made their decisions accordingly. Like Sir Henry Norris, a nice enough man but very close to the King. He was in his late thirties then, with greying hair and a spare figure. He'd become one of Anne's party in the early days. That was when she still looked to find allies who could speak to the King for her. Now, that wasn't necessary, but he was still one of her most constant companions. He was the King's groom of the stool, which meant he attended to Henry when he was emptying his bowels. This was a great honour, although Anne made fun of him.

"You are such a grand gentleman, Sir Henry, yet were your post for any other man, you would disdain it! Like me, you esteem *everything* about the King!" She would sail a bit close to the wind with Sir Henry. Her jokes about the King verged on the disrespectful. But she trusted those around her, maybe more than she should.

Sir Thomas Wyatt, though, had known Anne since childhood. He had been in love with her, maybe still was. But he'd accepted that Anne belonged to King Henry. He himself had a wife, although they lived separately. Now, he was just a friend to her, but a good one. She teased him without mercy, and yet confided in him. He was a handsome man, with his dark curling hair and soulful brown eyes. And he was popular with the ladies of the court, mainly for his poetry.

One afternoon, a group of us were sitting with Lady Anne.

Her mother, her sister, who had just come back to court, Sir Henry Norris, and Sir Thomas Wyatt. She was often left to amuse herself, as the King was like an idol, not involved in everyday life. I was sitting just behind the group, playing my lute softly. I remember this afternoon because they were composing poems about the ladies of the court. Anne was clever with words, and so was Sir Henry. But Thomas Wyatt was the poet, and his verses were the funniest and most skllful of all. It was a merry group, and the afternoon passed quickly. Anne's sister, Lady Mary Carey, was back at court, leaving her two children at home. We all knew that they were the King's bastards, and that five years ago the King had been in love with her. But no one said anything about it. This is the strange thing about court, daughter. People lived together in grandeur and pain. And sometimes people got hurt, or even killed. But after a few months, the people involved would come together again, drink and hunt together as if they were brothers.

A messenger entered the chamber, bowed and gave Anne a message. She immediately brightened on reading it.

"The King is back," she announced, a broad smile on her face. She waved me to stop playing and rose from her seat. Immediately, we all rose. We knew that soon she would be queen.

"I must go to my privy chamber and dress. The King expects me tonight. Gentlemen, you may go. And Kat, I shall not need you tonight." She walked out, closely followed by her mother and her sister, their trains swishing across the floor, leaving the scent of violets behind them.

"Kat, I have a poem for you." Thomas Wyatt was standing beside me. Sir Henry Norris had left, and we were alone together.

"A poem? Why would you write a poem for me?"

"I must pay my respects to beauty," he said. "I must admit I have only written the first line, but maybe you could help me write the rest? I sniffed. No one had ever written a poem about me before, and I must admit I was intrigued.

"So what is the first line?" Sir Thomas shook his head and grinned at me.

"You only get that if you agree to have a drink of wine with me before you go home." What was the harm? He had eyes only for Anne. So I went with him to the great hall, where the tables were empty after the midday meal. We perched on a bench, and Thomas called for a flagon of wine, which was set on the table in front of us. He poured me a goblet and handed it to me. I took a sip. He, meanwhile, took a large gulp of his.

"So here it is Kat. What do you think?" He pulled out a piece of paper from his pouch and read out loud,

"I know a kat whose bite is sharp but sweet...." I made a face.

"I don't like it. Why do people always compare me to an animal? And what do you know of my bite? I have never bitten you, or anyone."

"Kat, Kat, it is a metaphor. You have bitten me to the depths of my soul, with your wit and your beauty." He was very smooth, but his eyes were amused.

"Stop it, you're not taking me seriously!" He took another drink of wine and looked me in the eyes.

"Kat, you are wrong. I take you so seriously. You are one of Lady Anne's closest servants. You have known her since she was a girl. I take you seriously because I think you care for her, as I do." I thought for a moment, and then answered truthfully.

"Yes, I do care for her, although she is not the easiest of ladies to work for." He laughed out loud.

"That is your honesty Kat, and it's why I take you seriously. You and me, we must stay close. Anne has many enemies, and her position is perilous." I was astonished.

"But she is about to be Queen! How can she be in peril?"

"Think of the last Queen, who, like you, I loved and respected. Who was behind her? The Holy Roman Emperor, the princes of the Catholic Church, most of the court, and all the people. And yet, the King discarded her when he fell out of love with her. Now think of Anne. Who has she got behind her? Her family, yes. And her new friends, so long as they remain friends. If she fails to produce a son, do you think any of them will stay by her? I tell you, if there is no boy coming to save her, she will face a far worse fate than Queen Katherine."

"Oh, you are too dramatic, Sir Thomas! The King loves her. And she will produce a son, many sons!"

"Kat, you are full of hope. But watch over my lady Anne for me, I beg of you. And, Kat, call me Tom!" He grasped my hand and kissed it quickly. Shamefully, I blushed as I pulled my hand back.

"I will watch over her, I promise. You have no need to fear, Sir Thomas."

"Tom," he insisted.

"Very well. Tom."

We became friends then, of a sort. When Lady Anne was busy, Sir Thomas would scribble verses to make me laugh. He was always declaring that he loved me, but I knew he wasn't serious. Of course, Sir Thomas was a poet, and he tended to exaggerate things. Like George Boleyn, he was a good musician, and we sometimes played together. But he had never tried to force me, as George Boleyn did. There was a sadness in him, which never quite left him. I sensed a flame still burned in his heart for Lady Anne. He knew, of course, it was hopeless. But he found me a comfort to be with. Unlike the court ladies, I was not trying to follow Anne in his affections. I didn't hang around him in case he confided a secret about the Lady. So, we were easy with each other. Yes, he was an actor, whose affections were always larger than life. But he wasn't one of those who stabbed people in the back to get on. There were plenty of those at court. I didn't know how close I was then to someone who turned out to be Anne's most ruthless enemy. But I didn't know a lot of things then, daughter. When you are young, you take things at face value, and you believe that everyone who smiles is your friend. Yet, at court, they could smile at you as they pulled a dagger from their belt.

I realised very soon that I had been right to hide my identity. The long-lost daughter of Katherine of Aragon and King Henry! I would most likely have been laughed out of court or set to work in the kitchens where people could stare at me as the latest pretender. And that would not have been the worst outcome. That would have been if the court had accepted me as royal. Everyone would bow or curtsey. I would have fine gowns, jewels, and my pick of a stableful of horses. But those who would want rid of me would be waiting for a chance to destroy me. Anne Boleyn, Princess Mary, the King himself. It was safer to be an ordinary person in King Henry's court, far safer.

Lady Jane Seymour was a quiet girl with no pink in her face. It was difficult to see the colour of her eyes, as she kept them cast downwards for most of the time. She came up to me later, and asked me eagerly,

"So, did you pray for me Kat? You promised that you would." I vaguely remembered doing so, to try to comfort her. "Will I marry the love of my life, like you did?" It had obviously meant more to her than to me

"The love of your life, my lady? Yes of course!" I crossed my fingers behind my back. One was always meant to love one's spouse, and I am sure a good girl like Jane would do so. She tried so hard. She asked me once to teach her how to play the lute. We sat in the corner of the Queen's chamber, with me showing her a few chords on the lute.

"So, my lady, you see, if you place your fingers here... and here. Now try!" She strummed at it, and it made a noise that was not altogether unpleasant. I showed her the words to the Merrie Month of May and told her to sing as she played the chords. What a mistake that was. She had a terrible voice, and her wailing set the dog Purkoy barking, which in turn alerted

Lady Anne Boleyn, who was in an adjoining chamber. She strode in, book in hand, and turned a pitiless glare on me and Jane.

"Who is making that terrible noise? Kat, you are a musician, you cannot be producing such a din!" Jane looked very worried, so I decided to cover for her.

"Yes, madam, I am afraid to say that it was me. I have a sore throat today and cannot hit the notes right." I coughed loudly.

"Keep away from me then Kat! I do not want to go down with anything now. But it wasn't your voice. I would know your voice from anyone's." Jane shrank back a little and placed the sheet music on the table beside her. In a very small voice, she whispered,

"My lady, it was me. I am learning the lute, and Kat suggested I sing."

"Kat has no business to do that. You have no talent, no sweetness in your voice. Kat! I forbid you to give this howler any more lessons." I could see the tears starting in Jane's eyes. But Lady Anne didn't stop,

"I shall speak to the King. I do not wish for dull little women like you to be one of my ladies. I don't know why he allowed it in the first place. You are no ornament, more like a backward milkmaid. I cannot bear you to be around me." Lady Anne was in a foul temper. Maybe she'd had an argument with the King. She was often having arguments with him. She was tired of waiting for his divorce, and often argued he was not doing enough. And then he would shout, and she would cry and run off, taking it out on her servants. Two hours later they would be lovers again, and all the nastiness had been forgotten.

But Jane didn't forget it. She got up, trembling, and curtseyed shakily to Anne.

"In that case, my lady, may I withdraw? I would go to my father." Her face was wet now, and her voice nasal with tears.

"Yes, get out of the way! And Kat, you go too. I've had enough of the pair of you." Jane started to walk carefully towards the door. I followed her at a respectful distance. After what seemed like a long time, but was only a few seconds, we reached the door and went through it. Once the door was closed, Jane sank to the floor weeping.

"Why is she so cruel to me? I have done her no harm. And yet, every day she insults me, she tells me she doesn't want me. She laughs at me because I can't write poetry, and she imitates me when I speak French. She wants to bring me down Kat, but why?"

"She is just in a bad mood," I said. "She will feel better soon and forget all about it." Jane, though, was obstinate.

"But she shouldn't forget all about it. She shouldn't treat people like that and then expect to get away with it. I would be beaten if I spoke to people the way she does." I wondered if Lady Anne might be a little jealous. The King had complimented Lady Jane on her embroidery the other day, and Lady Anne had not been pleased.

"Now she'll send me home, and my father will be so angry," Jane sobbed. "I'd be happy to go home, I would. I hate it at court. But I daren't tell my father that."

"She won't send you home. She is hot-tempered, but she doesn't mean it." I reassured Jane. "And if you stay at court, you will find a husband, and that will make your father happy."

"But not me! I wanted to go into the religious life. I would have had a quiet life, praying and tending a herb garden. That is what I wanted." Jane's tear-stained face looked like a little girl's. It was almost as if she was stamping her feet because she couldn't have the sweetmeat she wanted. I felt sorry for her, a little. However angry her father became, she was always going to have the security of being part of the gentry, having a home, and knowing who her parents were.

I put my arm around her and let her cry on my shoulder. Although she was about the same age as me, she hadn't got used to the toughness of life as I had. Poor lady, she would soon learn.

"Jane, what is the matter?" A tall young man came over to us and pulled her out of my arms. He gave her a handkerchief, with which she wiped her eyes. For a moment we all stood there awkwardly, but then she spoke. Her voice was clear but faint.

"Edward, you do not know Kat. She is one of the musicians. Kat, this is Edward, my brother." I curtseyed deeply to the young man, who frowned in irritation.

"You should not be consorting with servants, Jane. Nor should you be crying in open court. What is the matter?" Jane sniffed, and then answered him.

"Kat was helping me. Edward, Lady Anne has told me she will send me from court. I am finished! Father will be so angry. I do not want to see him." Edward Seymour patted her shoulder placatingly,

"Don't make so much of it Jane. We all know Lady Anne has a nasty tongue. She will ask for you tomorrow."

"She called me a dull little woman, Edward! I know I am not stylish, or clever like she is. But she said she could not bear to have me around her." Edward pursed his lips and took her by the hand.

"That woman will come before a fall; she thinks she is a queen already. But she has not one ounce of the grace that Queen Katherine has! She will hit bad times, of that, I am sure. And there will be no one to take her part!" I looked a bit surprised at this. Edward Seymour's comment was savage. I looked around in case anyone was listening, but he had already noticed that we were alone.

"Edward, we can't say those things," Jane whispered.

"I know. For now, we must stay quiet and let her wreak her damage. But I tell you this, sister, there will come a time when she will beg for mercy. And there will be no one to give it to her." He turned to me.

"Now Kat, is that your name? You did not hear this, did you? For if you report it, I will make sure you are dismissed instantly." I took a deep breath. I didn't like this man at all. But he needn't have told me to keep quiet. By then, I had learnt to keep my ears closed and my mouth shut. The only way ordinary people survived was by ignoring what was going on around them. And that was what I did.

Later though, I did tell Will that Lady Anne was being hard on Jane Seymour. At a loose end since Lady Anne had sent me away, I had wandered over to Cromwell's office. Will was working there, as usual, but when he saw me, he put his quill down and came over to greet me.

"I don't usually see you at this time," he commented. "Is Lady Anne unwell?" I pulled a face.

"No, not except in her temper! I was teaching Lady Jane to play the lute, and poor Lady Jane, she is not a natural musician. Lady Anne got very angry and told us both to leave. Then Jane was crying and saying her father would beat her. She is a nice girl, but she's got no fight in her."

Just then, Thomas Cromwell put his head around the door. "Hello Kat, I thought I heard you talking. So, Lady Jane Seymour has felt the rough edge of La Boleyn's tongue?" He chuckled quietly,

"You will both be back before nightfall, I'll warrant. She will have had a love token from the King, and all will be well." He paused, though, and looked at Will and me. We were standing together, arm in arm, youthful and happy. He spoke slowly and deliberately,

"We are moving in the same direction as La Boleyn, you both know that. But don't forget, for us, the direction is not the King's marriage, it is the reformed church. And in time, La Boleyn will fall. Will, you will stick with me. But Kat, be careful. Do not hitch your future to her, my dear. For I tell you this: If she doesn't give the King what he wants, she will have a terrible end. And I will not be sorry."

CHAPTER 3

A few days later, Lady Anne Boleyn went out hunting with the King. I stayed in her apartment with a few of the ladies who had not chosen to go. I played a few songs and then put my lute down. No one was interested. Lady Jane Seymour came up to me, clutching her stomach.

"I have terrible pains this month," she confided. "And it is so cold outside, I do not wish to catch a chill." I smiled at her. At least she wasn't crying, which was an advantage.

"So, Lady Anne took you back?" I commented.

"Yes, indeed. I waited two days, then my brother Edward came with me to her chambers, and she welcomed me back in. It was as if it had never happened." She smiled, marveling at the inconsistency of important people.

"I came back the very next day, and do you know what she said? She told me off for being late! You know Jane, she has a harsh tongue, but she is not a witch, however much people may call her one."

"I know," Jane assented, "but she can be so difficult to work with. And I miss Queen Katherine so much!"

"I do too, my lady. I wish she were here today." I was honest. What I would have liked is to continue my work with Lady

Anne Boleyn as a musician but go home to Queen Katherine every night. Well, most nights. The two or three nights I spent every week in Will's bed were so sweet, and I could not manage without them. But talking about the Queen reminded me of one piece of gossip that I had heard from a chambermaid,

"Lady Willoughby is at court today," I told Jane. "You remember her, Maria de Salinas that was? Queen Katherine's oldest friend. She has come today to pick up some of the Queen's books for her. If we can catch her, we might hear news of the Queen." Jane looked at me doubtfully.

"Are you sure?" she asked. "Won't we get into trouble?"

"We can always say we were checking she didn't take any books that didn't belong to the Queen." I was eager to see what we could find out.

"It would be good to see her. I like Lady Willoughby. She was kind to me." I looked at Lady Jane and gave her a strained smile. We both knew that, unlike Lady Willoughby, kindness was not a great part of Lady Anne Boleyn's character. But, as she was out hunting, we were free to take a risk and look for Lady Maria.

We looked first all around the Queen's apartments, that Lady Anne was now living in. We checked every small chamber, opened every door, and looked out of many windows. There was no sign of Lady Willoughby. Suddenly, it came to me.

"Of course, she's not here! Do you remember, when Lady Anne moved in, she threw out most of the books? She said that they were all too gloomy and superstitious for her." Jane looked shocked.

"But they were religious books, holy books," she protested.

"You know what Lady Anne is like, she always wants new things," I said dismissively. I didn't know how much Lady Jane understood the direction in which Lady Anne was going. So, I moved quickly on, "There were a number of chests with books in them. The chamberlain ordered them to be put in the stables, out of the way. If Lady Maria has come to collect books, that is where she will be!" We both scrambled for our cloaks and made our way through the many royal apartments, down the stairs, and into the courtyard.

Outside the stables there was a wagon with two large horses stamping their feet in the cold. The drayman stood beside them, blowing on his fingers. We passed him and went inside. A stableboy looked at us curiously as we swept past the rows of empty stalls. Most of the horses were out on the hunting field. There were just a few stalls near the end, occupied by the less favoured nags. If I had gone hunting, it would have been one of these second choices that I would've ridden. I patted one sympathetically as we walked down towards the small storage room at the end. I remembered hiding in one such room many years ago, when I first tumbled out at the feet of Queen Katherine. For a moment, I allowed myself to miss her, and felt a pang of deep grief. I pushed it down and forced myself to concentrate. At one corner at the far end of the stables there were several chests leaning up against the wall. A woman was bending over them, with two manservants hovering behind her.

Hearing us, she rose and turned. It was Lady Maria, her face shrouded by a hooded cloak. But I recognised her immediately. She was older but still graceful as she moved towards us. For a moment she looked puzzled, and then a light came into her eyes.

"Kat! How wonderful to see you! And Lady Jane, how goes it with you?" She did not wait for me to curtsey but ran up to me and took me in her arms. Again, I remembered her scent of oranges and sandalwood. I hugged her closely. She had always been my friend at court, and I was pleased to see her after over a year. She pulled back from me, wiping her eyes, and then turned to Lady Jane and dropped a quick curtsey, which Jane returned.

"My apologies, Lady Jane. Kat and I are old friends, and I am so pleased to see her. Oh Kat, it has been a hard time, such a hard time!" Remembering herself, she looked round quickly to see if anyone was watching. All she saw was the two manservants who were watching with interest. Reassured, she turned to them and gave them their orders.

"Take these three chests here, on the left, and those two over the other side of the door. You may leave the other one – those books belong to Princess Mary."

"Yes, my lady," one of the men touched his forelock, and they moved together towards the first chest. "You take this end; I'll take the front." They picked up the chest and staggered through the door, leaving the three of us standing there. Jane reached out and touched Lady Willoughby's hand.

"My lady, you are freezing. Will you come inside and have some hot ale?" I had not thought to ask, but Lady Willoughby replied,

"I cannot my dear. It is so awkward. I do not wish to see the Lady Anne."

"She is out hunting," I said. "She won't be back till late. We won't go to her apartments anyway. We can find a seat in the hall." She looked doubtful.

"Oh, please, my lady. I would so much like to talk to you, and Lady Jane too." Jane smiled shyly and nodded her assent.

"I miss the Queen," she said, and her voice became thick with tears. Lady Willoughby, though, did not weep easily. She had been through too much. Briskly she let go of Jane's hand and moved towards the door.

"Very well, I shall come. But let us haste. We have not got much time." She bustled out of the stable, giving some more orders to the drayman and the manservants. Then she called to the stable lad that she would be back before nightfall to pick up her horse.

She knew the way. She had lived in this palace for years. We went quickly into the hall, past servants cleaning, lighting candles and kindling fires. We sat in a corner and Lady Jane called for three cups of hot spiced ale. As we were waiting, Lady Willoughby pulled off her fine leather gloves and laid them beside her on the table. Then she talked, her faintly accented voice spilling out all of the happenings of the last year, the inconveniences of Bishops Hatfield, where the Queen was living.

"But how is she? Lady Willoughby, how does her Majesty?" I demanded, dreading and yet longing for news. Lady Willoughby started to speak, but just then a boy appeared with three tankards of steaming ale. She paused until he had gone, took a sip of her ale, and spoke.

"My dearest Catalina, she is so brave. Day after day, she hears gossip from the courts. She is not allowed to see Princess Mary. You would think she would weep all day long. But no. She goes to Mass every morning. She sews shirts for his Majesty even though he will never wear them. She believes that he still loves her, you see. She thinks that he will realise the mistake he is making and take her back. Every time she hears of Lady Anne shouting at him, and making him miserable, it gives her hope. I tell you this, Kat. She still prays for him every night, you know that? And if anyone visits from London, her first question is always, 'How is my dear lord the King?' And she tells them to send him her deepest love."

I felt so much pain for her, "Why does she not just accept the divorce?" I whispered. "It would make her life so much easier. As it is, she is hurt every day." Jane's eyes looked moist, but Lady Willoughby shook her head vigorously.

"You never understood Kat, and why should you? This is her destiny, to be Queen. She will take no other course. She knows it is God's will." I looked down at my hands, and I felt so sad at the pain of it all.

"I just want her to be happy. She is so dear to me, dearer than any other human being." Lady Willoughby relented and put her hand over mine.

"And you are very dear to her Kat, she talks of you often and prays for you. But you know happiness is not what she seeks. She seeks God's will. She still studies her Bible. And she asked me to arrange the carriage of her books so that she had more to read." I took a deep draught of my ale and looked directly at Lady Willoughby as I spoke.

"She's such a fighter! I should have known she would never give in. And I can't blame her for it, it's what makes her amazing." Lady Willoughby smiled warmly.

"Aah yes Kat, what a woman! Don't think I have not wished she was otherwise. But that's my Catalina. She is of warrior blood." We laughed together. Lady Jane looked faintly shocked at our disrespect and muttered a quick blessing under her breath.

"Do you know what happened last month Kat? The King sent messengers to her, asking for her jewels. Told our dear Queen to give them up to that whore!" Lady Jane shushed her and looked around anxiously, but I was too intrigued to care.

"So, what happened?" I asked. "What did she do?" Lady Willoughby laughed loudly.

"You know what happened Kat. She shouted at the messengers and sent them away empty-handed. She told them she would not give up her precious jewels without a direct order from the King! Oh, he will do it, no doubt. But he will hate it. The parfait gentil knight, ordering his wife to surrender the jewels he gave her."

"So, what's happening now? Has he sent someone?" At this, Lady Willoughby's face fell. She looked down at the floor, and I could tell that she was struggling to keep her composure.

"He ordered me to leave Kat. He ordered me, Catalina's oldest friend, to leave her! How can he be so heartless? My heart is broken for her. I swore I would never leave her Kat, and that I would be with her until she died." She looked up at me directly, her eyes glittering.

"I hate him," she said flatly. "I hate and despise him." Lady Jane looked around again, this time very anxious.

"But he is the King," she whispered, terrified. Lady Willoughby nodded.

"He is the King, and he has my loyalty," she said. "But he will answer before God for what he has done to our Queen." I turned to Lady Jane.

"You know what all the Londoners are saying? They say she has been a good wife, and that he should not treat her so. I say to you he is cruel. Why else would he deny Queen Katherine the sight of her daughter and her friends?" Lady Jane muttered uneasily,

"I know what my old nurse says when I visit her. But I can't believe the King is so cruel. He is under a spell, and I pray every night that he recovers from it." Lady Willoughby raised her eyebrows.

"Better to pray for our Queen, that she may remain in the light of God's love. But then, she will never be deserted by our Lord in Heaven." She drained her tankard and set it on the table.

"I must go now. I do not want any of the hunting party to see me. I shall pray for you both in this godforsaken court." Jane and I thanked her. Who knows what good a prayer might bring? Lady Willoughby picked up her gloves and pulled them on.

"Oh, and please pray for me, my dears, that I might see my dearest Catalina one more time." With that, she stifled a sob and hurried away from us, going through the great door without a backward glance.

Jane and I remained silent for a few minutes. Truth be told, we had been so caught up in our own lives in Anne Boleyn's chamber that we had not wanted to consider how hard life was for Queen Katherine. But Lady Willoughby had brought us back to that reality, and we didn't feel comfortable about it.

Will came to meet me once he had finished his work, and we made our way back to Austin Friars. We took some wine up to our room and lay on the bed drinking. He was tired, but in a mood to celebrate,

"You know Kat, the King is giving Master Cromwell more

and more work to do. It's important work, to do with the divorce. So, I'm doing a lot more, and some of it is directly for the King! Master Cromwell tells me I am doing well, and, God be praised, he is putting my pay up by five pounds a year! Kat, it won't be long till we can have a house of our own, just you and me." He drank his wine and poured me some more.

"So I shall be away for a few days, from tomorrow," he said. "You can stay here if you want, but you will probably be busy at court. There will soon be something to celebrate!"

"How do you know? What is it that you are doing?" I asked eagerly. Nowadays Will heard more secrets than I did. But he didn't tell me, he just looked mysterious and whispered, "I can't tell you Kat, but if it goes well, I will buy you a comb set with mother-of-pearl. I shall watch you combing your lovely hair in the candlelight, before I take you to bed and ravish you!" With that, he started tickling me. I hit him hard to get him to stop, but before I knew it, we were kissing, and he was pulling me towards him. We were in a hurry that night, and it was cold, daughter. So, we didn't undress, he just pulled my skirts up and had me there and then, like an inn-keeper's daughter on a winter night.

I just could not resist him; I loved him so much. It was fast and frantic, but we both reached a climax and then lay in each other's arms. I fitted into the crook of his arm, where I felt warm and safe. Our breathing gradually matched each other's until we were almost one creature, curled up tightly against the cold.

It wasn't until we broke our fast the next morning that I remembered to ask him again. We were sitting in the corner of the kitchen, while the kitchen maid was busy baking bread.

"Go on, tell me Will, where are you going today? Are you on a diplomatic mission?" He shushed me and gave a warning glance at the kitchen maid.

"You won't get it out of me Kat, so don't try." I brought my lips close to his head, and whispered,

"Not even for a kiss?" He grabbed me and gave me a long and very ardent kiss. I felt the heft of him, his strength, and returned the kiss eagerly. But still, he did not give away any information.

"I shall be back within the week. I can maybe tell you more then," he told me, patting me on my backside. "Now get your cloak, Lady Anne will be expecting you." I pinched him in retaliation, grabbed my cloak, and wished him goodbye. I realised after I had left that I hadn't told him about my meeting with Lady Willoughby. I had a strange feeling that it was maybe best not to tell him. I trusted Will absolutely, but we thought so differently. I did not want another argument.

Lady Anne was pensive this morning. Her face was pale under her black French hood, and her eyes kept darting around the room as if she was expecting someone. She had dressed with her customary simplicity. Unlike Queen Katherine, she did not favour bright colours. Instead, she wore a gown of deep blue velvet, with tiny golden falcons embroidered at the hem. Her small waist was emphasised by the dark colour, and the gown's square neck perfectly presented her breasts, pushing them up just enough to be flirtatious.

"Kat, we are going to Calais soon." She hesitated. "That is, I have been told we are going." Her face was pinched, and she looked tired. "The King has not yet set the date, and I fear it will never happen!"

"My lady, it will happen, I am certain. Everyone is talking of it." I tried to be reassuring, but she wasn't calmed. She started to pull at a sleeve, finding a loose thread, which started to unravel.

"But he hasn't got the Queen's jewels yet. He says he wants to present me as his Queen, but how can I be that without the royal jewels? He knows that, but he just puts me off. He doesn't take me seriously Kat! I fear that he won't go through with it. He'll take me to Calais for a week, make me his mistress, and that will be the end of it." Purkoy, who had been sitting in her lap, fidgeted and whined, looking anxiously at his mistress.

"He won't do that, my lady. He cannot live without you!" I did not tell her that I heard many people saying she had put a spell on him.

"But if he means to marry me in Calais, then why am I not having the Queen's jewels? He says she won't give them up, but Kat, he is the King! All he has to do is order her, and yet he holds back." She brought her hands up to her neck and played with the rope of pearls she wore, with a golden B hanging from it.

"Kat, I have waited so long. I am afraid something will go wrong even now. And if it does, I am ruined." I thought she was being a bit over-dramatic but saw that she was genuinely troubled. It isn't often that a girl from a middle-ranking aristocratic family gets to oust an anointed queen. She still couldn't quite believe that it would happen. I often felt quite torn when I was with her. I loved Queen Katherine and wished that she could return, but I could not hate this turbulent woman who had risked so much. I tried to calm her a little.

"My lady, shall we go and look through the music room so that we can choose songs for the celebrations?" There was a small antechamber where I stored my sheet music, together with my records of what I had played for her when she was entertaining. She waved her hand distractedly.

"No, no. You go Kat. I am in no mood for that. Write me a list, and I will consider it later." I curtseyed and made my way through several chambers until I reached the music room, little more than a cupboard. But it was here that I had learnt my craft, and here that I wrote my simple compositions of which I was very proud.

I sat down with my lute and started playing different songs. Which ones would be fitting for this upcoming event that may or may not be a wedding? Some of the King's works would be called for, but which? O My Hart? Adew Adew Le Company? The trouble was, that some of them were written at the height of Henry's love for Katherine and maybe best avoided. I continued to play, and to experiment with my own compositions.

"Who is that playing?" A man's voice called out. A moment later, the door opened, and the King walked in. "I said, who is that playing?" he demanded. His face was very red, and he looked annoyed. "Who are you?"

I got up and dropped the deepest curtsey I had ever made. My forehead was almost touching the floor. I could not look him in the face, I had never been so close to him before, and he was quite intimidating. He poked me with his foot,

"Get up girl! Tell me, who are you, and what are you doing?" I scrambled to my feet and looked directly at him, blue eyes to blue eyes. I was surprised to see that he had been crying. I hated him for the man he was, and yet he was my King, and my father. I wished desperately that he was not my father, for that meant I was in some way like him. Of course, he didn't know about my birth. That was a secret between me and Katherine, Will and Thomas Cromwell.

"I am Kat Cooke, your Majesty. I am a musician for Lady Anne Boleyn." I did not think he remembered me from my years with Queen Katherine. He had seen me many times, but I was part of the furniture, like any other servant. It wasn't wise to remind him, so I didn't mention her.

"You've got that chord wrong," he said. "Let me show you." He bent over me and placed his hand over mine on the strings. I tried it, and he was right. He was a good musician, could have made his living at it, if he wasn't King.

"That's better, Kit, no Kat, wasn't it? You are not bad for a girl." He stood up again and wiped his eyes. "Kat, I am an ordinary man," he started. I did not know where this was going. He was anything but ordinary.

"An ordinary man, who is tormented and tortured by a

girl! Kat, you would not believe how she treats me." He took the lute from me and started strumming it. "I have given her everything, the queen's apartments, the dresses, the staff. But she has sent me away because she hasn't got the jewels. She has sent me away Kat! Her King! I can see that you can't believe it." Lady Anne had obviously been angry with him, and he was feeling like a whipped little boy. The tears spilled again from his eyes and splashed on the lute.

"She is such a saint, Kat. But she can be like a demon. I tell you, she screams at me, and kicks me. Yes, she kicks me!" Discordant notes issued from the lute. "I cannot bear it Kat, that she should treat me thus." I wondered whether I should remind him that Queen Katherine would never have kicked him and decided that this was not wise.

"I've told her, I am sending for the jewels. I have ordered Katherine to give them up. Anne will have them within the week. So why is she so hard on me?" He looked at me with those piercing blue eyes, as if I had the answer to all the vagaries of the female sex. I stumbled in my reply,

"Maybe, maybe... Your Majesty, maybe she sees the jewels as proof of your love."

He looked sharply at me, thinking that I was being critical. He thought for a moment, and then gave me the benefit of the doubt.

"She needs no proof of my love. I have made that clear to her for years, in my letters, my compositions, my dedication to her and her alone." It was true, from what I had heard King Henry had not slept with another woman for years. "No matter, I have sent some gentlemen to retrieve the jewels, by force if necessary. And at last, we may be moving forward." He handed the lute back to me and got up.

"Are you married Kat? Do you have a husband at court?" He was once more a King, fully in command,

"Yes, I am married, your Majesty. My husband works for Thomas Cromwell. His name is Will."

"I think I know him Kat. He is one of the gentlemen who has gone to fetch the jewels! Now I know he has a lovely wife; I shall tell him so when I next see him! I hope you are a good, obedient wife Kat; we cannot do with rebellious women."

I muttered assent to this, but his words had completely shocked me. So, Will has gone to force Queen Katherine to give up her jewels? How could he do such a thing, especially as he knows the Queen is my mother? The King moved to the door,

"You may get about your business now Kat and go to your mistress. Be sure to play her songs of love!" With that, he chuckled slightly and left.

I couldn't help thinking about what was happening to Queen Katherine. She knew Will, knew him from when we had got married. How could he treat her so harshly? I understood that he had to obey orders from Cromwell, but to seize the Queen's jewels, in the face of her defiance, was humiliating to her. Could he not have made an excuse? It was clear he was only going to provide the backup needed should the Queen have to be forced to give up the royal collection. It hurt me to think of her reaction when she learnt that her wishes were being over-ruled, that she was being treated with so little dignity, so little respect. Did I blame Lady Anne? No, I didn't. That might seem strange, but I was beginning to see that, like Katherine, she was a victim of the King's selfishness. He had promised to marry her and had then delayed. He had said he loved her, but certainly, at first, he had kept going back to Katherine. Anne wanted those jewels as proof of his honesty and intentions. The fact that he should not treat Katherine as he did, had nothing to do with her. And, as Tom Wyatt said, she was as powerless as Katherine, dependent on the King alone to realise her ambitions.

I waited for Will in Thomas Cromwell's office. I had heard from Jane Seymour that the jewels had been taken from the Queen, who had not resisted King Henry's direct order. So, I knew that Will would be home soon. It was getting late, and there were still some clerks working in the outside office, but I went into the small chamber where Will kept his files. I waited for some time, the peace only serving to emphasise the furious anger I felt. At mid-evening, just when I was thinking I should leave, he breezed in.

"Kat! How good to see you!" His face lit up. He looked tired though, and his clothes were dusty from the road. "How did you know I was back? Just give me a minute, and we can go home together." I stiffened my back and started to speak.

"I knew you were back because I'd heard the Queen's jewels were back. You went to get them from her by force, didn't you? I cannot believe you would do such a thing to our dear Queen. To humiliate her in front of all her staff!" Will came towards me and tried to put his arm around me. I shrugged it off immediately, and he stepped back, aware that I was very angry.

"We did not have to get them by force, Kat. The Queen gave them up without resistance. It was a piece of business, that was all."

"A piece of business! Taking all she had! I don't call that business, more like threats."

"We didn't take all she had Kat. Just the jewels. She still has the fine clothes, the house, the servants."

"Oh, and that's alright, is it? She's still got food on her plate, so it doesn't matter that you have seized everything the King ever gave her!" Will took my hands in his.

"Kat, you understand that I was just following my orders. You and me, we cannot make moral decisions. We do not have that luxury."

"I can make a moral decision!" I retorted. "I will leave you and go to live with Queen Katherine. That is the moral thing to do." Before Will could speak, I heard another man's voice. Thomas Cromwell was standing in the doorway. He gave me a bleak look, and for the first time I saw that his eyes were not kind.

"Mistress Kat, you would do well to listen to your husband." His voice was icy, silky, and it made me shiver. "You cannot go and live with Katherine. You are forbidden." I stared at him. This man, who had been so kind to me, who had never spoken down to me, was now giving me orders that I would be a fool to disobey. But I couldn't help it, I had to challenge him. Surely this man who had acted like a second father to us, would see sense?

"Who forbids me?" I challenged him, my hands on my hips.

"I do," he answered coldly. "Kat, we know you are the daughter of the Queen, and that you love her. But I cannot allow you to interfere in these matters, where the whole future of England is at stake. If you were to go to Katherine, would it not be likely that the story of your birth might come out? And then Kat, if you were to be seen as a second daughter for Katherine, I would not be able to treat you so kindly. You would add complications to the situation that would need to be, let us say, removed?" He didn't speak loudly, but I sensed the incredible determination behind his words.

"What do you mean?" I said. Will looked at me anxiously. Thomas Cromwell was on the verge of becoming the most powerful man at court, barring only the King. I knew it was no good for Will's career, or for mine, to make an enemy of him. By his kindness to us, he had made us dependent on him for our lives and careers. Maybe he remembered this, for the next time he spoke he was gentler.

"I mean, Kat, that we are in difficult times. You may be surprised to know that I like and esteem Katherine. She has a great spirit. But she is on the wrong side of history, and we cannot pander to her anymore. And Kat, if you come out in support of her, you are moving from the sidelines, where you are safe, to the circle of people that are closest to the King. And in that circle, a misstep, a word out of place, can lead to death. Do you understand me? If you were to do that, I would have to remove you." I stood there, stock still as if struck by lightning. Maybe he felt sorry for me because he held his hands up.

"Kat, Will, you know I love you both. Like me, you have both made your way through merit, not blood. It pains me to tell you the brutal truth. Kat, you are a brave, bonny girl. But you need to keep quiet about your relationship to Katherine of Aragon, and Will, you need to control your wife. If you reveal your true identity, you both will set yourselves against me."

He swept out of the office, leaving me trembling. I could not believe that this man, who had always been kind to me, had threatened me like that. I turned to Will, my face white, and he took me in his arms. We stayed like that, silent, shocked, until the great clock tolled eleven.

CHAPTER

4

It wasn't the same for Will and me after that. Oh, I knew, daughter that he loved me, but he was quite able to act in ways that I shrank from. We had always thought that working for Thomas Cromwell was a great advance for him, but to me it seemed that he had been drawn into a world of double-dealing, where previous friendships counted for nothing. I didn't like that about him, and I couldn't hide it. And for Will, my connection with Queen Katherine was dangerous, and he constantly warned me against it.

One evening, we were lying together in our chamber. We had just returned from the palace and were both tired. He was twirling his finger around a lock of my hair. Soothed, I lay there watching him.

"I do love you Kat," he whispered. "I don't want to fight with you." I turned on my side and looked him directly in the face.

"I don't want us to fight. I hate it that Cromwell thinks you should control me." Will laughed softly.

"As if I could, my love. I want you as you are, free and fiery." He looked thoughtful, "But Kat, please understand that my career is in the balance. If I do well over the next year, I will progress, and our lives will get so much better. We can't risk that by being linked to the old Queen's party. And it isn't just our jobs, Kat. It's dangerous, you know Cardinal Wolsey was set to be executed? Thomas More is at risk. The King puts people to death if they oppose him, you know that. You can't defend her. In fact, for now, try not to think of her. Once the King is safely married, it should get easier, I promise."

I kissed him on the lips,

"I know that Will, and I promise I will be careful." He smiled warmly at me.

"I trust you, my love, and we will get through this together." I leant over and kissed him. I felt him becoming excited.

"Come here and let's make a baby." He rolled over on top of me, and started to push up my night shift.

"Take this off. I want to see you, all of you." I pulled my shift off. "You're so beautiful, I love every part of you," he said, tracing my breasts, moving steadily towards my belly. I groaned softly and raised my hips up to him. I watched as he took his nightshirt off, shivering to see his erect penis. Even now, it was marvellous that this man loved me, and wanted to possess me. When I was in bed with him, I would do anything he wished. I adored the feel of his hard body on top of me, his penis pushing inside me. I twined my arms around him and pulled him deeper and deeper inside me. At last, shuddering, we both came to a climax. We both cried and kissed each other and eventually slept.

We were both still living at Thomas Cromwell's house at Austin Friars. We were amicable enough with him, although we didn't talk as much. But I could not forget what Cromwell had said to me. It was a threat, no doubt about it. A threat to harm me if I was to start openly supporting Queen Katherine, my mother. His words went round and round in my mind. Every time I saw him, sitting mildly at his table, drinking his favourite Italian wine, I would remember the cruelty in his eyes that terrible night. He had always been kind to me, amused by my forthrightness, and understanding of my intelligence. And he continued to be easygoing and pleasant when we spent time together. But I knew now I was right to be frightened of him. He was like one of the lions that lived at the Tower. They seemed gentle creatures, dozing in the heat. But give them a goat to kill, and they would tear it to pieces. I knew that if I went against him, there would be a terrible price to pay. I was too frightened to pay that price, so things continued much as they had been. But underneath the jokes, the generosity and the civility of the man, I saw a ruthlessness that scared me.

Will was kept busy by Cromwell, drafting parts of the legislation that would go before Parliament to end the right of appeal to the Pope, making King Henry the ultimate authority in the church in England. We didn't see each other much. When we were in bed together, we loved each other. The trouble was that it happened less and less. I didn't like to admit it, but I regretted giving him my word that I would not defend my mother. She, who was as much a part of me as he was. And I resented being made to choose. Oh, we didn't argue. But we spoke less and less. One afternoon, while I was playing in Lady Anne's chamber, a messenger came and told me there was a man asking for me. She gave me permission to go down,

"Don't be long! I need you here!" I hurried through the chambers, down the stairs, across the yard, and to the gatehouse. Tom Cooke was waiting there, Will's father and the man who had brought me up with Will. I felt a pang of guilt when I saw him. It had been several months since we met. Queen Katherine had encouraged him to visit me and had regularly asked me about him. But Lady Anne was a different woman altogether. Not that she was unkind. But her mind was so full of the great venture she was undertaking, that there was no room for consideration for others. It took all her energy to jump every hurdle that was placed in front of her. If she ever wondered if it was worth it, she would remember her mission, to bring reform to the church and to make the word of God accessible to everyone. She was completely sincere in this, I knew, but it left her no time for niceties. I decided that this time I would risk her displeasure. I rushed up to him and hugged him, then pulled him towards the Great Hall, where we could find somewhere to talk.

"How are you? It has been months since I saw you!" The words were tumbling out of me, I was so pleased to see him. But he looked older, and his hair was going grey.

"I am good, thank you Kat. Still working hard. But my master has engaged a young lad to work with me, and so I leave much of the heavy work to him." He looked at me with concerned eyes.

"Kat, Will visited me last week," he said heavily. I looked sharply at him. Normally, Will and I saw him together. Will had said nothing to me about this visit.

"He didn't tell me," I replied, "I would have come if I had known." Tom shrugged his shoulders,

"There was a reason he came alone Kat. He wanted to talk to me, as his father. He told me things are not good between you." I flushed and looked down at the floor,

"They have been better," I admitted, "but I am sure it will pass. We are both working so hard, we get very tired, and then cross words are spoken." Tom took my hands in his.

"Kat, remember that for me, you are still my daughter, and I will always love you as a father would. Today, I want to speak with you as a father would, when he sees that things are going wrong. Will told me how upset he is. You are criticising him and the work he does, and it hurts him." I sighed, wishing that Will had not involved his father. "Kat, he is working hard to build a future with you. That is what is most important for him. You may not like what he must do, but it is all for you."

"But he acts against Queen Katherine, whom I love dearly. I find it so hard to accept that," I cried out. Tom did not know that Queen Katherine was my mother. Will and I had decided that for his own sake, he should not be given that dangerous secret. Tom squeezed my hands tightly.

"Your loyalty does you credit Kat, and I love you for it. But remember, we are ordinary folk. What loyalty does Queen Katherine bear towards you?" I wanted to shout out that I would always be in her heart, but I couldn't. "We have to go with the tide. I loved Queen Katherine, as you know. But she is part of the past now. If Will wants to get on, he needs to work with Cromwell. And Cromwell, of course, is working to make Lady Anne the Queen."

"I just wish he had a bit more backbone about him and would turn down some of the jobs Cromwell asks him to do," I said petulantly.

"So, do you want to live like your mother lived?" He corrected himself, "Like Joan lived? Do you want to live in a tenement with no garden, no glazed windows, and people every side of you? Don't you understand Kat? Will is working so that you will never have to endure what she did." I felt a stab of grief at the thought of the woman who had brought me up as a mother, although she had not been my birth mother. She had never complained, although her life had been very hard.

"I know that Tom, but I wish it were different." Tom looked at me clear-eyed.

"Be more understanding," he said, "and remember that you too are working with Lady Anne. I can't see the difference myself."

"The difference is that I am not doing anything to harm Queen Katherine," I spluttered. "Surely you can see that!"

"What I can see Kat, is a young man working day and night to build a life with you. Some of the jobs he does are not to his taste. But Kat, it is only the rich who can afford to have morals. Remember that." He rose to his feet, kissed me on the cheek, and made to leave.

"He loves you Kat," he said. "I will see you together soon, I hope."

But I didn't see Tom again for a long time. I was working hard, in attendance to Lady Anne almost every day. She liked me to play in the background while she met with courtiers, wrote and read letters from her contacts. The meeting in Calais between the English and the French was very important to her. She was always a friend of France.

But it was about more than the country where she had spent seven years of her younger life. Lady Anne needed powerful friends abroad. The Holy Roman Emperor, Charles V, was Queen Katherine's nephew, and there was the threat of war if Henry did divorce her. But if Anne could persuade him to make an alliance with France, then Charles V wouldn't dare to send his warships. So, Anne, clever Anne, was working hard to become friends with the French ambassador.

Gilles de la Pommeraye was a small, wiry man with a short-trimmed beard and clean white hands. One evening after a hunt, where he had ridden with Lady Anne, I can remember playing for them both. King Henry was in a meeting with Cromwell, so it was just Anne and de la Pommeraye, with their respective servants. They had eaten and were drinking hippocras. The sweet almonds lying in a silver bowl were left untouched. Gilles did not enjoy them, and Anne was always careful not to eat too much.

"I have a surprise for you, Monsieur," Anne smiled and clicked her fingers. One of the ladies hurried out of the chamber and returned with a page who was carrying two large packages. The lady herself was burdened with a hunting horn.

"These are to remind you of our time together in the hunting field," Anne said, as the horn and the two packages were placed beside the ambassador. He clucked and laughed in appreciation as he discovered a green hunting coat made in the finest English wool and a hat to match.

"Madame, I thank you, you do me much honour," the little man said, holding up the coat in the light of the candles, so he could better examine it. "This is fine work indeed, and the cloth is the best I have seen." He was handed the horn, and blew somewhat weakly into it, yielding a sound that would not rally a puppy, let alone a pack of hounds. Purkoy barked angrily at it and made for the ambassador. Hurriedly, he put down the horn. Purkoy sniffed it and then cocked his leg. Gilles stifled a giggle and turned his attention back to Lady Anne.

"That is not all, ambassador," She pointed again to the page, who left the chamber quickly and returned a moment later, pulling a greyhound puppy on a leash. Immediately, Purkoy started to bark and ran over towards the small, shivering pup who was whimpering loudly. Lady Anne spoke above the fracas,

"Monsieur, meet Blanche, your new companion." Gilles looked nonplussed, and rather reluctantly reached out to take the leash. But then Purkoy jumped vigorously on top of little Blanche and put his front legs on her back. It wasn't clear whether he wanted to attack her or mate with her. Gilles made a sound of disgust and let go of the leash, looking as if this gift was not one he would relish. Purkoy dropped down from Blanche and both dogs ran madly around the room, barking loudly. I couldn't help it. I smiled. Luckily, Lady Anne didn't see me.

"She will settle down soon, I am sure," Lady Anne reassured him. But Gilles did not look convinced. Disappointed that her gift had gone down so poorly, Lady Anne called to the page, who captured Blanche and took her from the chamber.

"You may take her when you leave," Anne told him. Gilles looked uncomfortable but thanked her politely. He wiped his face with his handkerchief and took a long drink from his goblet. Lady Anne smiled, waited a moment, then moved the conversation on to the English visit to France.

"I am so looking forward to being in *la belle France* again, ambassador. For me, you are the most civilised country in Europe." Gilles de la Pommeraye nodded slowly, acknowledging the truth of what she was saying.

"You know that I was at the French court for many years," Anne continued, "and I look forward to meeting with old friends when I return." The ambassador coughed.

"I am sure there will be many old friends to welcome you, my lady." For Anne, this answer was not enough.

"I particularly hope to see some of the ladies of the French court with whom I spent so much time. I owe them so much." Gilles tensed up. I could tell he didn't want to have to tackle the subject in detail.

"I am sure you will, my lady, those ladies who are well enough to travel. It is a bad time of year for travelling, and the health of some ladies is poor." Anne frowned. She had been expecting this, and yet it was a disappointment. Being Anne, she didn't let it go,

"So, you mean that I will not meet with the French ladies? Is that so?" King Henry had told her she was going to France as his partner and would be received as such. But the reported reluctance of the French ladies to meet her suggested that they still thought of her as the King's mistress. Gilles spread out his hands and grimaced.

"My lady, you will meet with all of the French lords, every-one!"

"But not their wives and daughters! Why is that so, ambas-sador? Do they not think me fit to meet their women? Do they think I will dishonour them?" Anne's voice got louder, and some of the servants at the far end of the room looked up. "Is it because they think I am the King's mistress? Is that it? Because I tell you, ambassador, I am as pure as the day I was born. I am the King's love, not his whore!" Gilles flinched at that word and held out a soothing hand.

"I who know you, know that you are the most virtuous lady in Christendom. I will speak to the French King. Give them time, my lady." Anne pushed his hand away; her breath was coming in rapid gasps now. Purkoy came up to her, con-cerned, and she kicked him away.

"You, none of you, respect me. You do not believe me; you smile behind your hands at me. I tell you, I am the King's beloved!" Her voice was almost a scream. The door to the chamber opened, and Thomas Cromwell walked in without announcing himself.

"My lady, what is amiss?" he asked, scooping up Purkoy and holding the little dog in one hand. Anne was beside herself now,

"I have been told I will not meet the French ladies. I am to be humiliated! Cromwell, this is unendurable!" She jumped to her feet and started pacing the room. None of us approached her, we knew better than to do so when she was angry. Instead, we watched as Cromwell brought Purkoy to his chest and started stroking him gently. As the dog calmed, so did Lady Anne. After a moment, Cromwell spoke, quietly and deliberately.

"My lady, I came to tell you that the arrangements are well underway for the visit. You will be treated with every honour, I am assured. It is simply a matter of protocol. Once you are married to the King, every lady in Europe will be desperate to meet you." Anne clutched onto the back of a chair, trying to control her breathing.

"Here, boy, bring my lady some brandy!" Cromwell ordered, and a page boy vanished, only to reappear a couple of minutes later with a bottle and a small glass, which he set down on a side table. Deliberately, Cromwell set Purkoy down on the floor and took Anne by the arm. He brought her round to sit on the chair, and then poured her some brandy. Anne took it and started to sip. Without being asked, Cromwell took a chair and sat beside her.

"My lady," he said, leaning forward. "You should know that the King is ready to put the plan into action." De la Pommeraye started forward, looking at Anne curiously. But Anne ignored him and brought her eyes up to meet Cromwell's.

"You mean?" she whispered. Cromwell nodded grimly,

"You know what I mean, my lady. But we must, as always, proceed with stealth. Let us not be tormented over a few ladies." De la Pommeraye interrupted,

"Believe me, my lady. France will welcome you with open arms, as our faithful friend and ally." He smiled at her, twisting the end of his moustache with his fingers. Anne stayed silent for a moment, thinking. She was working out what would bring her the most advantage, I could see. Eventually, she spoke,

"I see, yes. Nothing must stand in the way of the alliance, even a few little minds." Cromwell smiled a little slyly, and de la Pommeraye stood up and bowed.

"As you say, my lady. Little minds. Let us be broad-minded about this, eh? You are a daughter of France; you know all about that!" Anne looked mollified and held out her hand to the ambassador. He kissed it, then turned to collect his coat and hat, carrying them out with the horn balanced on top.

"Don't forget your dog!" Cromwell called after him. He sounded so kind, so concerned. But I was certain he despised the little man for his inability to handle Anne.

After he left, Cromwell took Anne to one side, and they conferred quietly for a few minutes. As he spoke to her, her face became animated. I heard her say,

"So soon!" Cromwell replied,

"Indeed, my lady. You must prepare." He rose and bowed to her before taking his leave. As he left, he caught my eye and nodded towards the door. He wanted to speak to me. I felt my heart beating hard against my chest. I had done nothing, so why did he need to speak to me? I feared him now and did not wish to spend time alone with him. I followed him, unwillingly, until we were outside and out of earshot. Cromwell sighed and put his hands on my shoulders.

"Kat, I don't want to harm you. Believe me. Forget last time. By Jesu Kat, this woman is impossible! We don't need any more complications. That is why you can't come forward for Queen Katherine." He looked back towards the door.

"How is it the case, Kat, that I love and respect the old

Queen, although I despise her faith? I would rather spend an evening with Katherine, than five minutes with Anne. She lacks civility, and she unsettles the King." I could not believe what I was hearing,

"But you and she, you have the same aims, Master Cromwell. You are working for her to become Queen!" For a moment he smiled. My forwardness had always amused him.

"At this moment in time, we are working together. We both want a new church, a new England. But, by Jesu, she is difficult! I do not love her Kat."

"Why are you telling me this?" I asked. "Why are you trusting me?" Cromwell answered briskly,

"Very simple Kat. You cannot go against me, because of what I know. And, my dear, you have the spirit of your mother about you. No one else knows, but I see it in you whenever we talk. Watch over La Boleyn Kat; tell me whenever she is unsettled. I need to be informed." He took his hands off my shoulders.

"And make up your argument with Will," he ordered. "You are making him unhappy, and his work is suffering." With that, he bowed and went on his way, his footsteps echoing on the wooden floor.

Will and I did make it up, after a fashion. The attraction between us was so great that we couldn't stay away from each other for long. But we talked less about politics and religion. We didn't want to hurt each other, you see daughter. He thought I was being impossibly idealistic and should not prate on about loyalty and friendship. I thought he had betrayed his ideals by doing Cromwell's dirty jobs. One thing I didn't like to face up to was that we were both in positions where we had to keep our thoughts private. For we were both working within the court, where ideals were a glorious fantasy, withering whenever faced by the stark light of day.

I continued my friendship with Thomas Wyatt. I liked him because he did not lie about the strange circumstances of the court. He sensed the danger that surrounded us and spoke about it in his poems. But still, he was good company, funny and self-deprecating. He was not over Anne Boleyn, he still pined for her, so I filled a gap for him. Any court ladies would have been noticed, been significant. But I, a musician, could talk with him without anyone saying a word. Except that was, when they wanted music, and Thomas and I were sitting heads together, reading poetry.

"Hey Kat, do your duty! We should all be joyful now – we want some songs to celebrate." It was George Boleyn. He had never tried to seduce me again after the night he had attacked me. His sister Anne had been very angry with him about that, and it wasn't wise to cross her. At last, the wind had turned in her direction, and every day it seemed more certain that she would become Queen. Earlier that day she had been honoured by the King in front of the whole court.

We had all been standing in the grand hall of Windsor Castle, waiting for what seemed like ages. Thomas was standing beside me, and as usual he was making me laugh.

"I told my kitchen maid they are making her a Marquise," he whispered, "and she said, 'Poor lady, I never did like those sweetmeats with almonds'." I giggled. I was sure that Thomas had made this up, but I couldn't deny it was funny. I had wondered why the King was making Anne a Marquise. Why not a Duchess? It seemed that even now, he wasn't giving her everything.

"Don't tell Lady Anne that she said that!" I warned him.

"Do you think I am a fool, Kat?" I was very tempted to agree wholeheartedly. "Of course, I will not tell Anne that my kitchen maid thinks she is a confection made of almonds." Thomas loved Anne, but he was clear-eyed about her. Having known her as a child, he saw her as Annie, the girl he had once played with. He saw her with her tantrums and her tears, her cleverness and her sincerity. I plucked at his elbow.

"Sssh, something's happening now." There was a fanfare

of trumpets, and the doors at the end of the hall opened. The court musicians struck up a march as the King strode in. He created awe as he processed through the crowds, all of us bowing and curtseying to him. He was broader now, but it suited him. He was a large man in every sense, and every inch of him glittered, from his ruby-strewn bonnet to the gold embossed leather shoes that he wore. I had no liking for him; I never had, but he was the most magnificent man I had ever encountered. I found it hard to believe that he was my father. Whereas with Queen Katherine, I loved her and was overjoyed that she had proved to be my mother, for me, with the King there was only dislike.

The King took his place on his throne, sitting in front of the royal arms of England, the lion regnant, standing beside the Welsh dragon in a field of Tudor roses. His cloth of estate shone red gold over the throne. He looked around the room, fiddled with his sleeve, and then nodded. All at once the trumpeters started another lengthier fanfare, the noise echoing around the vaulted beams.

Standing on tiptoe, I could just see Lady Anne, a small, slender figure between two ample bejewelled ladies.

"Some of these matrons, they look like old horses," whispered Tom. It was true, there was a certain kind of aristocratic lady whose long face looked designed to be disapproving. But Anne was paying them no attention. Her dark brown hair hung around her shoulders as if she were a bride. Every inch of her gown was covered in jewels. It was as if she was a bauble herself, a precious jewel meant only for the King. As she went forward, step by step, her eyes were steady on the King. It was as if there was only them in the room.

Slowly, she approached him, and as she drew near, the musicians fell silent. Stiffly, she spread her heavy skirts and knelt at his feet. He stood up as the patents were read out, granting her the title of Marquise of Pembroke for herself and her descendants in perpetuity. Then he reached out to an attendant for the crimson robe of a peer and placed it carefully around her shoulders. The attendant hovered with a cushion, on which was a heavy golden coronet, too heavy surely for her fragile neck. The King took it and put it on her head, stood back, and then returned to balance it.

Then he took Anne's hands and brought her up to face him. The whole hall erupted in cheers. Thomas even whistled, along with George Boleyn and a few other young men of the court. They spoke quietly to each other for a moment before Anne cleared her throat and projected her voice to the very rafters.

"Your Majesty, I thank you for this great honour, and I swear that I will do all in my power to serve you and follow you for all of my life." Again the hall was filled with applause. Anne smiled broadly, and then took both her arms up to her head to remove the crown. She placed it carefully back on the cushion and then curtsied again to the King. She turned and waited for her attendants to move her train behind her. It was heavy and cumbersome, but she looked as if she was a maid on May Day, light-hearted and light-headed.

Anne processed back down through the hall, followed by the page carrying her coronet. Thomas looked at me and whispered,

"Best get back Kat. We'll be on duty now." Of course, he wasn't a servant, not like me. But he knew that for courtiers like him, there was always duty to be owed to the powerful. And so, while I played, he joked and played cards with the ladies, all sitting around Lady Anne.

She had taken off the state robes and was wearing a deep blue silk gown, which emphasised the darkness of her eyes and hair. Purkoy fussed and whimpered around her skirts, and every now and then she would pat him for a moment. She looked tired now, but triumphant. Unlike almost any other woman, she had been made into a peer in her own right. She was now of a status to meet the King of France. Everything was falling into place.

I didn't go with her to Calais, her party of ladies was very small. But Thomas Wyatt was part of the large delegation that went with the King. He had represented the King before in Calais, and he knew the French well.

They were delayed coming back from Calais, due to the bad weather I was told. The court was very quiet without them, and I spent more time with Will. But there was one thing that worried me. I was sleeping with Will, making love with him almost every night, but my courses continued. Every month I would hope that maybe they would stop, and I would be with child. But nothing happened. It wasn't that I wanted a baby straight away, but the thought that we couldn't have one was disturbing. I even remembered all the fuss King Henry had made about incest causing childlessness. But with Will, it wasn't incest. We had been brought up as brother and sister, but we were not blood relatives.

It was a month until I saw Thomas again, and he was able to tell me about everything that had happened.

"It was a strange time, Kat. There she was, beautiful Annie, but only a few fine ladies to accompany her! Many of them had made excuses, I hear. But Kat, she will be married soon, I would bet on it." His voice faltered.

"I hope he takes care of her, Kat. She has such a fierce spirit. I hope he doesn't crush it." I knew he feared for her as he watched, unable to do anything to protect her. "We were in Calais for a month. Oh, he went off to meet with the French King for a few days, but most of the time they were living together. They were at the Exchequer; I don't know if you know it, Kat?" I thought back to my trip to France for the Field of Cloth of Gold. It seemed such a long time ago, and I did not remember.

"It is a palace, Kat, but the royal apartments are smaller. And her chamber was next to his. I know he had her in his bed, Kat, I just know." He played with the silver falcon on the chain around his neck. It was a jewel that he had taken from Anne, I knew, and he wore it all the time. The King had not been best pleased when he'd seen it, but there was no intimacy between Thomas and Anne nowadays, and the King knew it.

Lady Anne swept into the chamber, followed by her sister, Lady Mary, and her mother. She commanded me to play and beckoned Thomas to sit by her side. From what I could see, they were writing couplets to each other, and then reading and laughing.

"Mary, I have a yen for apples," Anne said teasingly, "what make you of that?" Lady Mary smiled delightedly,

"Dear sister, I think that God has blessed you," she replied. I could never understand these courtiers. Lady Mary had been King Henry's mistress, had borne him two children and then been abandoned. I would not have expected her to be pleased that her sister was possibly pregnant with the King's child. But then, it was all about families. And while one of the sisters was in the King's bed, the Boleyn family would prosper.

Later, as I was picking up my music, Lady Mary came to sit beside me.

"Kat, it is such a long time since we talked. It is quite lovely to see you!" She sounded truly overjoyed. She was always the easier of the two sisters to talk to. "Do you remember those times we spent together when I was bearing the King's child? He's a bonny boy now and looks just like his father." She looked at me pensively.

"I did love him you know Kat," she said. "I am happy for Anne, but that time with him, it was love." I picked up my lute. "Come to my chamber and have some wine, Kat, for old times. Anne is far too grand nowadays." I thought for a moment. It probably wasn't a good idea to get close to Mary again, but on the other hand, she might tell me more about what had happened in Calais. And whatever Mary had done, she was always good company. So I went with her to her chamber, much less magnificent than her old one had been, and a long way from the King's. I sat on the bed while she poured two goblets of wine.

"So, tell me Kat, what have you been doing with yourself? Anne tells me you are her best musician now." I shook my head.

"No, my lady. It is just that I am there to soothe her when she most needs it. I am married now, you know, to Will Cooke, who works for Master Cromwell." Lady Mary made a face.

"Then he will be a clever man, your husband? They are always the worst!" She wrinkled her nose. "But try telling that to Anne." I plucked up courage.

"Are she and the King, are they, as man and wife now?" Lady Mary laughed. I'd forgotten how generous and happy her laugh sounded.

"Oh yes, indeed they are. It was the weather in Calais that did for her. They had all the ceremonial, and he went off to meet the French King, Francois, then the French King came to visit him. Oh Kat, it was magnificent. I was part of the group; she gave me a place. If all the ladies had been there, I might not have done, but so many of them turned their noses up! But Kat, she was amazing. She didn't show anyone who she was. There were six of us, all in cloth of gold, and we were all masked. The walls of the room were covered in cloth of gold, the plates were gold, everything was gold. We had to go up to the French gentlemen and invite them to dance. Anne got King Francois, of course. He knew who she was, well, who didn't, and they spent a lot of the evening talking together. But King Henry was desperate to have her to himself, and he kept on looking at her, looking so hungrily. It reminded me of when he was in love with me, Kat." She stopped for a moment and drank again from her goblet.

"But Anne is of different metal to me, Kat. Me, I loved the man, I bore his children, and then I let him go. I wouldn't cause trouble. But Anne, she has always known that she wanted more, and now she would hold out until she got it."

"But they are not married yet, are they?" I asked.

"No, but he is too deep in to change his mind now. She is on the world stage now, as his consort. He is committed to her."

"So when did it happen?" I was curious, as was almost every other person at the court.

"We were all going to come back to England. All the ceremonies were over, we'd said goodbye, but then the most terrible storms blew in. What could they do? You cannot risk the King of England on a rough sea. So, they were stuck in that house, just the two of them, at night, with the wind howling around her bedchamber. She told me that she was having nightmares, that she was frightened about what she was getting herself into."

"She said that to you?" I was incredulous.

"Don't forget, I am her elder sister, I carried her around as a baby. She may think I am feckless, but she cannot keep a secret from me, not if she is troubled."

"But she is frightened?" Lady Mary laughed.

"Of course, she is. She has made herself into the most important person at court, apart from the King. She knows that position is risky." Mary drank again from her goblet.

"That night, she couldn't sleep, and he came to her and comforted her. There wasn't any intention to yield to him, but in the end, she told me that was what happened. He can be a kind man, often, and she needs kindness." I glanced at Mary.

"She has everything anyone could want; how can she lack for kindness?" Mary sighed.

"She is not like me, an unimportant girl who can be kissed and forgotten. Yes, she has the King of France, she has us, her family. But she knows that we are fair-weather friends, even me. She has made herself too important for our kindness, and she knows that."

CHAPTER 5

Anne was pregnant. She was eating apples by the pound and her face was rounder. But any softness in her expression was not echoed by her temper. The legislation to make Henry the leader of the church in England was still going through Parliament, and as far as we knew, no marriage had happened. Thomas told me that he suspected they had married privately, but could not make it public, as Henry still happened to be married to Katherine. So, Lady Anne was still uncertain, and three months pregnant with Henry's child.

She took it out on everyone. One afternoon I was playing the lute, a soft and gentle Benedictus by Isaac, to lull her and the baby. She sat back in her chair with her eyes half closed. All at once, the atmosphere changed. She sat straight upright and pointed straight at me.

"Kat, how dare you!" I stopped, confused by her sudden accusation. "How dare you play that lute? It is desperately out of tune! Every note hurts my ears. I cannot bear it. You would imagine that you of all people might have some musical intuition and avoid this assault." She got up from her chair and strode over to me, grabbing the lute from my hands and throwing it on the floor. It crashed and splintered. I was dumbfounded, and near tears. That lute was mine, and my dearest possession. And she had destroyed it. Yes, I could use the lutes that were in the cupboards of the court, but they didn't have the mellow tone, the silken feel of the wood, that my own had.

"That is the trouble with all of you! You make me suffer; you do not help me as you should." Purkoy jumped up and started barking. He barked loudly at the window, then turned and ran up to me, snarling at my skirts. Thomas Wyatt looked at me concernedly and made to pick up the little dog. He took him, holding him at arms' length and went to the door.

"How dare you manhandle Purkoy?" Anne screamed at him. "Put him down at once!" Thomas put the dog down, stepped back and bowed his head. He knew Anne, and he knew that arguing with her when she was like this had no point. I, however, was not as wise.

"My lady, I am sorry, but the lute was in tune." I knew that what I said was true.

"But it was not in tune for me, Kat, and you are supposed to be my musician! I hate you, always creeping about. And you are too friendly with Thomas Wyatt. Don't think I haven't seen you skulking in corners!" All the ladies were transfixed by the scene, watching Anne intently as she berated me. "That is it, you are not fit to be a musician. Leave me – I never want to see you again!" I felt anger rise within me,

"That is unjust! I have served you loyally, and what am I to do now? Live on the streets?"

"Be a spy for Thomas Cromwell," Anne shouted. "You are one already. I hate you!"

I started to cry. I felt as if she had hit me in the stomach, it was the intense physical pain of being attacked. I was defenceless, paralysed by the shock of what had happened. Shaking, I stood there looking at her. She could not do this to me. She could not hurt me so terribly. Staring at me, she saw that I was crying. I curtseyed shakily and made for the door. I thought that I would never see her again. I was telling myself that it was for the best, that I couldn't serve someone who hurt me like that, and that Will and I would find a way to survive. My mother would never have treated me like that. She would never have treated the lowliest chambermaid like that. I felt a hatred towards Anne overtake me, and I longed to reject her publicly. I went to pick up my lute, then remembered its mangled remains were on the floor. Slowly, I walked through all the ladies to the door. I remember that their faces were cold. They did not feel anything for me. Another servant that could be summarily dismissed.

I opened the door and walked through it. There were two guards on the other side, and I passed them without a glance. I got into the next chamber before I really broke down, sinking onto the floor and weeping. What was I to do now? My relationship with Will was up and down. I had lost my lute, and with that, my means of earning a living. And I had lost all connection with the court. I sat with my skirts spread out on the rushes and sobbed for everything I had lost.

"Here, Kat, come here." Thomas Wyatt was standing over me, his hand outstretched. "Hush now, come with me." His eyes were warm, and full of concern. I felt stupidly grateful to him for his humanity, but my pride had been deeply hurt.

"Go back to Lady Anne, Thomas. It will do you no good to be with me. We are too close, she says." He pulled me up and gently used his hand to wipe my tears from my face. Then, as delicate as a breath, his lips brushed mine. Being hurt, I felt his affection warming me, and I welcomed it. But he was a courtier, he would hurt me like Anne had.

"Don't stay here with me. Get back to your lady!" He shook his head and smiled.

"I won't go back without you, Kat." I started to protest, but he shushed me,

"Lady Anne has sent me, Kat." I stared at him in disbelief.

"You heard what she said, Thomas, she doesn't want to see

me again." He took my face in his hands,

"You know what she is like, Kat. She is so scared, and her temper is frayed. She lashes out, like an animal at bay. And then, minutes later, she regrets it. She is waiting for you in her privy chamber. Please come with me, Kat, she is calling for you."

"She doesn't want me; she just wants someone she can shout at." Thomas kissed me again on the lips. For a moment, he lingered, and then he said quietly,

"No, Kat, she trusts you. You're not one of these court ladies who would stab her in the back as soon as Henry tires of her."

"She thinks I'm a spy for Thomas Cromwell," I said, unwilling to be brought round.

"She doesn't! She admitted to me just now that she didn't think that. Yes, you are his protege, but why should that be a problem? Soon, he will make King Henry head of the church, and she will become Queen." He took my hand and spoke beseechingly.

"Please, Kat, come and see her, for me?" I allowed him to lead me through the chamber, back to the door, and past the guards. I followed him with the eyes of all the ladies watching me, not acknowledging them, my head held high. Then we were in Anne's privy chamber.

She was lying on the bed, her face buried in the pillow. Her silken skirts were crumpled, and her hood was crooked. Thomas shut the door.

"Kat is here, my lady. She has agreed to come and talk with you." There was a sniffle of tears coming from the bed. "I will leave you now." Thomas bowed and went to the door.

"No!" I cried. I didn't want him to leave us alone. He held up his hand and spoke firmly,

"Kat, I must go. Lady Anne wishes to see you alone." He opened the door, gave me a small smile, and left.

I stood beside the bed for some minutes, watching the

huddled figure on the bed. Outside, there was the hum of the courtiers' voices and some laughter. But within the room, it was almost silent except for the muffled sounds of tears. At last, her head rose from the pillows, she turned and looked at me. Her eyes were red and puffy, her cheeks tear stained. She looked a world away from the grand lady she was. Rather, she was like a little girl who'd had a temper tantrum. I waited.

"Kat, come and sit beside me." She sat up and patted the bed. I was hurting too much.

"How can you expect me to do that, my lady? You've told me you hate me." Anne's face crumpled.

"Kat, I am sorry. I didn't mean it. You know, sometimes, when passions stir inside me, I cannot help it. I hit out at people. I do it to the King even, and sometimes he runs from me because he cannot stand it." I stood stiffly by the bed, refusing to sit down. Anne flinched at the sight of my face and started to cry again. I would not go to her. At that moment I wanted nothing more than to be away from her, this woman who had wounded me so badly.

"Kat, have I hurt you? Please don't say I have. I hate myself!" I sighed. I'd seen her like this with other people, but she'd never attacked me before. No wonder her emblem was the falcon, for she was fierce. "Please, Kat, come here. Have some wine." I shook my head.

"No, I don't want anything." Her face was desolate, utterly miserable.

"Kat, I will buy you the best lute in all of England. I will have a master craftsman to make it. And I will tell him to make you two, so that you have one for here and one for home." I turned to her, tears pouring down my face.

"You think that would make it alright? You are rich now, and you think you can buy me? I always believed in you. You talk about the equality of people's access to God, and I thought that you valued me as a person, in spite of the difference in our rank. But you don't really believe that, do you? Queen

Katherine may hold old-fashioned ideas, but she would never treat me like that!" I thought that Anne would jump on me for mentioning Katherine's name, but she didn't. She looked down at her hand, covered in rings except for the all-important gold wedding band. Then she started talking, very quietly, almost as if to herself.

"She was brought up to this. She has the family, the tradition, the power, all behind her. She can afford to be kind. But me! I have no one at my back. My family will support me so long as the King stays sweet. The French will do the same. But if I lose the King, then they will be turning their backs, and it will not be long before they are ordering assassins to find me." She sounded so bleak that despite my anger, I could not help but interrupt,

"No, my lady, they would not do that. They esteem you highly." Anne wiped her eyes and looked directly at me.

"So long as the King loves me Kat, so long as he loves me..."

"But he does love you," I said, aware that I didn't sound very certain.

"Yes, for now, he loves me. But will he love me tomorrow? That is why I must marry him, have a son, establish a new church, all in five minutes! If I can do that, then I will be safe. But you can see, I am impatient. I don't know how much time I have, and at night I don't sleep for the thoughts that race through my head. That is why, Kat, I was so unkind. Your lute was out of tune, just a little." I wanted to tell her that it was her hearing that was out of tune, but my returning good sense stopped me. "Normally, Kat, that would not offend me. I know how to be gracious." I knew I had to assent to this,

"Yes, indeed my lady. You have been very gracious to me."

"But Kat, when I haven't slept, and I am wondering when he will marry me, the slightest scratch, the smallest squall, brings my panic to the surface. I feel like my head has been taken over by it. I cannot help it, Kat, please believe me." She made a regretful face at me, like a small girl who didn't know what she was doing. I had to forgive her.

The thing was, daughter, she was not a bad woman. Passionate, intelligent, more principled than all those around her. But she was playing a dangerous game. And it told on her, yes, it told on her.

In due course, two beautiful lutes arrived for me, one made of yew and one of still-scented rosewood. The rosewood lute had a wonderfully mellow tone, and I kept it at court, where I could serenade lovers and intriguers. The yew, more service-able, stayed at home, where I used it to try out compositions and, occasionally, to play for the household.

Will and I lived more or less contentedly. We were inti-mate sometimes, but less often than before. We didn't talk to each other much. We were often tired, and our hearts were full of what was happening at court. We wanted a baby, but one didn't seem to be coming. We were sitting in the kitchen one day, drinking small ale and eating freshly baked bread, when he asked me about my courses,

"Were you not due this week, Kat? Has there been no sign?" I was surprised. I didn't think he was that involved with my cycle. But I had to disappoint him.

"There was nothing till this morning; I was just a few days late." He put his arms around me and kissed me briefly on the mouth.

"It will happen soon enough, my Kat. Maybe it is good that it has not happened yet. The King's Great Matter has pre-occupied me for so long. But soon he will be married, and we can get back to a normal life. Imagine it, Kat. We can have our own house, with a small plot at the back for herbs. On sunny evenings, we can walk down by the river, sometimes go to a fair. We will have a good life Kat, I promise."

The truth was, although Will and I wanted children, we were both relieved that I hadn't fallen pregnant so far. Will's dream of our own house didn't call me then. I had served

Queens. It felt like a step downwards to serve my own husband and children. And Cromwell's instruction to Will to control his own wife made me feel very uneasy. Of course, Will was definite that I could do as I pleased. But I had seen often enough what happened to women when babies arrived. And I didn't want it, not then. Don't feel that we didn't welcome you when you arrived, daughter, despite the difficult circumstances of your birth. But we wanted to build an ordinary, stable life for you to grow up in, not a life dogged by plots, religious disputes and hurried love affairs. We wanted what Tom and Joan had enjoyed, a life of love and hard work. The only problem with that was that, as with all ordinary people, their lives were dictated by forces greater than them. When the sweating sickness came to London, Joan could not leave for the country, as the moneyed classes did. And Tom had to follow his master and live away from his family. Sometimes it seemed that no matter what you had, or where you were born, an ordinary, stable life was only a pleasant dream.

Nobody knew exactly when Anne and the King were married. It was sometime in the first months of the New Year, and it was before the legislation had passed through Parliament to enable Henry to do as he wished. But he knew that he could not afford to wait until then. Anne's pregnancy was beginning to show, and she was alternately furious and exultant in mood. The King treated her with exaggerated courtesy, and would not gainsay her, no matter how unreasonable she was being. He saw her belly, and he knew that she was carrying his heir. Nothing could be allowed to upset her or cause any problems in the pregnancy. And by Easter, the formalities had been completed, and Henry acknowledged Anne as his queen.

"He's told Queen Katherine she will be called the Dowager Princess of Wales," Lady Jane Seymour whispered to me. "Lady Willoughby told me. But Queen Katherine will not accept the title and expects all her staff to call her Queen." Jane and I still referred to Katherine as the Queen. We had served her so many years and respected her greatly. We could not change the habits of a lifetime in five minutes. Of course, when anyone else was around, we did not talk of Queen Katherine, but when we were alone, we did. We remembered her dignity and her kindness. Life had been so different then, without the screaming matches, but also without the passion. For the King and his new Queen were overwhelmingly, crazily, in love. And now they no longer had to hide they kissed and flirted in front of everyone. Henry would tease Anne about her status as a Marquise and tell her that he was simply her poor servant, whereas she was so very wealthy,

"And all in your own right, Madam." He grabbed her hand and kissed it longingly, staring into her eyes. These newlyweds ignored their most powerful and respected courtiers, advisers and families. They had waited more than four years for this, and now it was all opening up in front of them. It was as if they were both twenty. But had they forgotten? Henry was in his forties, and Anne had passed her thirtieth birthday. There was no time to waste.

So, at Easter, Anne went to Mass as Queen, in cloth of gold. Just as Katherine had been, she was prayed for and deferred to. No one in the land could touch her now.

By Whitsuntide, Anne was six months pregnant, but there was one more ceremony to go through before she could withdraw and rest before the birth of her baby. It wasn't enough that Queen Anne was now acknowledged as the King's wife. She must be crowned, and anointed, just as he and Katherine had been at the beginning of his reign.

I tell you, daughter, I have never seen such a display on the Thames as when Queen Anne was carried, with the tide, from Greenwich to the Tower of London. There were hundreds of crafts, about one hundred larger boats, including Anne's own barge, the King's barge, the Lord Mayor's barge, and the barges that the lesser ladies and servants were carried in. Then there were over two hundred smaller boats all tagging along beside.

I was in one of these, with Thomas Cromwell and his household. As a musician, I was not part of the new Queen's retinue, but in Thomas Cromwell's barge, we were able to come close to the royal barges, and see what I couldn't have seen if I'd been crammed in behind or one of the thousands of people lining each bank of the river Thames, children on their fathers' shoulders, women standing on tiptoe, all to catch a glimpse of their new Queen.

"She is big with child," Cromwell observed. The rich red gold gown she was wearing did not conceal her growing belly, rather it emphasised it. It was her triumph. Helped on by some ladies, she took her seat in the main body of the vessel, underneath a canopy bearing her coat of arms. Cromwell commented wistfully,

"I remember when my Lizzie was pregnant. She was sick all the time. She could not have borne the motion of the water." Cromwell looked very sad. His wife, whom he had adored, had been taken by the sweating sickness four years ago, followed soon after by his two daughters. Only his son, Gregory, remained, sitting near the front of the barge now, shouting and singing along with the King's musicians. That was one reason why Cromwell had been so kind to Will, and to some of the other young men in his household. Apart from Gregory, they were his family now. He had been such a devoted husband and father. I wondered what losing them had done to him. Of course, he didn't show it, but life can become very cheap when you have lost those you love. "Will she get through all the ceremonies," Will asked, "being so great with child?" He looked at me, maybe hoping that I would soon be in the same situation. I smiled tensely at him, and he squeezed my arm apologetically.

"Soon, Kat, soon," he whispered. Cromwell smiled cynically and clapped Will on the shoulder.

"She will get through every ceremony, that one. She will get through anything to get what she wants." I knew Cromwell was right, and now she was so close to being an anointed queen, she would not falter.

Daughter, I will be frank. I have never liked the Tower of London. It was dark and inconvenient, unlike the lovely Greenwich Palace. Even then, before King Henry's murderous sprees, it was associated with death. The little princes, who vanished fifty years ago while held there. The mad King Henry the Sixth, killed in his sleep. The young Earl of Warwick, killed for no other reason than his royal blood. But it was a royal palace, as well as a fortress, and the tradition was that the king or queen to be crowned would spend the night before the coronation there. Actually, Anne was going to stay there for two nights, closeted with the King. Wanting his consort to be housed magnificently and with all due honour, he had ordered the renovation of the queen's apartments. But still, it was surrounded by high walls, and the pleasure gardens were sparse and neglected. When Anne looked out of her window, all she would see was a grey fortress, built in an earlier age, and weathered by many wars. Did she enjoy that time with Henry, worshipping her every move? Or was she plagued by sleeplessness and fear? Knowing her, I thought that it was probably both. She was eager to be recognised as Queen, eager to change the things she knew needed changing. But she was leading a lion by a silken rope, daughter, and she knew it. I would not have been surprised if she had seen those nights out, wakeful and on guard.

Although the King had been with her at the Tower, he did not take part in the Coronation itself. She carried all of that herself, brave, six months pregnant and triumphant. Will and I watched from the street, along with all of London. Some people were exultant, heralding a new beginning. Others said vile things about Anne, calling her the greatest whore in Christendom, or the King's Concubine. But whether you were for her, or against her, the one thing you couldn't do was ignore her.

On that day, she dazzled. Her litter was open, carried by white horses. She shone inside it, like a jewel in a satin casket. She was wearing white, which was shot through with gold, shimmering and catching the sunlight. Her coif was in the French style, white satin, crisscrossed with gold. Over it, she wore a golden coronet. She was smiling and looking all around her. There were cheers, some people were holding back, but she was pleased to acknowledge them.

As I watched her, she suddenly sat up straight and looked directly at me. She waved for a moment, and then made a motion of strumming a lute. Again, she smiled at me. Ever since she had attacked me and then wept her repentance, she had given me special attention. It was as if I was bound to her, that because I had forgiven her, she considered herself in my debt. In this way, she was very different from many other aristocrats. She had treated me appallingly, but she had rec-ognised that, and felt bad about it. And although I had been terribly hurt by her, in the end it was easy to forgive her. Like Thomas Wyatt, I was enthralled by her.

Cromwell was invited to the Coronation. Some courtiers were reluctant to go, but not him. He would not turn up this invitation, and the chance to move yet higher in the King's estimation. But his wasn't an uncritical eye. He told Will, who later told me, that when Anne prostrated herself in front of the altar, she looked, "as like a spinning top with her belly on the floor and her arms and legs splayed out like wings. But" he said, "she behaved with dignity and some grace. Now she is in place, and Cranmer is the Archbishop of Canterbury, let us hope we can proceed apace with reform."

Lady Jane Seymour was less diplomatic. Like me, she loved the old Queen. Katherine of Aragon was in internal exile, and it was as if she had never occupied the throne. But Jane remembered her. For Jane, Katherine was the only true queen, and Anne Boleyn was indeed a concubine. There were others who agreed with her.

"Half the ladies of the court found some excuse not to be there," she told me. "The King's sister, Mary, stayed away with her daughter, and I couldn't see the Duchess of Norfolk. They are refusing to acknowledge her! They will stay away from court until she falls from grace. It won't be long." I protested,

"Jane, that is an unwise thing to say. Don't speak to anyone except me in this way. You could be in danger. She is the Queen now."

"Don't worry. I am careful. You don't count, Kat." I smiled sarcastically.

"Yes, I know. I am just part of the background."

"I didn't mean it like that, you know. I mean I can trust you." She smiled at me, and for a moment her plain face looked almost beautiful.

"Did you know the King commented on my Coronation gown, at the banquet afterwards? He said that the green silk matched my eyes. I was so embarrassed." She blushed a deep red. I wondered if she had ever received a compliment before.

"Just be careful Jane. The King is in love with Anne, but if she catches him flirting with you, it will be you who suffers."

"He likes me, I think. But don't tell anyone else!"

"I don't repeat what you say, Jane. But you should still be careful."

"I will, I promise." Jane clutched at my arm and suddenly whispered to me,

"Kat, you should have seen her Coronation robes, that red, it made her look quite washed out. And then, you know what happened? It was at the end of the ceremony, when she was processing out. She couldn't see her feet with the baby bump, and she trod on the hem of her robe. She pulled the gown up, and it tore, Kat. It wasn't a large tear, but still. Oh, she carried on as if nothing had happened, and everyone was looking at her crown. Not many people noticed, but I did. It is an omen, Kat; I am sure of that."

"That's just superstition, Jane. It wasn't an omen. Her

gown was a touch too long, that was all." Jane wouldn't agree, "I know you are against superstitions and saints and omens – but Kat, this means something. I am certain of it." I didn't challenge her. Lady Jane Seymour was very much a traditionalist. She wouldn't put herself in danger. She would always go along with whatever the King decreed. But for her, deep in her heart, she loved the Old Queen, the old religion and the old certainties.

CHAPTER 6

Queen Anne was not well. Her ankles had swollen, and she kept fainting. She could not keep food down. Along with all her household, I suffered. She never attacked me directly again, but she would set me to play some music, then change her mind and tell me to stop. Later, she would ask me to play again. I remember one afternoon, when, thinking I had been dismissed, I had gone to find Will, only to be tapped on the shoulder by one of Anne's ladies, who said she was asking where I was, and who had given me permission to leave. I shrugged my shoulders and returned, and she did not upbraid me. Instead, she called out to me as I entered,

"Kat, where have you been! I am desperate for dancing!" She ordered all the ladies to get up, and I played Tandernaken, a lively tune by Agricola. As I played, she tapped her foot vigorously to the music. I have often wondered whether it was listening to dancing while in the womb that led to her daughter, Queen Elizabeth's love of dancing.

But there, I've jumped ahead of myself. The truth was that the King and Queen were both certain they were having a boy. King Henry had ordered great celebrations to be in place when the prince was born. He spent much of his time with

Queen Anne, treating her as if her belly contained his greatest treasure. Which of course, it did. Every time he saw the material of Anne's skirt jump, as the baby kicked at the wall of the womb, Henry would clap, and roar,

"He is a jouster, our son. See how he kicks on his horse." Anne looked none too pleased at being compared to a horse, but she was too tired nowadays to make a scene. Henry surrounded her with an obsessive caution, forbidding her to walk outside, telling her not to eat red meat, "as it makes the babe too restless." He had always been interested in herbal remedies, and spent many hours concocting infusions for heartburn, headache, and an easy labour. These he would present to Anne each morning and expect her to drink them immediately. Screwing up her face, she normally obliged, except one morning when she had a headache. He brought her a bottle of crushed lavender, rue, and sage. She poured it into a glass, sipped a little and then wrinkled up her nose.

"This is disgusting, I cannot drink it." Henry looked crestfallen. His potions were what was going to keep the unborn prince healthy.

"Try to drink it, sweetheart. It will ease your head." Anne sipped again, and then pushed the glass away. Immediately she got up and ran out of the room. When she returned it was clear that she had been sick. She glared at Henry, took the bottle and poured it out over the floor. He looked as if he was about to burst, but he knew the importance of keeping a pregnant woman calm, so he just shrugged his shoulders.

"I will find something else for you, sweetheart. I have several other prescriptions to try. But now I must go, I am meeting with Cromwell. Rest, sweetheart, do not exert yourself today." A flicker of irritation crossed Anne's face, but she suppressed it quickly. Soon she would be giving birth to her prince, and then she would be safe. Able to show annoyance at Henry's over-attentiveness, able to fly into a rage with him as she used to do.

I remembered that day when I first met Queen Katherine of Aragon, fifteen years ago. I had witnessed King Henry telling her not to hunt because of her pregnancy. She had shown her irritation then, and I had tumbled to her feet in surprise. But although she was a dutiful wife, she was always able to sway him. She had no fear in disagreeing with him because her position was unassailable. How wrong that was.

It was strange to me to see King Henry fussing about the pregnant Anne, just as he had fussed around Katherine when she was with child. Turning away from history, it was as if nothing had changed, only the face of the pregnant queen. And Katherine, where was she?

Lady Maria Willoughby kept us up to date with news about our beloved old queen. Not officially at court, she still had friends, who she visited, and when she was around, she would call myself and Jane Seymour to meet with her. She wasn't allowed to see Katherine, but she had contacts in the staff, who passed on information to her. Our dear mistress was now living at the Bishop's Palace in Buckden and suffering from the damp. She did not acknowledge King Henry's recent marriage, and she was still refusing to be called the Princess Dowager of Wales.

"Why do you not write to her, Kat?" asked Maria. "You are one of the household she misses the most. I hear she talks of you often." I shifted uncomfortably in my seat.

"What could I say to her, my lady?" I said. "My life here is the same every day. I have no news for her." I couldn't say that the reason I did not write was that I knew any letter of mine would be read by the King's agents. Any communication could throw a shadow on Will's career. And, even worse, if I was open about my relationship to the Queen, I was putting myself and her in danger. I wanted, above all to call Queen Katharine my mother, but I could not do that in any letter. And without doing that, what was the point of writing? It felt like King Henry had cut me off from my own mother.

"I cannot write," I said. "It is painful for me to remember the old days."

Lady Jane Seymour looked at me strangely, and then at Lady Willoughby.

"But why should Kat write to the old queen? She was just a serving maid then. Surely the Queen does not remember her?" Lady Willoughby looked seriously at her.

"The Queen does indeed remember Kat," she said, "she remembers all who served her." With that, she glanced at me, and I knew, I just knew, that Lady Maria Willoughby had been taken into the Queen's confidence. She knew my secret. She knew that I was one of Queen Katherine's babies who had been left for dead, found by the midwife, and adopted by ordinary people. If the Queen was going to tell anyone, it would be this woman who had been with her all these years. I had to ask her; I knew that. But how to get rid of Lady Jane?

I fixed Lady Willoughby with a glare and spoke briskly to her.

"My lady, I found a book of Queen Katherine's in my lodging the other day. I borrowed it. If I give it to you, will you be able to ensure she receives it?" Lady Willoughby nodded.

"Of course I will," she said. "She will be pleased you are thinking of her."

"May I meet you here tomorrow to give you the book?" I had to return to the room where Will and I slept to find it.

"I will be here tomorrow, at daybreak." I knew Lady Jane liked to lie abed in the mornings, so the earlier I could meet Lady Willoughby, the better.

"Can't you make it later?" Jane asked. "We could go for a walk by the river."

"No, it has to be early, otherwise the Queen will miss me," I insisted.

"The Queen?" said Lady Willoughby with a tired smile.

"My lady, we must be careful what we say here at court. You know who the Queen is in my heart, but here at Greenwich, it is Queen Anne." Lady Willoughby smiled, acknowledging the sense of what I said.

"Of course. We must be careful. We'll meet tomorrow, Kat."

It was the end of August, and the morning sunrise was beautiful. The sun still had its warmth, but there was the barest chill underlying it, hinting that the summer would not go on forever. I met Lady Willoughby outside the great hall. She was dressed for riding and told me she was going home that day.

"But I will be seeing my contact from Buckden soon, and will give him the book," she told me, looking expectantly at me. There was no book on my person.

"Lady Willoughby, I need to talk to you. I think you know what it is about." She looked at me as if I was stupid.

"Talk Kat? What about? You know talk is dangerous." She pulled at her riding gloves impatiently.

"You know, don't you?" She paused and looked me directly in the face. "You know," I repeated. "You know why Queen Katherine prays for me and talks of me almost as much as she talks of Princess Mary." Lady Willoughby's face froze, but I continued. "I think you overheard something, because the Queen wouldn't have broken my confidence. You know that I am her daughter."

"Be quiet Kat!" Lady Willoughby glanced all around her, but there was no one about. She softened a bit, "We don't know who is listening now. Come, let us walk to the stables."

We walked away from the hall and into the centre of the great yard in front of the palace. In this space there were no niches or archways to hide in. Lady Willoughby stopped still.

"Pretend to fix my bonnet," she ordered. "We will say a feather came loose." I stood over her – like Queen Katherine she was tiny – and fiddled with her hat. She spoke quickly,

"I did not overhear anything, Kat, I do not listen at doorways. But Kat, I guessed. It is not that difficult. Look at you, you are the image of your father, and you have your mother's spirit. And the Queen loves you more than any other except Princess Mary and the King. I am not stupid, Kat, I realised quite soon that she must be your mother. But then I thought, how can that be? I cast my mind back to those births. Did all the babies die? And then I thought, maybe one had survived, by some miracle. I asked the queen about it one night when we were alone together. At first, she denied it, Kat, but you know she cannot lie. She shared it with me then, after I had given my word not to tell another soul."

"And so, why did you seek me out? Surely, it is best to leave things as they are."

"It may be so, Kat, but the Queen is not well. I do not believe she has long for this world." I felt as if a giant charger had kicked me in the chest,

"But surely, she will recover? She will have the best of care." Lady Willoughby looked grim.

"Not anymore, she won't. Kat, you have not seen her recently. She is in prison now, guarded by strangers who do not care for her. She does not get the best care anymore. Indeed, it would suit the King well if she was to perish." Lady Willoughby pushed my hand down from her hat and picked up her skirts.

"And so, Kat, you should know that if her life nears its end, I am determined to be there. And you should be ready to come too, if you love her as you say you do." With that, she swept off to the stables. I called after her,

"Godspeed my lady." My voice was shaky. Maria Willoughby had forced me to confront the fact of my mother, the Queen's ill treatment. And she had forced me to consider what I would do if she died. I had been so involved in the court, and yes, so loving the freedom of being a musician, that I had pushed my mother to the back of my mind. But now she was in the fore-front, my dear mother. My dear, sick mother, who had given me so much. Maybe soon, I would be called upon to repay some of the love she had shown me. And that would put my job and my marriage in jeopardy. I bowed my head, overcome with the magnitude of what I had just realised.

"Hey Kat, why so miserable!" It was Thomas Wyatt, up early to join the morning's hunt. He was dressed in green – these nobles liked to pretend they were Robin Hood – and he looked impossibly handsome.

"I was thinking of the past, Sir Thomas, and it made me sad." He looked at me seriously, and said,

"Don't do that, Kat, it will not serve you well. Come and have a drink of wine with me before the hunt. That will cheer you up!" We walked to the great hall where wine was being served to all the hunters and their attendants. Noise and laughter echoed from the rafters, and it was hard to hear what he was saying. I leaned closer to him.

"I said, Kat, that you look most fetching in that new coif." He pulled at one of the strings of my buttercream coloured silk cap. He didn't have to reach forward far to kiss me. I jumped back from the taste of his lips, but he caught me and pulled me towards him again. For a moment, it was very sweet, but then I remembered myself and pushed him away.

"Behave yourself, Sir Thomas! You will ruin my reputation!" He grinned and bowed. I cannot tell you, daughter, how much this meant. A gentleman did not bow to a servant, however pretty he found her. It just wasn't done. But he bowed to me, a great courtier's bow. And I couldn't help it, daughter, I was flattered. He had paid me the compliment of seeing me as his equal, and I could not but smile in delight.

"You should not have done that, Sir Thomas," I said, "I am just a musician."

"One must always salute beauty," Sir Thomas looked me up and down, "and when that comes with intelligence and wit, it would be a crime not to recognise it." I flushed and then bobbed him a curtsey.

"I must be off, Sir Thomas; the Queen will be waiting."

"I keep telling you I'm Tom! Now be off with you," and

he turned abruptly and started speaking with another gentle-man that he knew. Daughter, that morning will remain with me all my life. I had heard that Queen Katherine still loved me and prayed for me. And I had learnt that Sir Thomas Wyatt admired me. But I had also been issued with two challenges. The first was, should Queen Katherine become very ill, would I go to her? And the second was, should Sir Thomas become serious, would I go to him?

Fortunately, there was little time to consider my challenges. Queen Anne asked for me every day, needing my soothing playing to comfort her when she was feeling huge, sick and frightened. Like most mothers, the first baby's birth is an anxious time. Daughter, for me, your birth was frightening. But as with most mothers, including Queen Anne, when the baby arrives, you feel nothing but love for him or her. Just as I did for you, my dearest daughter.

The day came when Queen Anne retired to her private chambers to give birth. As with Queen Katherine, these were dark, secluded and warm. No men were admitted. All that served the Queen at this time were women. I was included. Queen Anne loved music, and of course none of the male musicians were allowed into the chamber.

In some ways, it was different from Queen Katherine's confinements. There was no girdle of the Virgin for Queen Anne to clutch, no assorted relics to pray to. But again, it was just us women. This was our business, and the men had no part in it. We slept and ate in turns. The Queen would never be left alone.

It was early in the morning when I woke to hear moaning. Lady Boleyn pulled me from my pallet and told me to put on my gown,

"She's gone into labour, and she needs soothing. Get you to her, now." I remembered that it was Lady Boleyn who had been so unwelcoming to me at Queen Katherine's confine-ment. But now it was her daughter giving birth, she wanted every comfort to be available for her.

Daughter, you might remember that I had not been present as Queen Katherine gave birth. So, Queen Anne's labour was the first I had witnessed. I was excited but also a little fearful. This experience lay in store for all married women, including me. I knew there would be pain involved but didn't know how much. And I knew that usually at the end, there would be joy, but I didn't know that sometimes there would also be disappointment.

Daughter, I played and played that day. First, Queen Anne listened, sometimes singing with me in a soft, quiet voice. Every now and then she would tense up, and become silent, her mother sponging her face with a damp cloth. But as the day proceeded, the silence was replaced by screams, and the moments of calm vanished. The midwife was at the bed, with several ladies beside her. She was talking loudly to the Queen, telling her to breathe through each pain. Now, the midwife was just an ordinary woman, and the Queen was the Queen. But in this circumstance, the midwife was the one in charge, and the labouring Queen had to put herself and her baby in this woman's hands.

Midday passed, and the screaming became louder. Food had been brought to the doorway of the birthing chambers, but no one went to eat. We were all focused on that bed, that woman screaming, and the baby that was making its way out of her womb. I was not playing now, it seemed wrong to be doing so. I was just outside the birthing chamber, listening and fetching water when asked. It was hard to tell exactly what the time was in there. It was dark except for one small open window, but the sunbeam that fell from there became golden.

Now daughter, imagine. I had never seen a babe being born. It was one of the main concerns of women, but I had not yet experienced it. What do you think I did? Of course, I made my way inside, standing unobserved at the edge of the group of women crouching round the bed. I knew that childbirth was painful, God had decreed it to be so for women. But the look of terror on Anne's face was frightening. Could something be about to go wrong? But the women around her seemed unworried. Now two women were holding her legs apart, high up in the air. The midwife was sitting between Anne's legs, rolling back her sleeves, and yet another woman was wiping Anne's brow with a damp cloth. All of the aristocratic ladies formed the next layer of attendance. They were not involved in the messy business of birth, but were there to pray and to exhort Anne in her labours.

It was a noisy business with the screams, the prayers and the crying. Anne looked across the room at her mother and cried,

"I can't do it, Mother. I can't do it!" She was panicking. Her mother was not sympathetic. She spoke harshly,

"Of course, you can. It is what women do. Stop crying and do as you're told!" Her sister, Lady Mary, who might have been kinder, was in the country. But even she could not have helped. For Lady Anne's labour was the hardest work of her life. Every woman in the room understood that and understood that it had to take its course. There was no freedom in the birthing room.

A calm voice stilled Anne's crying. It was the midwife, her voice authoritative.

"Now, your Majesty, you will have to do what I say. When I say push, you must push down with all your might, as if you were pushing out a stool."

"I can't do it, I am frightened!" Anne called out.

"Yes, my dear, you can do it. Just breathe, breathe in and breathe out. I can see your baby's head. You're nearly there. Nearly, nearly."

"It's so hard." Anne was whimpering like a trapped animal.

"It is hard, your Majesty, but you can do it. Now, now PUSH." The midwife was an officer on the field of battle, and

Anne was the infantryman. I noticed a doctor had entered. He was standing towards the back of the room, looking away from Anne's outstretched legs.

"PUSH!" I noticed a scrap of ginger hair in the space between Anne's legs.

"I can't, I can't."

"Yes you can. Good girl. Now he's coming. His head is coming, your Majesty. Your prince is coming." The midwife's tone became excited. For a moment, Anne opened her eyes and looked down.

"Is he really?" she asked.

"Just one more push, my dear, that's it. PUSH PUSH PUSH." With a scream of anguish, Anne pushed a bloody bundle out onto the sheets. The midwife took the baby, wiped off the blood and wrapped it in a linen cloth. There was a silence in the room as she placed the baby in Anne's arms.

Anne relaxed, and a look of inexpressible tenderness crossed her face.

"My little prince," she said. "Welcome my lord." The midwife cleared her throat.

"You have a fine princess," she said, "the first of many healthy babies, your Majesty." Anne unwrapped the baby and saw that it was indeed a girl.

"A girl," she said flatly. "A girl." There were no tears as the midwife set about delivering Anne's afterbirth and then cleaned her up. The baby was placed in the ornate cradle, and there was a flurry among the aristocratic ladies as Lady Boleyn left the chamber to inform the King.

"A royal princess!" King Henry held the little girl up to his eye level. "A fine, healthy girl! Well, well. No need to be downhearted. She is healthy, and many other babies will follow. Congratulations wife." Anne, sitting up against her pillows, feigned a smile.

"Next year, it will be a prince, your Majesty," she said. "I am made for princes."

"Indeed, wife, you will be the mother of many. And you, are you well?" There was concern in his face, but I wondered if it was for Anne's childbearing prospects rather than Anne herself.

"I am very well, your Majesty. I look forward to rejoining the court after I am churched."

"Good, good. We shall celebrate when you return. Let us call her Elizabeth, after my mother. The Christening will take place tomorrow, but no need for the jousts that we planned. More fitting for a prince, eh? We can dance for our daughter when you are recovered."

And so, the birth was celebrated, not with tears, but with a cut-down Christening and a promise of princes to come. Anne recovered quickly. She knew that she had to be healthy to go back to the King's bed, and so she did as she was told by the ladies looking after her. She drank broth, she ate eggs and honey, and she sent up prayers of gratitude every hour.

She soon got over the disappointment and was a very attentive mother. Of course, little Elizabeth was breastfed by a wet-nurse, but Anne insisted on having her cradle in the chamber with her, and she continually looked over to her, watching the little red-haired girl as she slept. I was put to work playing lullabies while Anne sang softly.

"Lullaby, lullow, lullay lully,

Beway bewy, lullaby lullow

Lullay, lully

Baw me bairne, sleep softly now...".

It was an old song, and it stirred memories in me, of Joan, the woman who had brought me up, rocking me on her knee. My real mother, Katherine of Aragon, had never sung me a lullaby. She hadn't known me until many years had passed. I felt a wave of great sadness pass over me, missing both of my mothers.

The King's voice sounded loudly outside the chamber. He was visiting the baby princess every day and becoming gradually more enamoured of her. He burst into the chamber while

I was playing, and the midwife was examining Anne.

"Your Majesty, I am attending the Queen," she said. "Shall I return later?" King Henry waved her aside,

"Go with the Queen to the antechamber," he ordered, "I shall wait here with the babe." Anne raised her eyebrows at the midwife but got off the bed and walked slowly to the next chamber, followed by the midwife. I heard the sound of their voices from next door, talking quietly. I guessed the midwife might be exclaiming that the King should have moved, not his wife, and Anne smiling and answering that we have to humour the King.

He sat perched on the bed, looking large and out of place. Leaning over, he tickled the baby under her chin.

"Good morning, my little sweeting," he whispered. "I am your papa. Let me see you smile, my darling little one." He leant over and picked baby Elizabeth out of the crib. Started, she let out a wail, her little legs kicking against the swaddling. But he wasn't put off. He held her to his chest and soothed her, "There, there, my little princess. You are your father's girl, with my hair and my voice too!" I continued playing softly.

"You there! Stop the music. I want to hear my daughter breathing," he ordered. I stopped and stood there, unsure of what to do next. He put his giant head up against his daughter's chest, and then listened.

"Such strong little lungs," he whispered, "such a strong little girl, my Elizabeth." Then he looked at me.

"Who are you anyway? You have a look of someone? But no, it can't be." I knew that he was seeing my resemblance to Katherine of Aragon, and to my sister, Princess Mary. But he would never know that.

"I worked as a maid for Queen Katherine," I said. He grunted, annoyed.

"The Dowager Princess," he corrected me.

"Yes, I am sorry, your Majesty, the Dowager Princess. I got accustomed to the wrong form of address... it was so many years." He nodded approvingly.

"So many years of sin, and we didn't know it. You are excused, maid. I sometimes make the same mistake myself." He gently placed the sleeping baby in the cradle.

"But it was sin, and we got no heir together. With Queen Anne, there will be many babies in the cradle. Elizabeth is but the first."

I saw him sitting there, gazing at his daughter, and I felt almost sympathetic to him. This is the man I hated for the way he had treated my darling Queen Katherine. But it was clear he loved his daughter, just as he had loved Princess Mary. Now I have you, my own daughter, I know how strong that love can be.

Foolishly, I said,

"Elizabeth will make a great queen, your Majesty." He nodded and rose to his feet.

"We will see if we can match her with a king," he said. "She will make a great alliance." Now, daughter, you will know how I say things without thinking. And even in front of this terrifying, powerful man, my tongue ran away with me.

"Your Majesty, she may even be a queen in her own right," I said. "Any daughter of yours could run a kingdom, no doubt about it." He tutted and looked at me angrily.

"I'll have none of that nonsense here! Katherine was always going on about how Mary would make a good queen. Why don't you women understand? It is not a woman's place to rule, not in England." I don't know why I said it, but I replied,

"But your Majesty, the Dowager Princess Katherine led an army of English soldiers while you were campaigning in France." His face darkened and he came and stood directly over me. He was so large that he blocked out the light, and all I could see was his massive chest, rising and falling in anger.

"Why speak you for her, girl? I will not have this in my court. You are the musician for the Queen, not the old woman that clings on to life far away." I realised that I had made a bad mistake.

"Your Majesty, I know that. And Queen Anne has been so good to me. She is so clever; I love working for her. But I know we women will never match the abilities of men. We are so weak compared to you." He snorted and then clapped his hand on my shoulder.

"So, what about the Princess Dowager?" he asked. "You know that she was simply following my directions. She did as she was told and did it passably well. She did not lead England."

"Oh no, your Majesty, I understand now. You must excuse me. The Princess Dowager was limited in her leadership. She was weak and emotional. My reasoning is but a woman's and I did not understand what is needed for statecraft." He removed his hand and grunted.

"Very well. Watch your tongue in future." He walked out of the chamber, calling out a farewell to Anne in the further room. I stood there shaking. I had challenged the King of England, the man who could have me put to death in an instant. Why had I done it? Maybe it was because, somehow, I felt connected to him, and able to say what I meant. After all, although he didn't know it, he was my father.

But, in the end, I did as all women had to, and most men. I submitted to the King and denigrated myself and all other women to calm him down. Why did we have to do this? Because it worked, especially in those days. Queen Katherine was the worthiest leader I had ever met. But the King could never admit it. I must admit I was relieved to have escaped without punishment. But I was also deeply ashamed of myself.

CHAPTER

The problem was Princess Mary. Of course she was now called the Lady Mary since she had been rendered illegitimate following the annulment of her parents' marriage. King Henry was convinced that happiness would follow if only Mary could be brought into line. Preferably installed as a junior lady at court, submitting to her father's headship of the church and performing obeisance both to him, and his new Queen. But Mary was as obstinate as her mother. She would acknowledge her father, nothing and no one else.

Now Queen Anne did try. I know that the talk was that she hated Mary. But it was the King who raged and threatened Mary, not her. I know because I heard him. It was the day that the baby Princess Elizabeth was being moved to her own household, out of London, at Hatfield House. As befits the heir to the throne, she was moving with a governess, nursemaids, a Chamberlain, stable hands, horses, tapestries and furniture.

Queen Anne had dreaded that day. She had never been the kind of woman who clucked over babies, but she had a fierce love for her angry little scrap of a daughter, and she did not want to be parted from her. In the weeks before she left, Queen Anne spent every spare moment in the nursery, singing and playing with her baby. She would sit on a chair beside the cradle, rocking and singing, often dangling her pearls to attract Elizabeth's eye. Sometimes she called on me to accompany her on the lute, because she said I would not frighten the babe as some of the male musicians might. But on that day, it was the entry of the King that made the infant scream in fear. He was viciously angry, punching the wall and shouting at the Queen.

"She will not submit! God's blood, she is in league with her mother. She deserves a horsewhipping, and I have a good mind to give it her."

"You know that she threatens my position by doing this? She is making herself the focus of every malcontent who doesn't like me." Anne spoke rapidly, angrily.

"Are you not her father?" she asked. "Can you not control her for my sake?" Henry roared his reply,

"I will teach her a lesson she will not forget, and I expect you to support me in this." Anne looked non-committal,

"She is your daughter," she pointed out. Infuriated, he picked up a goblet that was on a side table and flung it across the floor. Queen Anne leant protectively over the cradle, shielding the child from the sight of his red face and spittle-flecked mouth.

"Don't, you will scare the child," she spoke softly, but with force.

"And you should not order me what to do! Am I not a King? Is it my fate to be surrounded by intransigent women? What do I have to do to get some peace?" He reached out and slapped Anne across the face, leaving a brutal red mark. Anne stiffened in shock, and I stopped playing. Elizabeth woke and started to whimper. Without a word, Anne picked the baby out of the cradle and took her next door, to where some ladies were sewing. Then she returned, shutting the door behind her. Neither of them seemed to notice me, and it was too late to go and join the other women.

"How dare you treat me like that? I am not some labourer's wife to be cuffed around the head by her drunken husband! I am your Queen, and I am worth more, so much more!" King Henry put one hand over her mouth, the other behind her head, restraining her.

"Now listen to me," he whispered. "You are only Queen because I wish it. I can change my mind in the blink of an eye, and don't you forget it!" Anne did not move. She stood there rigid until he released her.

"I am not worthy of this ill treatment," she said quietly. "What has happened to us? You swore you would love me forever." Henry flinched at this, as if it were a blow. His face became concerned, tender.

"I will always love you, sweetheart. I will never stop loving you! Do not fear me. I have been vexed today because I heard from the Lady Mary that she will never accept me as head of the Church. I have offered her money, a new house, a father's love, but she casts all of that away." Anne was silent, putting her hand to her cheek, which was still stinging. She looked around, and saw me, cowering in a corner.

"Kat, will you come with me? I need to walk," she ordered. She came and took my hand, which was unusual.

"Stay sweetheart, stay a moment," said Henry. "I came to tell you that I will make the Lady Mary do as she is told. Tomorrow, Princess Elizabeth will be moved to Hatfield, and do you know what I shall do?" Queen Anne's voice was muted,

"No, your Majesty, I do not know what you will do."

"I will order her to Hatfield to serve your daughter, Princess Elizabeth. She will be made to curtsey to your daughter. She will be made to follow at the end of her train, and she will be taught her place." The cruelty in his voice made me shudder inside. I had not particularly liked Princess Mary, but for a father to treat his daughter so, I found despicable. I couldn't help but wonder what he would do to me, if he ever found out that I was his daughter also. It seemed to me that he cursed every woman he was close to.

"Very well," Anne said icily. She was not ready to forgive him. "So, Elizabeth is to go tomorrow? Kat, walk me back to my chamber, I need some time to prepare myself." He grunted something, which she took to be an adieu, we both curtsied deeply to him and left the chamber. Once we were out of ear-shot, she started to cry. It wasn't elegant crying, with a dainty tear in each eye. No, she was howling, her nose running, tears staining her cheeks. I hurried her back to her chambers, ignoring the strange looks we were getting from passing courtiers and servants.

When we got back, she flung herself on her bed while her women rushed to her side. I had seen her like this once before, just after she had attacked me. It was as if she was overtaken by a storm..

Anne continued crying. I could do no more. I left her and went through to sit in the presence chamber and practiced a few of the chansons that she liked.

"Hey Kat, how goes it?" Sir Thomas Wyatt was standing in front of me. I grimaced and pointed to the door, from whence came the sound of muffled crying. He looked longingly at it, and then sat down beside me.

"She does not wish to lose the princess," he observed. "She has become more of a mother than she expected." I gave an emphatic strum on the lute.

"She is angry that Lady Mary will not acknowledge her," I told him. He put his hand over mine to still the noise,

"Yes, she is angry, but her anger is mainly fear Kat. She knows there are people that hate her, and Mary is a focus for them. The King is volatile, don't forget. In time, he may turn against Anne, and then Mary will become his heir again." I looked unconvinced.

"You really do love her, don't you?" I asked him. "You will always find an excuse for her." He raised my hand to his lips and kissed it.

"Yes, you are right Kat. Until the day I die. But I know her well. She would be friendly with Mary, if only Mary could accept her as Queen. She has tried." I pulled my hand away.

"Stop it, Tom, you are such a flirt!" He laughed and seized my hand again. "So, I'm Tom now, am I? That's good Kat. I am getting somewhere at last." He leant forward and kissed my cheek.

"Don't worry, I will leave you now. I must go to see the Queen. Be ready for when she calls you." I watched him stride across the room and go through the door. I couldn't help but notice how handsome he was. It wasn't something I was aware of normally, but on that day, I realised that I was attracted to him. It was a disturbing realisation. I knew it was because the relationship between myself and Will was strained. But what could I do? At least I knew that Thomas Wyatt loved only Queen Anne and was not about to proposition me. It was just a flirtation, and one which kept a much-needed smile on my face.

After a few months, Queen Anne decided to visit her daughter at Hatfield House. We were to ride there, spend a couple of days, and then return to London. For the first time in many weeks, Anne was beaming. She was ordering wooden toys, tiny jewel-encrusted gowns, and a small horn book, "so she can learn her letters." Lady Boleyn, Anne's mother, laughed at her.

"She is but six months old, your Majesty. She is too young to learn her letters."

"But my daughter is very clever, Mother, you know that!" Lady Boleyn shrugged.

"Well, I suppose she can cut her teeth on it," she agreed, stowing some baby night shifts into the chest for her granddaughter. The King was merry again, and that helped improve the atmosphere. He was laughing at Anne's jokes again, and I heard from Jane Seymour that he was visiting the Queen's chamber most nights. Everything seemed set fair again. All

Anne needed was to fall pregnant.

So, it was a happy procession that made its way along the great North way towards Hatfield. Anne rode a handsome bay horse that the King had given her, accompanied by around twenty ladies and courtiers. Then there were the soldiers that guarded her, and finally, the servants, me included, who were at the rear. I was riding, but most of us were in wagons, perching at the front, with the Princess's presents stowed behind. There was also, of course, a convoy of wagons carrying the essentials that Queen Anne needed for a three-day stay.

It was near eventide when we reached Hatfield, and we were happy to be riding up Fore Street to the palace. We passed through the gatehouse and made our way tiredly up to the main entrance.

It didn't stop then for us. We had to join with the servants of the house to finish the preparations for the Queen's visit, to unpack her wagons, and to put out everything she needed. She had wanted to run to the nursery as soon as we arrived, but Lady Elizabeth's governess, Lady Margaret Bryan, made it clear to her that the princess was sleeping, and could not be disturbed until later. So, Anne asked me to play while she waited in her chamber to meet her daughter, and her daughter's court.

That evening, after she had eaten in her chamber, Queen Anne went into the presence chamber. All her ladies were standing behind her. I was in a corner, playing my rosewood lute. There were no trumpeters with us this time. We were, after all, coming to visit a baby. Anne waited, drumming the fingers of her hand on the arm of the chair. After a few moments, the door opened and a small procession entered, led by Lady Margaret Bryan with a squirming Princess Elizabeth in her arms. Queen Anne jumped up and held out her arms,

"Give her to me. Oh, my baby, my darling girl. How I have missed you!" Princess Elizabeth turned her brown eyes upon her mother and smiled. Everyone clapped, enchanted. Anne kissed the top of her head and sat down with Elizabeth on her lap.

"See, look, she sits up so straight, just like her father!" Anne was overjoyed to see the changes in her daughter. "And she is so big now, I wonder if she will fit the gowns I have brought her." Lady Bryan curtseyed and said,

"I can always have them altered, your Majesty. Her Grace the Princess is a good eater, and she still drinks plenty of milk from Mistress Ocle." A matronly woman with a white apron curtseyed deeply to the Queen.

"See that Mistress Ocle is well rewarded," Anne instructed. "She must be paid a retainer, for I shall need her again!" Mistress Ocle blushed and looked pleased. But Anne's attention had already moved on. For at the back of Princess Elizabeth's small retinue was an awkward teenage girl. Short of stature, and vanishingly thin, I still recognised the girl I would always know as Princess Mary. While the other ladies were crowding round, watching Anne and her daughter, Mary was a lonely figure, hanging back as far as she dared. But Anne wouldn't let her go unremarked upon. She handed Princess Elizabeth to Mistress Ocle, stood up from her ornate wooden chair, and walked over to the girl. We all held our breath.

"My lady Mary," Anne said, holding out her hand. "Will you spare me a moment for some conversation?" Mary ignored Anne's hand but nodded sulkily. Anne ushered her away from the Presence Chamber into a small side room. The door was closed quietly. For a moment there was silence, and then the sound of awful, angry weeping. Anne appeared at the door.

"She will have nothing to do with me, Lady Bryan. She is a disobedient girl who is not worthy of her father's love." Lady Bryan immediately apologised,

"Your Majesty, she has lost her manners recently. I am sorry. But she is missing her mother, and she has nothing in common with a six-month-old baby." Anne snapped back at her,

"With a Princess! Elizabeth may be a baby, but she is a Princess!" Lady Bryan smiled, acknowledging her mistake.

"Of course, your Majesty, and what a delightful Princess she is! She loves your visits, she knows her mother, I can assure you." She looked over towards Elizabeth, who was blissfully unaware, sucking vigorously at Mistress Ocle's nipple. Lady Bryan continued tentatively,

"It may do the Lady Mary's temper some good if she were to see her mother, perhaps?" Anne cried out,

"Jesu, these two Spaniards! It is not my fault she is not seeing her mother! If they would only accept the King is head of the church, and that I am Queen, then she can see her mother every day of the week if she so wishes!"

"It is your fault! You bewitched my father and took him away! You will never be Queen. My mother is the Queen, and you are not fit to kneel at her feet." Mary was standing there at the door, her small frame shaking with the intensity of her feelings. "I can tell you this: I despise you, Anne Boleyn! I will never recognise you as Queen. Never!" With that, she ran through the chamber and out of the other door. Lady Bryan made to go after her.

"No, leave her!" Anne ordered. "She is a wicked little girl, and she doesn't deserve your sympathy! I shall expect her to stay in her chamber tomorrow. I do not wish to see her. I don't trust myself not to wring her neck!"

With the argument ringing in everyone's ears, the household made ready for bed. We were all chastened, and not a little sad. What had been meant to be a joyful reunion of mother and child had turned into something a lot nastier. I slept with the maids that night, but I was awake all night. I did not like Mary, she had not been kind to me. But the way Anne treated her made me feel very uncomfortable. She was only a girl, and she was missing her mother. Could Anne not have a little pity?

As it turned out, she did try again. After a day of dandling

Elizabeth on her lap, playing peek-a-boo and discussing wean-ing foods, Anne got up from her chair.

"I am going to see Mary," she informed the ladies. They scrambled up to go with her, but she waved them back. "No, it is best I go alone." She walked out of the chamber. We could hear her skirts swishing as she made her way away from us all. We waited. No one said anything, so I played a little to ease the mood. But it was no good.

After half an hour, Anne was back. She sat down and looked at all the expectant faces turned up at her.

"Well, I tried. And I did not shout. I did not scream. I told her how she would be welcomed by me and her father, and how she would have all due honour at court. How she could see her mother, spend time with her." Lady Bryan looked enquir-ingly at her, "but it is of no avail," Anne continued. "She will not acknowledge me as Queen, and she believes her father to have gone against what she calls the Holy Church. There is no point trying with her, she is her mother's daughter."

Later that year, King Henry and Queen Anne went on a progress around the West of England. It was a way of showing themselves to the populace, and of rewarding favoured aris-tocrats with a royal presence at their stately homes. This was nothing like the simple retinue that had accompanied Anne to Hatfield. This was a court on the move, and the train of horses, litters, wagons and carts was so long it took a good twenty minutes to pass. Almost everyone went with the prog-ress. I was there. My sex meant that I had never been one of the King's official musicians, but I was accepted as Queen Anne's favourite minstrel, asked to play every day in her pri-vate chambers. Around that time a new musician arrived. He was called Mark Smeaton, and he tried hard to ingratiate him-self with Anne. She was amused by him and flirted a little. But I knew I need not worry. Anne was too careful of her reputa-tion to allow any man into her private chamber where she was at her most unguarded. And so, my position remained secure.

One morning, King Henry and most of the gentlemen went hunting, one of the great joys of the summer progress. Anne told me that she and a small party were riding over to visit Hailes Abbey. One of the largest abbeys in England, it possessed a relic of such power, that people flocked from all over the country to see it and be cured by it.

"It is said to be the blood of Christ," Anne told me. "And these monks are charging the poor to come and see it! How can it be the blood of Christ after fifteen hundred years? I detest these practices!" So, we rode over to meet with the Abbot, who welcomed Anne with wine and patronising deference. I smiled to myself. He obviously didn't know her. She was nobody's fool.

"And so, may I see Christ's blood?" Anne asked, sounding eager. "I am told it will cure all ills."

"Oh yes, your Majesty, it has brought comfort to so many. The sick, the lame, those wishing to conceive…" he glanced over at Anne. She was preparing for battle, I knew. He escorted her to the chapel where the relic was placed in a large bottle, held in a silver clasp.

"See, your Majesty, the blood liquefies, it is miraculous," he said, looking down at her in a fatherly way.

"So, how much do you charge the poor souls who come here?" Anne asked in a deceptively soft voice.

"We do not charge people," the Abbot confided, "we just ask for donations. We are here to serve, not make profits."

"That is strange," Anne remarked, "as the dame I spoke to on the way here told me she had sold her cow in order to meet your demands." Thomas Wyatt was standing behind me, and he whispered in my ear,

"Skewered!"

The Abbot started to protest that the woman was telling lies, "She must have been trying to make you feel sorry for her, your Majesty. If you point her out to me, I will make sure she is punished." Anne bent her head gracefully towards him.

"That will not be possible, Lord Abbot. Because I gave the woman some money and sent her home."

"Home? But she was coming to the shrine!" The Abbot sounded a little uncomfortable now. Anne spoke very sweetly,

"I told her that her son's coughing would be better treated with meat and good food. In my opinion, Sir, that is more efficacious than a pot of honey, coloured red."

"Your Majesty, you cannot mean?" The Abbot was blustering now.

"Yes, I do mean. The blood of Christ!" Anne's voice rose now. "Do you think I am stupid? How can blood remain, in essence, the same for hundreds of years?"

"But that is the miracle, your Majesty. The holy blood of Christ does not behave as normal."

Anne started to shout,

"You are a charlatan, Lord Abbot. And you and your predecessors have been bleeding the poor of their money in order for them to see a pot of honey coloured with saffron! That is what I have been told! And where does all that money go, Sir?" The Abbot stammered,

"To the glory of God, your Majesty. To praise and worship him."

"To praise and worship him with the finest wine, the softest wool habits, and the sweetest meat," Anne shouted. "You are a disgrace to the church, Abbot! Rest assured, reform is coming, and you will not be allowed to continue, that I promise." With that, she swept out, leaving the Abbot wringing his hands.

"By God, she means it," Thomas Wyatt said to me. "The one thing you can say about Anne, she never did refuse a challenge."

The progress continued without further incident. I was pleased to learn that we were heading for Wolf Hall, the house of Lady Jane Seymour's family. She had left the court early to visit her family, and I was looking forward to seeing her again. The country life suited her. Her cheeks were pink and rounded. We stayed with her family for two weeks, and Jane and I fell into our old friendship easily. I worked most days, but Queen Anne had precious little private time, with all the dinners and dancing she was entertained with. So, we had time to catch up, and to gossip.

One morning Jane led me out of the house, along a lane, to a small row of cottages. It was September, and the brambles by the side of the lane were full of blackberries. The sun was warm, and we both felt carefree.

"Where are we going?" I asked her.

"I want you to meet someone," Jane said. "She has been like a mother to me." She stopped at a cottage with a tiny front garden full of vegetables and pot herbs. The front door was opened before we had even had a chance to knock. A little old woman, red-cheeked and smiling, rushed out and embraced Jane.

"My sweet girl, have you brought your friend?" Then she remembered herself and curtseyed to Jane. "My lady," she murmured. Jane pulled her up.

"Don't be silly, you must not curtsey to me. May I introduce Kat, who works at court? Kat, this is my old nurse, Mistress Ashdown. She brought me up." The old woman reddened a little,

"I wouldn't say that, my dear. You saw your mother, maybe, every evening. But enough, come in, come in." The room inside was tiny, its floor thoroughly swept, a small fire in the hearth. "Sit down dears and have some mead. I make it myself."

"Mistress Ashdown's mead is renowned," said Jane. "You should never drink it all night, or else you will end up being very foolish." This was a side of Jane I hadn't seen. She was relaxed, jokey. "I used to call her Mistress Mead because she was sweet to me, like honey."

I tasted the mead carefully. It was sweet, and strong, and had the scent of chamomile.

"Aye, you can call me Mistress Mead if you wish. I like the name." She beamed at both of us. I could feel the mead relaxing me.

"So, what was Lady Jane like as a little girl?" I asked.

"Oh, she was bonny, and kind. Not like her brothers! They were a handful! But Lady Jane now, she was my favourite." She jumped up suddenly and reappeared with two bowls containing stewed apples with blackberries, covered with thick cream. "Eat this, my dears, I made it last night. I hoped you would come today."

And so, with the berries and the mead, we spent a happy couple of hours with Mistress Mead telling me all about Jane's childhood. She tutted in sympathy when Jane told her that I was a foundling, and her eyes filled with tears.

"Must have been hard for you, dear. But you've done well for yourself." At last, we got up to leave, and she opened the front door for us. "Jane, make sure you come back before you go to London!" Jane cried out,

"You know I will! I can never forget the childhood you gave me, Mistress Mead." The old woman chuckled. "And Mistress Kat, you are welcome, if ever you are in the area, please knock on my door. I will give you another beaker of mead!" I laughed. In truth, we were all a little merry.

"I will indeed," I assured her as Jane and I tumbled into the lane, whispering and giggling to each other. We stopped to pick some cow parsley, and I put sprigs of it into our hair.

"There now, we are like maids of the May," I cried. "Let us dance!" And we linked arms and kicked our feet in the air as if we were just simple country girls.

We heard the sound of horses' hooves galloping along the lane. Turning, we saw several men, all mounted on large, powerful chargers.

"It is the King," whispered Jane. Immediately, we stopped dancing and stood by the side of the lane. He approached, accompanied by around ten courtiers, all men. We must have looked like hoydens, with our hair all undone and our faces flushed. We curtseyed to him, a trifle unsteadily. He looked down at us with mock severity.

"Lady Jane, is it not?" He spoke to her. It was accepted that I was of no account. "You are a merry maid today. Does your father know you are out on the highway?" She cast her eyes down.

"Yes, your Majesty, he does. He gave me permission to visit my old nursemaid. And you see, I have a companion." The King took no notice of me.

"If I were your father, I would give no such permission," he said, and then with heavy gallantry, "a beautiful woman like you could come to harm." Jane blushed but said nothing. There was a moment's silence, when all we could hear were the horses puffing and pulling at their bridles.

"And such a pleasure to meet a quiet woman," the King observed. "It is restful after all the debates and conversations I have." I knew he was referring to Anne, who, when she wasn't arguing, or loving, would always be wanting to discuss issues of the day, or the latest theological work.

The King jumped down from his horse. "I cannot allow you to continue, Lady Jane. Ride with me on my horse, and I will get you safely home." Jane cast a sideways glance at me, but I could do nothing. He walked over to her and scooped her up. He placed her at the front of his horse and then jumped up behind her. For a moment, he buried his face in her hair, but then he remembered himself. They all trotted off, the King making lively conversation, and Jane replying in monosyllables. I was ignored, standing still in the middle of the lane. But it wasn't that which bothered me. It was disturbing to see the King flirting with Jane. I told myself I should ignore it. She wasn't going to become Henry's mistress. Her father would not allow that. Best then, to forget it. I picked my skirts up and started the walk towards the large house that lay in front of me, and my mistress, the Queen.

CHAPTER 8

Maybe the holy blood of Hailes Abbey had worked its wonders, as Queen Anne announced she was with child just after her visit. This time, it would be a boy, she was sure. She was doing God's work, pushing reform in the church, and surely God would reward her with the prince that would guarantee her safety? She was in a sunny mood and determined that her prayers would be answered.

Christmas at Greenwich was riotous. Without Queen Katherine's moderating influence, the younger courtiers let themselves go. The Lord of Misrule, whose job it was to subvert all the normal rules and regulations, told them to dance and be merry, and who were they to disobey him? Anne reigned triumphantly over it all. In the past, she had been absent from court, unwilling to defer to Queen Katherine. But now she was mistress of all, and she shone brilliantly amongst the crowds of courtiers, advisors and servants. She danced with Sir Henry Norris, who was holding her carefully. He did not want to be responsible for any ill coming to her or the baby. But she pulled him around the floor, laughing at his reluctance. Then she turned to her brother, George Boleyn. The two of them were well matched as they led the dancers in a stately pavane.

Both tall, slim and graceful, they moved instinctively in time. I was watching, and I knew I could never move with such grace. But George and Anne were so close, they almost thought as one.

The King moved to ask Jane Seymour to dance with him. Blushing deeply, she accepted and allowed him to guide her round the floor. She had none of Anne's style, but I could see that Henry liked her adoring eyes. I'd asked her about what happened when he took her back to Wolf Hall on horseback. She'd looked down at the floor.

"Nothing happened. Why should it?" she said defiantly. "The King told me about the hunt that day, and he said that I should accompany him another time. But you know, they left the day after, and he hasn't said anything since. I know that the Queen is not hunting now because of her condition, so he may wish for ladies to accompany him."

"You in particular," I said, and she looked crossly at me and pursed her lips.

"You know Kat, you are very irritating! I would do nothing improper, and you know it. Anyhow, it is Christmas, and everyone is dancing with each other." She glanced over towards the floor, and I saw Queen Anne, this time hand in hand with William Brereton, dancing and laughing as he whispered into her ear. As I had experienced earlier in my life, Christmas is truly a time for flirtation.

I was allowed to go back to the home I shared with Will the day after Christmas Day. When I arrived at Austin Friars, it was already getting dark, and I found Will and Thomas Cromwell sitting companionably in the kitchen, beside the fire, drinking mulled wine. The applewood on the fire crackled, and the room was full of the scents of Christmas. I particularly noticed rosemary, for remembrance. Cromwell would be mourning his wife and daughters, that they were no longer here to dance a Christmas jig with him. But when he saw me, his face lit up.

"Kat, come and sit by the fire. I have work to do. Will needs some company. Pour yourself some mulled wine." He pointed at the iron pot hanging over the fire. "Plenty there to keep you merry tonight," he said heartily. Then his face dropped, and he looked incredibly sad. I realised he was remembering past Christmases with his wife singing and his daughters dancing around his hall. "Be kind to each other, children," he said, and got out of his chair, gesturing to me to sit in it. "I will see you tomorrow," he said. "I am glad you could come back tonight, Kat."

Will poured me some wine and handed it to me. It smelt green and spicy, to me the essence of Christmas. I sipped it, puckering my lips at the heat of it.

"We should not fight Kat," Will said, leaning forward and taking my hand. "You know I love you above all other women."

"I know you do," I acknowledged, "but I get so angry with you – you are trying to keep me from my mother, and you promised it wouldn't be like that." Will started tracing a circle on my palm, round and round and round.

"Kat, you know why I do that. It is dangerous for us, particularly for you, to be associated with her. When we married, I promised that I would accept you as Katherine's daughter. But you can't become a rallying point for her. We can't risk being identified with her; bad things are happening to those who do not conform to the King's will. Soon, when we have enough money, we will buy a house. If you want, I will set up on my own and move away from Cromwell. Then you can be more open."

I started to cry, "I don't know why you love me, Will, if I put everything at risk?"

"It is because you are a woman of principle, and a brave one at that!" he said, "I tell you, Kat, I would rather have you, with your spirit and your fire, than all the fancy little mistresses at court. I haven't changed how I feel about you, you know." I drank again from my goblet. "I have a present for you," he said, "but it is up in our chamber. I did not know if you would get away tonight."

"But the day for presents is New Year's Day," I pointed out. "And I have nothing yet for you."

"I want to give it to you tonight," Will said. "Who knows what you will be doing on New Year's Day? Come, my wife, come with me." He looked at me and gave me a tentative smile. He was very handsome tonight. I leant over and kissed him on the forehead. Then he stood up, pulling me with him, took me in his arms and kissed me long and hard on the lips. I found myself responding to him, clinging to him, wanting to feel his arms around me, his man's body on top of me. I could never say no to him. We walked tipsily up the stairs, holding each other around the waist, stopping to kiss every couple of steps.

In our small room there was a fire burning. Will sat me on the bed, went over to the chest and opened it. He pulled out a large bolt of sea green silk, as iridescent as a magpie's wing.

"Will, that is beautiful," I whispered, hardly believing that it was for me.

"For a gown, for May Day, we can get it made up," he said. "My beautiful wife, I am so proud of you." I started to cry.

"No one has ever given me something so beautiful," I rubbed at my face with my hands. "I cannot believe it is for me. How much did it cost you?"

"Be quiet! Master Cromwell got a discount for me on it. But I am not going to tell you, not ever, so stop asking questions, wife!" With that, he sat beside me on the bed, then pushed me back, his mouth on mine, his hands pushing my skirt up, feeling remorselessly along my legs to what was between my thighs. Not that I resisted him, no – I loved him, and I wanted him so much that night.

Daughter, I have said before that I must tell you everything. The relations between a man and woman are usually private, and I will not go into details. But it is important that you realise that Will and I loved each other, utterly and completely.

As Will had guessed, I was back at court a day later, busy playing for Queen Anne while she gossiped and played cards with her friends. Sir Henry Norris was there, and William Brereton, but George Boleyn had gone to the country. Mark Smeaton kept hanging around, trying to muscle in on my job, but Anne still preferred me, I was glad to say. She would allow him to play occasionally, when I was away, but that was all. And when she retired to her privy chamber, it was only me who was allowed in to play.

The court was still feasting, and I was tuning up my lute in Anne's chambers when a maidservant came in and beckoned me to the door.

"Mistress Kat, there is a lady asking for you," she said quietly to me. Then she looked around and whispered, "It is Lady Maria Willoughby. I remember her from before. She is down by the stables, she wouldn't come in. She wants to talk with you." I thanked the maid and grabbed my cloak. It was cold down by the stables.

Lady Willoughby was waiting for me, blowing on her hands to keep warm. When she saw me, she opened her arms and embraced me.

"Kat, I have bad news. The Queen is very unwell. She worsened over Christmas, and now the fear is that her time is short. I am going to ask the King if I may go to her. As you are her daughter, I think it fitting that you should come. Shall I ask the King for you also? I shall say I need a maid. You do not mind if I describe you as such?" I stammered a reply,

"Of course I don't, but what ails the Queen?" Daughter, I felt as if I had been kicked in my stomach. I hadn't seen the Queen for a long time, but I always believed I would see her again. She was my mother, remember, and I owed her everything. But somehow, I had thought she would always be there whenever I was free to go and see her. But now, Lady Willoughby was telling me that she would soon leave this earth. I cannot describe the desolation and shock that hit me just then.

"She has such great pains in her stomach, and she cannot eat, I hear," Lady Willoughby said. "The doctor has said that this is her final illness. We cannot let her die alone, Kat. We must go to her." I nodded my head vehemently,

"Of course, but how can we? We are not allowed."

"Leave it with me, Kat, I will ask the King. Meet me here tomorrow at nightfall, and I will tell you what to do."

I hurried back to Queen Anne's chamber, my mind in a ferment. I could not, would not leave my mother to die alone. But going to her would imperil my post at court, my friendship with Queen Anne, and most terrible of all, my relationship with Will. He wanted me to forget Queen Katherine, something which he accepted I couldn't do. But what would he think if I galloped off to be with her at her deathbed? There would not be an easy way back for the two of us, I knew that. So, maybe I shouldn't go? But then, I remembered how Queen Katherine had cared for me, had looked after me, long before she ever knew I was her daughter. Did I not owe her for that? Could I bear to let her leave this world without bidding her farewell? I knew that I couldn't. So, I would have to meet with Lady Willoughby tomorrow, and if she was able to go to Queen Katherine, then I would go too.

I arrived early the next night, but she was already waiting, pacing up and down the yard in front of the stables. Her face was hidden by her cloak, but I could tell it was her. The slight figure and the quick movements gave her away.

"So, shall we go?" I asked, without even greeting her. She didn't answer me directly,

"I spoke to the King this morning. I asked for a special audience with him and told him it was about Queen Katherine. I was admitted. Maybe he hoped that she had changed her mind and was accepting the situation after all these years. But yes, he agreed to see me. He was so disappointed when I told him that the Queen was of the same mind as she ever was and that she would never accept Queen Anne as her successor."

"Doesn't he know her? That is the last thing she would ever do," I commented. Many of us had tried to change Queen Katherine's mind on this, but no one had succeeded.

"I told him that she was dying, and you know what, Kat, he smiled. That man smiled! You would think he might show some sadness after all the years they spent together. But then I asked him, very humbly, if he might allow me to be with Queen Katherine during her last days. I reminded him that I was her oldest friend and had known her since childhood." She shook her head despairingly. "That man has no pity, Kat. No mercy, no love. He denied me! He told me that Katherine should die alone. He said she deserved this fate because she had made him suffer. She had made him suffer! I could scarcely contain myself. But I had to Kat, for her sake. So, I asked him again, for the love of God, and as a merciful sovereign, to allow me to go. But he refused and called the guard to take me away." She looked so sad that I reached out to her.

"I am so sorry, Lady Willoughby, so very sorry."

"Call me Maria, we must forget the formalities now," she told me. "I am going to ride to Kimbolton Castle, where she is, and force my way in. I shall not take no for an answer. Are you willing to accompany me?" I didn't pause.

"Yes, Maria, I will." Although all sense was against it, I knew in my heart that this was what I must do. I loved Queen Katherine, and I owed her this last service.

"Very well. Meet me by the gate tomorrow at eight, just as the sun rises. You need a horse, a good one." I had to confess,

"Maria, I have never owned a horse."

"No matter. You can ride?"

"Yes, of course. I am a good rider."

"Very well, I will bring you a horse. Kat, you know this will change everything for you. Are you sure you want to do it?"

"Yes, Maria, I am more certain than I have ever been."

I could not tell anyone in the Queen's household, or at Thomas Cromwell's house. To do so would have meant we would be stopped. I left court early, excusing myself by saying that I had a bad headache. When I reached Austin Friars, I surreptitiously gathered a clean linen shift, hose, bread, some cheese and cold meat and put them all into a bag. This I placed in the chest in the hall, beside the entrance door, ready for my escape.

I rose early, leaving Will still sleeping. I knew I should have told him, but that would just cause more conflict between us. He might have tried to stop me, and I couldn't risk that. Instead, I blew him a kiss as I stood at the door before creeping downstairs and retrieving my bag.

As I got to the gate of the palace, I saw Lady Willoughby already seated on her horse. Beside her, there was a groom holding the reins of two other horses.

"Kat, this is John, my groom. He has your horse for you." John nodded at me, took my bag and stowed it in the saddlebags one horse was wearing.

"Here he is, my lady," he said, "he's a good steady one, won't throw you." He helped me onto the horse, a large dark brown beast with gentle eyes. Then he mounted the other horse and doffed his cap to Lady Willoughby.

"John will be riding with us to Kimbolton," Lady Willoughby told me. "He will see to the stabling of the horses and provide us with protection." With that, she gathered the reins of her horse and led us on through the city.

Daughter, we were on the road for thirty-six hours. We didn't stop, except for brief breaks to eat and rest the horses. Lady Willoughby was not a young woman, but she set a pace that even young knights would find hard to match.

"My lady, we should find somewhere to sleep the night," John said to her that evening.

"No, John, we cannot afford to waste time. I cannot let my Catalina go without me." She looked over at me.

"Kat, are you strong enough to continue?" She needn't have asked. Like her, I could not let Katherine of Aragon,

Queen of England, and my mother, leave this earth without saying goodbye. So, we continued to ride. It was the middle of the night, and the road was merely a rough track, when Lady Willoughby's horse stumbled on a rock. A younger person could have stayed on the horse, but Lady Willoughby was the same age as Katherine of Aragon and riding side saddle. She fell off into a muddy puddle. John and I both dismounted and rushed to her aid. She seemed a little dazed, but after a moment scrambled to her feet.

"My lady, let us find an inn," John tried again, "you need to rest yourself and put on clean clothes."

"No. Catalina is waiting. We have no time to waste. Help me up John." She mounted the horse again and continued to ride on, without complaint or tears.

It was New Year's Day when we reached Kimbolton Castle. Lady Willoughby sent John away, first giving him a pouch of money. "That is for your service, John, and also enough for you to find shelter and food on your way back to London." Then she turned to me.

"Kat, you must dismount and stay some distance behind me. Take both horses." I did as she told me and watched from a distance when she went up to the great gateway and banged loudly on it. A manservant appeared.

"Good sir, I ask for your help. I am a woman alone, and I've had an accident. I fell off my horse, and I think my ankle is broken." The guard looked at her doubtfully, and then said,

"No one is to enter without a licence. Get you on your way, mistress." But Lady Willoughby was made of sterner stuff. She sat down, just inside the open door, and started to cry.

"Oh, the pain, it is too much. I cannot ride anymore. Leave me here, good sir, I will die quietly." The guard looked flustered, turned and spoke to his colleague.

"I've sent for the steward, Sir Edward Bedingfield," he informed her, "you can speak to him." Lady Willoughby groaned and lay full length on the ground.

"Thank you. I can barely move," she said, looking directly up at him. "You are a kind boy, I can tell."

Sir Edward appeared in the doorway, bringing a waft of winey breath, his face pink and his stomach protuberant. He recognised Lady Willoughby at once.

"My lady, what are you doing here?" He looked down on her with a worried face. She was trouble, he knew that.

"Sir Edward, please help me. I have had a fall from my horse, and I can barely walk. I need to rest and have medical attention for my leg." He shifted uncomfortably.

"Lady Willoughby, you are here to see the Princess Dowager, do not deny it."

"I don't deny it at all," she cried out. "I have permission from the King to visit her. But on my way, my horse threw me, and I am sorely injured." Sir Edward grunted and leant forward to pull her up to a sitting position. Slowly, she sat up, wincing with pain.

"Show me your licence to visit," he said, "then I can admit you."

"I have it somewhere," she said. "I had a pouch with it in. Look on my horse." The guard looked towards me.

"Yes, that is my horse. My servant wench is holding it. Go and see." Sir Edward nodded, and the guard came beside me and started rifling through our saddle bags. After a few minutes he looked over to Sir Edward.

"There is no licence here, Sir." At that, Lady Willoughby started to wail loudly.

"Of course there isn't. That pouch was lost when I was thrown, it is somewhere on the road. I couldn't see in the dark."

"My lady, without a licence I am not allowed to let you enter." Sir Edward shook his head and started to withdraw.

"Kat, come here!" Lady Willoughby called me. "Hand over the horses to be stabled." I handed the reins to one of the guards, who took them sheepishly.

"Sir, you will at least allow our horses to be fed! And, as for me, I shall perish here, for I cannot move elsewhere."

Sir Edward was restless, wanting to get back to his New Year celebration. He sighed.

"Very well. For a few hours only." He turned to the guards. "Let them in and take them to the kitchens for food. I don't want to see her again, is that clear?"

"Thank you, Sir. May God bless you." Lady Willoughby beckoned to me, and I helped her up. She leant on my arm and hobbled slowly through the door. Sir Edward vanished through a further door, and a maidservant came forward to help us.

Once she was sure he had gone, Lady Willoughby's gait changed considerably. She straightened up and started to walk so quickly up the stairs that I found it hard to keep up.

"Where is the Queen? In these apartments?" She gestured ahead to the state rooms. The maidservant, puzzled, said,

"Why yes, if you mean the Princess Dowager, she is housed in the best rooms, believe me." With that Lady Willoughby brushed past her, marched along the gallery and towards the ornate door that was the entrance to the state apartments. I followed on, dodging the maidservant, who looked more puzzled than anything else. In a moment, we had passed through the door, and Lady Willoughby had pulled the bolts across it, locking us in.

She strode into the chamber, scattering ladies and maidservants in every direction.

"Where is the Queen? I want to see the Queen." One woman pointed at a further door.

"In there." I didn't know the woman. I didn't know any of them. They had been chosen by the King because they were not friends of Katherine. All of us had been barred.

No longer. Lady Willoughby, Maria by now to me, swept through the door and slammed it shut. The key turned in the lock, and I was left standing outside with a group of women I didn't know or respect. I decided to wait.

I was hungry by then, and I asked one of the women if she could bring me some food. She looked sulky and told me they only had bread and cheese.

"That is all I need, and some small ale, if you please." She went out and reappeared a moment later with a hunk of cheese and a small loaf of bread. I sat down to eat, realising how hungry I was.

I could scarcely believe that my mother, the Queen, was behind the door. I had not seen her for more than two years. Would she still be the same? Would she be pleased to see me? Would I even be allowed to see her? As I ate, these thoughts circled me. I was lost, just as I had been all those years ago when she had discovered me in the stables. I needed her now, as I needed her then.

As I was finishing the last of the bread, the far door opened. Maria beckoned me to come into the chamber. I stood up, brushing the crumbs from my skirt, and walked slowly and steadily towards her.

She ushered me into a chamber that was dark, lit only by a few candles and a flickering fire. I couldn't see anything for a moment, until my eyes got used to the dark. I could just make out the bed, up against the far wall, and inside that bed, a small pale figure propped up against the pillows. A maidservant tended a pot that hung over the fire, but there were no other staff in the room.

She whispered in French through the silence,

"Kat, my Kat, is it you?" She sounded much weaker than she had before, but her voice was still clear. I made my way to the bed and sat beside her. I was shocked to see how much she had changed. Always plump, she was now as thin as a sparrow. Her face, once so pink, was sallow and lined. But her smile was the same. She had always beamed at people, making them know that she was delighted to see them. But I felt that her delight at seeing me was real, and I basked in it for a moment.

"Your Majesty," I whispered, "I am sorry you are unwell." She smiled wryly.

"But my illness has brought me you, my dear girl, and my oldest friend Maria. I thank you both so much for coming to see me. It must have taken much courage." She spoke with an effort, and it made my heart lurch to hear her.

"Are you happy, Kat?" she asked, "I have wondered about you, how you have borne what you lost. My princess, with no one to recognise you." I took her hand in mine. It felt bony and fragile.

"Your Majesty, I am happy. From what I have seen, being a princess is not a destiny to be envied." She nodded.

"But Kat, never to know what it might have been like! Do you not imagine yourself living as you were born, as a princess of the blood?" She lay back against the pillows, exhausted.

"Come child, lie beside me, as you did before." I lay down, facing her, and started to stroke her hair.

"Mother," I was still speaking in French, which the maid would not understand. "You brought me up. You loved me as no one else has ever loved me. I was lucky in that I had you. And my sister, Princess Mary, had to leave you. If I had to choose between being a princess and being able to be with you, I would choose you every time." I leant over and kissed her on the cheek. It was wet with tears. For a moment I held her.

Maria, Lady Willoughby came up to us.

"Her Majesty is tired, she needs sleep," she said. "Come with me, Kat, we need to draw up a list of provisions which the servants can buy for us." Queen Katherine lay back with a sigh. Maria and I moved over to the other side of the room.

"She has not eaten for days," Maria said. "She can keep nothing down, and they persist in giving her heavy food. We need to make her some custard, and some chicken broth. We can do it over the fire."

"Why not in the kitchen?" I asked.

"The Queen is afraid that she is being poisoned. We must watch over her, and the cooking of her food, every minute." We worked out a rota so that one of us would always be with her. I was the first to be able to sleep, so I found a pallet bed and lay down. I fell asleep almost immediately.

I woke up to the noise of a party of men arriving at the castle. Maria opened the door a crack and asked the maidservants what was going on.

"My lady, the King has allowed Chapuys, the ambassador from Spain, to visit. He is here with a body of men and some representatives from Thomas Cromwell." Maria's face was first overjoyed, and then angry,

"So, he allows Chapuys to visit, at the very last minute. But he is to be spied on every moment. And your sister, Princess Mary, is forbidden from visiting. What a cruel man the King of England is."

Maria admitted Chapuys to the room, and he went quickly to speak with the Queen. They were old friends, and her face was animated as they talked. Meanwhile, Maria was making a custard, with fresh eggs and milk, sweetened with honey. Her face was red as she stirred the pot over the fire, but she wouldn't allow anyone else to do it. When it was ready, she swept Chapuys away from the bed, and fed the Queen spoonful by spoonful with the delicate custard. At first, Katherine was reluctant, but the custard was so easy to eat that she took about half of the bowlful. Maria looked triumphantly at me and Chapuys.

"See, they have been making her eat heavy, fatty meat. No wonder she is sick! But this simple custard has stayed down. She has not been sick since we arrived. Indeed, the Queen was lying against the pillows now, looking as if she was about to fall asleep. She looked just like a little girl, laying there so trustingly.

Over a couple of days, our care of the Queen led to an improvement in her condition. She started to sit up and comb her hair. Then she ate a bowl of stewed apples with cream, and some colour returned to her cheeks. Chapuys, who had spent many hours sitting with her, noticed these signs with relief.

"She is recovering, thank God," he said. "This is not the end of things." He left for London, absolutely certain that Katherine was out of danger.

But he was mistaken. That night she felt worse. I was sleeping beside her, and she woke me and asked for her confessor.

"My time is near, Kat," she whispered. "I must make my peace with God." And so the priest came, and she received extreme unction for those who are facing death. Maria was sitting on one side of the bed, and I on the other. Towards the back of the room, a group of the ladies were waiting, hushed and expectant. They were joined by the maids, and I noticed that some of them were crying openly. Queen Katherine was forever popular with the servants, for her kindness and piety.

I sat beside her as her breathing became more and more laboured. Maria held her hand while I stroked her hair. We sat like that for hours as she breathed, stirred, and breathed again. At one point she opened her eyes and looked at me.

"Ma fille," she said in French. "My daughter. May the Virgin Mary watch over you, and keep you safe for all of your life." I choked with tears.

"Maman, mother, you are everything to me." She smiled and made the sign of the cross on my forehead. Then she turned to Maria.

"Tell Princess Mary that I bless her, and I know that she will follow God's will for all of her life. I have had many children, and I have loved all of them. Be sure to tell Princess Mary that I loved her. But tell her to be brave, and to resist her father's sinful plans. She is my daughter. I know she will keep the faith. I pray for my husband and my King, that he resumes his rightful mind. And, Heavenly Father, I pray for my soul. Please forgive my sins and allow me to enter Paradise, where I may know your glory." And then she closed her eyes and lay back on the pillow. Everyone was crying now, even the women who had been her guards. Maria started praying, tears streaming down her cheeks. I joined in, begging the Lord God to bring my dearest mother to Himself without fear or pain.

Katherine lay there, pale and still except for the faint breaths that still came from her mouth. She looked so peaceful, and I knew that God was answering our prayer.

Just before two o'clock that afternoon, she passed. A Queen who had done no harm, and much good. A witty and clever woman who could take on the cleverest men and win. A lady who did not deserve her fate but lived bravely through every setback. And so England lost a queen and I lost my mother.

CHAPTER 9

We rode back to London a few days after Queen Katherine's death. This time, we were a lot slower, both hardly speaking. We were mourning her and unable to find the spirit to even converse. But when we got to London, Lady Willoughby asked me what I was going to do.

"I will go back to the court, my lady. I hope Anne Boleyn will take me back." Lady Willoughby tightened her lips.

"The concubine! Kat, should you ever tire of working for her, you must come to me. I will find you employment. I cannot let my Catalina's daughter starve. You and I, we are part of her, and always will be." I was heartened by this. Lady Maria Willoughby was married to an English peer, her household was a great one. But she was not in the King's favour. Living with her would be nothing like as exciting as being at court.

"She is ill-used by the King, as Queen Katherine was," I said. Maria snorted.

"That is her own fault, Kat. I have no sympathy!" But her face had softened. Like me, she detested King Henry. Maria could not help but feel some satisfaction that he was now abusing the great concubine, Anne Boleyn. And that somehow lessened her dislike.

"If her pregnancy produces a prince, she will be safe," she said. "Otherwise, she is a sitting target. Go, if you must. But remember, you will always have a place with me if you need it."

I arrived back at Greenwich with my excuses prepared. I decided that I would tell the truth. Queen Anne knew that I had served Queen Katherine, and I hoped that she would accept that I had gone at Lady Willoughby's entreaty. At the very least, the news that Katherine was dead should lessen her annoyance.

When I arrived at the Queen's apartments, Queen Anne was not in her Presence Chamber. It was strangely deserted except for a few servants passing through with firewood, candles and brushes to sweep the floor. I caught up with a footman carrying a barrel of ale through from the cellar.

"Where is the Queen?" I asked. He smiled.

"Why, she is with the King. They are having a party." I was puzzled. Christmas and New Year were now well over.

"What is the party for?" I asked.

"It is to celebrate the death of the Dowager Princess." He bent and whispered to me, "The old Queen as we know her. They are mad with joy. The King is making merry with the whole court." I followed him through the palace to the King's Presence Chamber, the largest and most magnificent in the whole palace.

The hall was blazing with candles, and noisy with music and laughter. People were calling out for the King and the Queen to lead the next dance, a spirited galliard. I made them out from among the crowds of people, making their way to the head of the hall. It was not hard to find them. They were both dressed in yellow, and the King had a large white feather in his cap. Still grieving for Katherine, I saw this as it was. A gratuitous insult to a great lady. I was so angry. I wondered if I should go straight back to Lady Willoughby. Everyone I knew here was happy that Queen Katherine had died. I felt more alone than ever before.

As the musicians were tuning up, the King clapped his hands.

"Let the lords and ladies dance late into the night tonight! For, thank God, we are now free of any fear of war." Of course, he had risked war with the Holy Roman Emperor by divorcing his aunt. Now she was dead, politics could continue as usual, unswayed by any family feeling. All the courtiers clapped him enthusiastically, and I sensed a feeling of great relief amongst them. Henry turned and held out his hand to Queen Anne, radiant in saffron coloured silk. He led her out in front of the others, and the musicians struck up a lively tune. I noticed Mark Smeaton and wondered if he had usurped my place already. George Boleyn was there, the Duke of Suffolk, Henry Norris and William Brereton. Sir Thomas Wyatt waved at me as he led lady after lady onto the floor. And so, the court danced while Queen Katherine was barely cold.

I could understand the relief, though. Everyone had wanted Katherine to compromise, and she hadn't. She had sworn, though, that she wouldn't ask her nephew to invade England on her behalf, and she had kept her word. But the fact that she was now dead removed the last impediments to a glorious new age, of a baby princess and a prince to come, of the reformed church, and of an English King no longer subject to an outside power.

Later, the King fetched Princess Elizabeth, and showed her round the room, tickling her and feeding her with sweetmeats. I noticed Lady Bryan standing there, frowning slightly, no doubt hoping that she could bring her charge back to Hatfield tomorrow, where she could resume her routine. But on that night, she stayed up late, spoiled by her father and mother, and every courtier in the room.

Queen Anne withdrew early to her chambers, curtseying to the King. He nodded indulgently. He would not want her to get overtired with the baby prince she was carrying in her womb. I followed her procession and caught her as she entered her privy chamber. She sat down, took off her hood, and put her hand in the small of her back.

"My back hurts," she complained. Then she saw me.

"Kat Cooke, where have you been? I have not seen you for days." I took a deep breath.

"Your Majesty, I was asked to accompany Lady Willoughby to Kimbolton." Anne sat up straight.

"What? You went to that old woman? How could you be so disloyal? You have betrayed me, you viper! I've a good mind to charge you with treason. Begone Kat, I don't want to see you. You are no longer in my employ. Leave my service and go home to your husband's service. Your very presence disturbs me." I stood there for a moment, stock still. I could not blame her. But naively, I had hoped she would understand. I should have known she would respond with bitterness. I curtseyed, turned on my heel and left. Remembering what she was like when she lost her temper, I decided I would sleep in the maids' dormitory tonight and go to see Will tomorrow. I would have to tell him I was coming to live with him. But how would that be possible in Thomas Cromwell's house? He had already made it plain that if I identified myself with Queen Katherine, I would become his enemy. I went to the office where Will worked early the next morning and waited for him. I knew he was always the first in, and so I hoped to catch him on his own. Just before daybreak, I heard his footsteps approaching the door, quick and business-like as always. He opened the door, started back in surprise, and then spoke,

"Where in God's name have you been? I have been searching for you, and nobody knew anything. Tell me, what have you been doing?" He gripped the edge of his desk, and I noticed his knuckles were white. He looked angrier than I had ever seen him before.

"I'm sorry, Will, I couldn't tell you. I couldn't tell anyone, or else we would have been stopped."

"Stopped? What do you mean? Were you doing something

for the Princess Dowager?" His voice was like ice. I tried to pacify him,

"Only my duty as a daughter. Will, please understand. I had to see my mother before she died. Lady Willoughby told me she was very ill, and you must know I had to say goodbye." Will took a deep intake of breath.

"So, let me be correct. You went with Lady Willoughby to see the Princess Dowager on her deathbed?" I nodded, and he looked at me angrily.

"And in doing so, you went expressly against the King's wishes? You also risked your position with Queen Anne, and you laid us open to Cromwell's revenge. You know that he warned you against going to Katherine. Good work Kat! You have ruined my future, put yourself in grave danger, and are likely to be charged with treason!"

"Treason?" I gasped. "Surely not? We were doing no harm." Will looked at me, his brow furrowed.

"Katherine was seen as being in league with the Spanish. Any contact with her could be seen as traitorous. Don't you understand, after all we've been through?" He took my arm and pulled me to the door.

"Kat, we must find somewhere quiet to talk." He dragged me along the corridor until we reached a richly appointed office.

"Cromwell is with the King now. We won't be disturbed," he said. "Sit down!" He sat on the chair behind the desk and gestured me to a stool.

Will leant forward and grabbed my hands in his. Staring into my eyes, he spoke,

"Kat, I know you loved her. But you know that Cromwell and Lady Anne will not welcome any show of loyalty to her. Either we are on their side, or we are their enemies. Do they know?"

"I told Lady Anne yesterday," I said.

"And?"

"She dismissed me. She said I was lucky not to be charged with treason. I have to come to Austin Friars." Will shook his head.

"Can't you see that's not possible? Cromwell won't shelter you. Remember what he said. He might come after you, me, both of us. You have not done well, Kat."

"So what shall we do?" I said. Will frowned. For once, he looked defeated.

"So, I will leave Cromwell's service and ask my father if he can find me work in a kitchen somewhere." Despair seeped from him. I could see how painful it was for him to give up his hopes.

"Is that necessary? Can we not carry on as usual but move out of Cromwell's house?" Will stood up and started striding around the room.

"Don't you see? Cromwell will not employ anyone who threatens his plans. It doesn't matter where we live. He won't trust me, being linked with you."

"Well then, don't be linked with me!" I cried out. My temper was up, and I could not accept what was the truth. If Will was to make his way in the world, he had to stay on the right side of Cromwell. I could see how much it cost him to give that up, and it angered me.

"Do you mean that?" he asked coldly.

"Yes, I do! I cannot be responsible for you losing your job. Leave me!" I knew I was challenging him to walk away. But I did not expect him to accept that challenge. He spoke rapidly,

"You are still my wife, Kat, but you're right. We can't live together." I felt winded, as if he had hit me in the stomach. I immediately regretted what I'd said and cried out,

"But I can't live without you, Will! I love you."

"But you went behind my back, Kat. That's what hurts me." His voice had softened a bit, and I started to realise how much he was suffering.

"I'm sorry, Will, but you would have stopped me, and I had to go."

"Kat, whenever you have to choose between your royal mother and me, she wins. You never really treat me as your husband, you don't think of my interest. I wonder if you ever will."

"You expect too much of me, Will! Yes, you are my husband, but when do you put my interest first?" Will shook his head angrily.

"You know that I have accepted that you work at court. I trusted you, but then you let me down. I know you love me. But you had no thought for me when you did this. You didn't discuss it with me. Can't you see how that hurt? I deserved better Kat. You've admitted as much. Look, go to Lady Willoughby, your fellow conspirator. She will take you in."

"But what about you?" I asked.

"I will tell Cromwell we have separated, and that I am no longer responsible for you. I hope that will be enough." Will sighed and sat down. "Go to Lady Willoughby for now, Kat. Leave me, Kat. Do not come back to Austin Friars. Cromwell will not forgive you."

"But I can't do without you!?" I cried out. A passing page looked curiously at us, and then hurried on his way.

"You say that now! You betrayed me, Kat! I begged you not to get involved with all of this. But no, you had to do it. You didn't even stop to ask me. The truth is that she was more important to you than me. I think you don't care about us at all."

"No, no, that's not true," I cried out, but Will didn't stop.

"You didn't think about the effect on us, did you?" I shook my head, feeling very guilty, but then the anger overcame me once more.

"Don't you understand? I just lost my mother! The best queen England ever had." Will tensed up and put his hand over my mouth.

"For God's sake, keep quiet. You do not know what danger you put us in. Look, I know you are grieving, but by your actions you have made it impossible for me to comfort you. You know that if Lady Anne wants revenge, we could both end up in the Tower?" I shivered at the thought. Will continued in a calmer tone. "I can't just walk out like you can. I have to make a life. We must hope that Cromwell is too busy to deal with us both. You must avoid him, don't remind him of your presence. Now go, Kat, if you have any love left for me. Go to Lady Willoughby and keep silent." With that, he gave me another push and then slammed the door shut.

Daughter, I cannot tell you how desolate I felt. I ran back towards the Queen's chambers, not thinking straight but going instinctively to where I had always felt safe. By my stupidity, I had lost Will and all that he meant to me. But a part of me felt angry with him. Yes, I had been reckless, but surely, he should understand that I had to be with Queen Katherine as she passed from this life? He had disappointed me, and I thought less of him.

Nearing the Queen's apartments, I put down my head and ran. I could barely see for the tears that were coursing down my cheeks, not that it mattered. I could find my way to the Queen's apartments in pitch darkness.

"Hey, Kat, what is the matter?" I had run into a man's chest. Taller than me, he had put his arm around me, and was looking down with concern.

"Tom!" I gulped. "I am lost. I've lost Will, I've lost the Queen. I will have to leave court; I cannot bear it." When I said I'd lost the Queen, I was meaning the old Queen, but Tom took me to mean Queen Anne.

"Whatever has happened, Kat? We can sort it out, don't worry." The tears started again at his kindness, and I clung to him, breathing in his scent of cedarwood and pine. He moved quickly.

"Kat, come. We cannot talk in front of people. Come to my chamber, it isn't far." He steered me along through numerous chambers, some humming with people whom he ignored.

Through the yard, and up some stairs, then through more chambers, and then at last up a small spiral staircase. At the top, he paused and opened the door,

"Here, Kat, you are safe here." There was a manservant laying a fire, and Tom sent him to fetch bread, meat and cheese. There was already a large flagon of wine on the sideboard, with several goblets standing beside it. Tom sat me down on the settle by the fire and poured me a large goblet of wine. The servant returned and gave me a platter with spiced meats, cheese and freshly baked bread. Tom waved him away and told me to eat.

I hadn't noticed how hungry I was. I hadn't eaten properly since Kimbolton. I tore into the bread, tears still running down my cheeks. Tom sat sipping his wine, waiting for me to finish.

Eventually, I pushed the platter away from me.

"What has happened?" he asked. "I haven't seen you for days, and now I find you weeping as if your own mother had died." I couldn't tell him that was exactly what had happened. But I had to explain what I had been doing.

"You know I served Queen Katherine before? Well, I went to see her before she died. Will is very angry with me about it. He says I am risking his career at court. He has sent me away, Tom. He doesn't want to see me again." Tom looked troubled.

"He must be careful, Kat. We can't afford to be human while we are at court." I sobbed out loud.

"But why? All I was doing was seeing a dying woman! Tell me what is wrong with that, Tom? What hurt does that do to anyone? Queen Anne called me a viper." Tom raised me up and took me in his arms.

"You have been hurt by this circus, as I have Kat. Don't give up. We need real people in this place. Real, sweet people," and he kissed me full on the lips. Daughter, please do not blame me, but I felt so alone. I returned his kiss, desperate for some affection, someone to tell me I was worthy of love. Will's rejection had left me aching, and Tom was offering to soothe that ache.

He took me over to the bed, and we lay down together. It wasn't frantic or intense. It was just like two friends, kissing and talking, talking and kissing.

"You are an artist, Kat," he said, delicately kissing the tips of my fingers. "With these sweet digits you bring delight. You are the best musician I have ever heard. You would go far if you were not a woman."

"I wish I wasn't a woman. Then I would be able to make my own life like you." Tom laughed softly.

"I do not make my life, none of us do. And it would be such a loss for you not to be a woman. You are the very sweetest, most delicious woman I know, and you are in my bed. God is kind to me tonight." He pulled my coif off and worked to undo my braids. After a few minutes, my hair was down my back, red gold in the firelight.

"Kat, you are so beautiful. May I take off your gown so that I can see you, all of you?"

Daughter, I should have refused. But he was so charming, and I needed to feel loved that night. So I stood up and let him unlace me. I stepped out of my gown and pulled my shift over my head.

"Kat, you are Venus, the goddess of love," he breathed, taking off his own clothes and flinging them on the floor.

And then, daughter, we made love. I refuse to be ashamed of it because he was kind, and he brought me great pleasure in his bed. I knew that nothing serious could ever come of it, with him being a gentleman and me a lowly lute player. But for that night, we were equals, and we gave and received pleasure equally.

The next morning, I woke up to see Tom pulling on his clothes. He saw my eyes open and leant over to kiss my nose.

"Get dressed now, Kat. We will go to see the Queen. I will make things alright."

Tom was still close to Queen Anne, I knew that, and when he ushered me into her presence, she smiled to see him. But when she turned to me, her face was grim.

"Your Majesty, I have found a lost lute player," he said, bowing. I curtseyed and kept my eyes on the ground.

"I told her to go away," Queen Anne said. "She left my service without any notice. That is enough! But then, when she told me she had gone to see old Katherine, the Princess Dowager, that was a knife to my heart! Is that not the action of a viper, Tom? You tell me!" She looked challengingly at Tom Wyatt. He started talking to her softly, as maybe he had in the past.

"Your Majesty, I know you have the kindest heart. I have often depended on you, and you have never let me down." Anne pursed her lips and nodded.

"And so?" she asked.

"Mistress Kat is deeply sorry for her action. It was a foolish thing and influenced by an excess of feeling and loyalty which she possesses in great measure. Your Majesty, you know deep in your heart that Kat is loyal. She was loyal to Katherine when it only brought her trouble. She will be as loyal to you." Anne looked at me consideringly.

"I am full of remorse at what I did," I said, "and I prostrate myself to beg your pardon." I knelt in front of her, as Tom had instructed me to do.

"And, your Majesty, Kat is setting some of my poems to music," Tom told her. I stirred a little. I did not know of this. "We wish to perform them for you to celebrate when your prince is born."

"Tom, you know you to twist me round your little finger. Oh, do get up, Kat! Very well, you can stay, but one more foot out of place, and that will be it!" I pulled myself up, stammering my thanks. She took one look at me and my dishevelled state and waved imperiously at me.

"Now go and clean yourself up! Get out of my sight!" I

backed quickly out of the room before she could change her mind. As I left, I heard her asking Tom to walk with her in the gardens and entertain her. He answered cheerfully, the relief permeating his voice,

"I shall be honoured, your Majesty."

So, I didn't need to retreat to Lady Willoughby. I rejoined Queen Anne's household, trying to merge into the background as far as possible. As soon as he saw me, Cromwell cornered me.

"Kat, you must be the greatest idiot at court," he hissed. "I told you to keep away from Katherine. Do you want to force me to stop your silly plotting?" I didn't cower. I looked straight into his bloodshot eyes.

"You know my relation to the lady," I said, "and you know how close I was to her. It was my duty as her daughter and her friend." He looked exasperated.

"Will has told me that the pair of you have separated. You know you cannot come back to Austin Friars now?" I nodded.

"I should charge you with conspiracy, along with Lady Maria. But the King wants no more reminders of his old wife. He wants to move forward with his new love. I told Lady Anne to dismiss you, but she said that Thomas Wyatt pleaded your case with her. Did you flutter your eyelashes at him, make him feel sorry for you? He has an influence on Lady Anne that few of us do. I do have close bonds with Sir Thomas, but he was being unduly sentimental. So be it. I will leave you in place for now, because if I removed you, questions would be asked. But if you ever line yourself up with the deceased Princess Dowager again, I personally will throw you in the Thames."

Anne was a little distant with me, but not unkind. Her mind was occupied much more with her pregnancy and her swelling belly. While I played, she would call out when the baby was moving, getting her mother to come and feel it kicking. She rested often, but that didn't stop the terrible sickness that assailed her, as it had done in the past. She gained some relief from drinking an infusion of ginger, but the rich foods that were served to the court often made her retch.

She was determined, though, to go to the jousts that King Henry was competing in. It was January, so she was wearing a green velvet gown lined with soft white ermine and scattered with diamonds. Her cloak was of sable, the most expensive and exclusive fur there was. Although her face was worn and tired, she looked every inch a queen.

I was left behind in her apartments. I did not enjoy jousting, particularly when the weather was cold. I had hoped to speak with Tom, but he was outside cheering at the sport. We were still friendly, and I knew in him I had an ally. But the night we spent together had not been repeated. I think we both knew that it wouldn't go anywhere. I was happy to keep it as a special memory of love between friends. If it had continued, there would have been so many risks: disgrace, losing my post, even pregnancy. So, without speaking about it, we had both gone back to the way we were, without any recriminations or blame.

I plucked listlessly at my lute. I had a composition that I had been working on, and I couldn't get it to go right. I wanted it to be joyful and full of zest. I hoped I could play it for the Queen on May Day. Absorbed, I didn't notice at first the clatter of feet running up the stairs. It was only when Tom burst in that I looked up. His face was ashen.

"The King has had an accident. He is not moving. I fear he is dead." I jumped up and ran to him.

"What do you mean, Tom? What happened?"

"His horse threw him, then fell on top of him. They took him from the field, but he wasn't moving, his eyes were closed." I shuddered at the thought. The men in the joust were all wearing heavy plate armour, as were the horses. The weight of all of that falling on a human body, heart, lungs, stomach. It was inconceivable that anyone could survive.

"Where is the Queen?" Such a sight must have been deeply

shocking for her. Her husband, the father of her unborn child, killed in plain sight.

"She is with him now. The doctors are trying to revive him. I fear it is in vain. She is crying, and praying, but to no avail."

There was a flurry outside the door, and Thomas and Elizabeth Boleyn came in. They had been made Earl and Countess of Wiltshire now their daughter was the Queen. But I could tell by their faces that they were scared that they might lose everything.

The Earl of Wiltshire closed the door behind him and turned to his wife.

"He's dead. He hasn't moved for two hours. He's gone, wife."

"So, what are we going to do?" Elizabeth, the Countess cried out.

"We must think carefully. We will need a temporary regency until Anne gets to her term. If it is a boy, then he is the King, otherwise it is Princess Elizabeth who will be Queen. Either way, we must maintain control of Anne, and of Princess Elizabeth. We should send out George and some men to take control of Hatfield House. Where is George?"

"He's with Anne," whispered their mother, "she is in his arms."

"He hasn't got time for that," the Earl snapped. "He must muster some men and go now." The countess sat down heavily.

"What about Princess Mary?" she said. "There will be many who say she should be Queen."

"All the more reason for George to go to Hatfield. He can take custody of her as well as Elizabeth."

"Mary is of age, and her mother was well respected. All we have is an unborn babe and a toddler. She is very dangerous to us." The countess was very scared. She knew what would happen to her family, should powerful nobles install Mary as queen.

"We will keep her a prisoner, don't worry," her husband said. "And we will remind everyone that she is illegitimate and in thrall to Spain. Once we have our baby prince, people will forget all about her. England wants a boy, and that is what we will give them."

"Go then, and find George," the countess told him. But before he could move, there came a sound of unearthly wailing from outside the door. It burst open and Queen Anne rushed in, followed at some distance by her ladies. The screaming was as if she was in agony, which she surely was. She was shaking uncontrollably, and her face was white, except for her red, swollen eyes. Two ladies approached her and tried to get her to sit down, but she fought them off like a wild cat, clawing and pushing them away. Her mother went up to her and slapped her hard across the face. A wave of shock went through the room at this assault on an anointed queen. But it made Anne pause for a moment, standing there gulping for breath like a little girl who has been overtaken by her temper.

"Anne, remember the baby," her mother said. "You must not upset yourself." Anne turned on her and beat her around the head. Her father intervened and pulled her back. But she turned on him,

"Remember the baby! Remember the baby! Is that all that matters? My life is ruined, and all you can say is remember the baby." The countess went back to her and managed to steer her to a settle beside the fire. Then more tears came, this time without sound. She looked utterly desolate as she sat there, turning away all offers of comfort. At last, she looked up at all of us and wiped her eyes with a handkerchief.

"I must tell you that the King is dead. And so, everything will change."

CHAPTER 10

The Duke of Norfolk, Queen Anne's uncle, entered her chamber, for once without any fanfare. He saw Anne sitting exhausted by the fire and walked over directly to her. He did not bow.

"Anne, the King has been pronounced dead by doctors. His body will be removed to his apartment shortly. We must move swiftly to assert our power." Anne's father called over to him,

"We have discussed this. I will send George to take control of Princess Elizabeth and the Lady Mary."

"That is good," said the Duke of Norfolk, "but we must also move here. I will announce that I will take up the Regency until Anne's pregnancy has come to term. Whether the baby is a boy or a girl, will make no difference. The country will need a regent for many years, and as the premier Duke of England, and the heir's great uncle, I am the only one who can take this on."

"Wait Norfolk, do not assume power you are not entitled to." The Earl of Wiltshire, Anne's father, was not best pleased. "I am the grandfather of the heir; my daughter is the Queen."

"But you do not have the influence, Thomas," the duke said patronisingly. "I am the only one who wields the power to control this situation."

During their argument, Anne sat quietly by the fire, staring into the flames. Suddenly she looked up.

"No," she rapped out, "I am the highest ranking here, or did you forget? I am the Queen and the mother of the heir. I will be the Regent, and you will support me."

"Now, Anne, don't be unreasonable," her father said. "It has to be a man."

"I have men aplenty who will support me," Anne countered, "and any move against me would be counted as treason." The Duke of Norfolk bent over her, and threatened,

"You will be controlled by me, madam, or you will end up in the Tower!" Anne's mother and father hastened to defend her.

"We can work something out," the Earl of Wiltshire said, "Anne will be the figurehead, and we will make the decisions, it is workable."

Before Anne could respond, the door to the chamber opened and Master Cromwell walked in. I noticed the look of dislike on Queen Anne's face. He was one who would not last long, I thought. He bowed deeply to the Queen, and to the two noblemen. He was puffing, and out of breath, and for a moment he was silent. But then he spoke, hoarsely and urgently,

"He is alive, your Majesty. The King is alive. He is conscious once more and has been taken to his chamber." Queen Anne collapsed and started to weep,

"Are you telling me the truth, Cromwell? Do not be cruel. Is he truly alive?"

"Truly, he is alive, your Majesty." A look of immense relief came over Anne's face. She was safe again. She glared at her uncle, who had dared to disrespect her, and then spoke,

"So, lead me to him, Master Cromwell. I must see him." She got up from the settle and stood up straight, her back slightly arched.

"Your Majesty, I will, once the doctors have finished with him. But I can tell you that he sent you a message."

"What message? So, he thought of me?" Cromwell smiled wryly.

"Indeed, he did Madam. He said he is stronger than any horse, and you must not distress yourself. He orders you to rest and protect our unborn prince." Anne made a face as Cromwell withdrew. As he passed me, he looked me in the eye and muttered,

"For God's sake, Kat, make your peace with Will! I am tired of him weeping every night!" I tried to respond, but he was already walking towards the door. Of course, now that Queen Katherine was dead, I presented much less of a threat. Cromwell had his mind on other things now. He left without a backward glance.

It took two days for the King to recover. I was told that at first, he forgot peoples' names, and called Queen Anne by Katherine's name. Unsurprisingly, this did not please her, and it also renewed fears in the Boleyn faction. Was the King indeed recovering? Or was he about to relapse into some kind of seizure? The King was always being observed, but now it was with fearful eyes. The Duke of Norfolk, the Boleyns, Master Cromwell, all of them watching with quick, greedy eyes. But on the third day, he walked from his apartment to the Queen's chamber. Yes, he lent on a stick, but this King was far from a dead man. His brilliant blue eyes darted around the courtiers as he walked. I wondered if he knew how they had been plotting, and realised that yes, he probably did.

As he entered, Queen Anne rose from her seat and swept him a deep curtsey.

"Your Majesty... Henry – I rejoice in your recovery! The Lord God has blessed us indeed." Henry looked at her with some irritation.

"Get up, get up! You were foolish Anne to believe I was near to death. I heard that you were wailing and crying! What faith does that show in me, eh?" Anne flushed.

"Your Majesty, you mean so much to me, I was so worried – but I was foolish, I should have known that you are invincible." So now she is playing Katherine's old game. The game of pacifying him, making him feel good. She was not strong enough now to shout at him.

"How goes my prince?" Henry patted her small belly proprietarily. For just a moment a look of distaste crossed her face, but she quickly recovered. Smiling, she said,

"Your prince is most mighty, your Majesty. He will be a warrior, of that, I am sure." The King beamed.

"Just keep resting, my dear. And don't do anything foolish." And he turned on his heel and swept out of the chamber.

As it happened, it was not Queen Anne who did something foolish, but the King himself. The next day, while resting as instructed, she heard his voice in the outer chamber. I was playing sweet, soothing music to her, but his laughter cut through it.

"You're a funny little thing, and no doubt! I think I shall call you my mouse!" A woman's voice answered softly. Queen Anne frowned and propped herself up on one elbow.

"Is that the King?" she asked, still hazy with sleep.

"Yes, it is your Majesty," I answered. "He sounds well and strong." Queen Anne looked thoughtful. Again, the King's voice intruded,

"So, what will you do if I set the cat on you, my little mouse? You will need me to protect you from her claws." Queen Anne struggled to a sitting position, swung her legs over the side of the bed, and stood up. One of her ladies rushed to offer her an arm, but she ignored it.

"The King is happy," she said, "I must see what makes him smile." She swept out into the next chamber but paused, frozen, in the doorway. I came up behind her, and I saw the King sitting on a great chair, with Lady Jane on his lap. He was holding her and tickling her, and she was lost in fits of giggles.

"You little whore! How dare you entice my husband so?" Lady Jane stopped giggling and pulled herself out of the King's embrace. He tried to pull her back, but she freed herself and curtseyed to Queen Anne.

"I should have known something was going on," Anne muttered grimly. "Lady Jane, you are dismissed from my service henceforth," I saw that Lady Jane was starting to cry, "and don't try that on me, girl! You should be grateful nothing worse is happening to you!" At this, the King stood up, and faced up to the Queen,

"Madam, you will not dismiss Lady Jane from your service. I forbid it." He turned to Lady Jane. "You see, mouse, I said I would protect you from the cat." Lady Jane gave him a small smile, but the Queen was overtaken by a mounting fury.

"You have betrayed me, Henry, and now you order me to keep your mistress on! I tell you I will not do it, I will not!" The King took her by the arm, and she flinched at the tightness of his grip.

"You will turn your head and smile, madam, as your betters have done before you." Her face went white. All it had taken was for Katherine of Aragon to die, and she became a new stick with which to beat her successor. "Lady Jane Seymour will stay in court, and she will be welcomed by you. Kiss her on the cheek, Anne." We all held our breath. Anne was not going to do this, I knew.

I was right. Anne spat on the floor in front of Lady Jane.

"That is your kiss! I cannot prevent you from being here, but know that I hate you!" Before the King could remonstrate with her, she gathered up her skirts and ran back into the next chamber. We could hear her screams and cries, until they were muffled as her mother hurried in to quieten her.

King Henry took Lady Jane by the shoulders and planted a kiss on her forehead.

"Don't worry, little mouse. I will protect you; I promise." He glared around the room at us all.

"If anything happens to this maiden, you will all be punished!" Spittle from his lips hit Lady Jane's face, but she appeared to welcome it, and smiled weakly at him. He turned, kissed her hand, and strode out of the chamber, leaving the rest of us speechless.

I asked her about it later. She had become very coy and would not speak about the King, but she did say that his interest in her was a spiritual one. She told me it was a shame that Anne's jealousy was putting the wrong light on it.

"Kat, you know I am not the King's mistress, nor will I ever be!" I liked her, but she wasn't clever. Like most of the women at court, she had no power to choose. So, I was still friendly with her, although many of the Queen's ladies had become cool. Queen Anne herself was icy, demanding that Jane perform the most menial of duties. She was sent to carry messages, to clear out cupboards, to stitch on her own a mountain of shirts for the servants. I came across her, crouching outside the Queen's chamber, afraid to go in.

"My lady, what is the matter?"

"That is the third time she's told me to go to hell. She hates me Kat! I don't think I can take anymore. I will ask the King if I can return to Wolf Hall. I am tired of the court, and I want an ordinary life."

For me, the court was the most exciting place on earth, but I couldn't blame Lady Jane for wanting to go back to an ordinary life. Sometimes at the moment, it was what I wanted. To seek out Will and go back to an ordinary life with him. To forget being a court musician and become a contented lawyer's wife, with a baby in my arms and children around my skirts. It was a lovely dream. But then something happened that would make it even more unlikely.

It was in the evening, five days after the King's accident. I was in the Queen's chamber, playing softly as she and her ladies played cards. The atmosphere was subdued. The King had not forgiven Anne for her outburst, and so had not visited her since. The excuse he gave was that he did not wish for her to become distressed again. That was him, always wanting to be the saintly husband, even though I knew him to be a demon.

Increasingly courtiers were sensing her loss of importance. Anne felt herself surrounded by people who wished her harm. And she had some reason to think that. Even her beloved Purkoy had been found dead on the ground outside having supposedly fallen from an upstairs window. As a small lapdog, it was hard to work out how Purkoy could have possibly reached that window unless, of course, he had been helped.

Queen Anne threw her cards on the table and got up.

"I am so bored," she complained. "Ladies, will you dance with me? I need something joyful." Of course, all the ladies laid down their cards and stood up. I changed to playing a lively galliard. Queen Anne stepped out to lead the dance, and all the ladies lined up behind her. Suddenly, she gave a cry and sank to her feet. I stopped playing immediately, and her mother ran to her.

"Anne, what ails you? You must not dance, it is foolish." I will never forget Anne's face when she looked up at her mother. She was very frightened. She let out another scream, this time long and agonising.

"Mother, I had not started to dance... this happened. I am in so much pain, I cannot stand!" Her mother and two other ladies picked her up by the arms and dragged her to the bedchamber. She screamed at every touch, and with every step. I have been in some birthing chambers before and since, daughter. But none of them were as pitiable and as terrifying as this one. Anne's screams were not just at the physical pain, but also the mental agony. She knew she was going into labour. But her baby was not yet viable, and she knew that. Her mother sent for the midwife,

"Tell her it is just for her advice. Her Majesty is not in labour." She was hoping desperately that a herbal infusion, some prayers and the midwife's gentle advice might work. Queen Anne could not be losing her baby. It was a difficult pregnancy, that was all.

But Anne's screams continued and rang through her apartments. I knew that people would be whispering, and soon the King would know. The midwife came, felt Anne's forehead, and then her stomach. She looked grave.

"Her Majesty is in labour," she asserted, "and I am sorry to tell you that nothing can stop it."

"Nonsense!" Anne's mother said. "Why, when I was pregnant with George, I nearly lost him, but I took some herbs, and the pains stopped." The midwife shook her head.

"I am sorry, my lady, but nothing will stop this labour." At this point, Anne let out an earth-shattering cry that must have sounded through Greenwich.

"Let us pray to the Virgin Mary!" The Countess of Wiltshire was desperate. "If only we had her girdle to protect my daughter." Anne turned on her mother, her face contorted with rage,

"Have you learnt nothing? That was superstition! That was what I wanted to change!" She howled, and then the midwife took control. She parted Anne's legs and bent between them. Grabbing a clean linen cloth, she put it between them.

"Now, your Majesty, the baby is coming." After another terrible cry, Anne grunted and strained hard. I didn't look but a moment later the midwife showed us all the cloth. A small red mass lay there, recognisably a baby, although far too small to survive. The midwife wiped it off and showed it to Anne.

"A boy, your Majesty, but born too soon." She motioned to a servant to take away the cloth. I felt a pang. I could not help but remember that when I was born to Katherine of Aragon, they had thought I was dead, and taken me away like that, like rubbish. It was only later that the midwife saw me breathing, and by then it was too late. I was adopted and never knew my real mother until much later.

Anne lay there silently while the midwife cleaned her up.

There was no hope that her little boy could be alive. It was far, far too early. Her mother was crying silently, her back to Anne. It struck me that there is no one more alone than a queen who has just miscarried a boy. To lose a girl would be tragic, but to lose a boy, especially now, was calamitous.

The King came to visit the next morning. He was subdued, and his entrance was without the normal grins and jokes he made when moving around the palace. For once, he took no notice of Lady Jane Seymour, who was standing alongside a group of ladies. The chamber was in near silence as he walked through the door to where his wife lay. The door closed, and we were left wondering what was going on.

Lady Jane nudged me. "Now he will have less patience with her tempers, and my life will get better." I wondered what she meant by telling me her life would get better. Was she plotting to become Queen? But no, Lady Jane was not a plotter, even if her brothers were. She turned and smiled at me, her plain face almost beautiful.

"The King has told me to go to him if she is cruel to me. Now there is no baby he will be able to be strict with her." Poor innocent Jane! All she was thinking about was how to stop Anne's bullying. I would swear on my life daughter, that she did not imagine that she would be our Queen before the end of the year. Nobody did. Maybe her brothers had hopes, but none of us could foretell what was going to happen over the next few months.

The door to Anne's chamber opened, and the King appeared. He paused at the door and said,

"When you are up, I will speak to you." His voice was cold, colder than the icy January morning. He walked out among us, and we all made our obeisance. As I rose, I saw that he was looking directly at Lady Jane. There was no desire in that look. Instead his face was calculating, weighing up the odds. He caught my eye and looked away towards the main group of ladies.

"I see God will not give me male children," he said, loudly enough for Anne to hear. He looked back at her door sourly, and then made his way out of her apartment.

It was another week until I saw Queen Anne. For seven days she remained closeted in her chamber, huddled against the cold winds that whipped around the palace. With her was her mother, and her friend Margaret Wyatt, Sir Thomas's sister. Every few hours food was brought into the chamber, and later removed less than half eaten. She was in deep stages of grief and shock, and she didn't want music, she didn't want poetry, or cards, or even a priest. Even her mother despaired of bringing her out of her misery.

Tom Wyatt told me what he knew. His sister had been present when the King visited, and according to her, there had been a bitter exchange between the couple. She had blamed him for her miscarriage, telling him that the sight of him flirting with Lady Jane Seymour had brought it on. He rounded on her for that, telling her angrily that she would do well to ignore his flirtations, as her jealousy was unattractive.

"No man loves a scold, Anne. You must know that." He'd spoken with a chilling objectivity, as if imparting some valued piece of learning. But she had wept when he spoke, and had declared her love for him,

"Sire, I am sorry I displease you so. It is because I love you more than life itself." Tom Wyatt's eyes filled with tears when he told me this. I knew he was remembering the times when she had told him she loved him. Those times were gone, without the possibility of return. He must wonder if Anne loves Henry, I thought. Would it be better for him if he thought she had fallen into marriage against her will? Or was it easier to believe, as I did, that Anne genuinely did love the King? Apparently, she'd told him that her love for him was so intense it was impossible for her not to feel jealous when she saw him flirting with another woman. She compared herself to, "those who marry to make alliances, who can afford to turn a blind eye to their husband's affairs." I knew she would have meant Katherine of Aragon here. She was saying that Katherine and Henry's marriage had been a political one, where no love was involved. Therefore, Katherine did not feel the pangs of jealousy in the same way as the wife in a love match. She was clever alright, and there was a time when Henry would have been influenced by her argument. But now Katherine was dead, making a comparison with her had become a lot less profitable.

Another visitor was the Duke of Norfolk, who was bawled out by Anne,

"You told me the King was dead, and then you plotted to unseat me!" She paused for a moment, and then cried out,

"Family or no family, you will stab me in the back, I can foresee it." Stony-faced, he muttered,

"That is nonsense, Anne, and you know it. I had to make plans, and you were a part of them." He bowed, took her hand and kissed it.

"There is no point in reliving what has gone before. We were faced with an emergency and had to act quickly. God be praised, the King survived, and the emergency was averted." At this point Anne had broken out in weeping, and the duke had withdrawn with as much haste as was decorous. He paused in the outer chamber, his face grey with stress, and spoke to Anne's mother.

"Try to get her to eat something, sister. We must get her well and back into the King's bed as soon as possible."

"That is easily said, brother. But you know Anne was always an obstinate one. Fiery in her love, desperate in her misery. She will only eat when she is ready."

"Heaven help us," said the duke, "we are dependent on the whims of a mad woman! Talk some sense into her and get her up and churched as soon as you can."

"I will do my best," she replied, "but I do not know how long it will take. She has just lost a baby!" The Duke of Norfolk bowed briefly, and left, shaking his head at the intractability of women.

I sought out Sir Thomas Wyatt. I wanted to talk with him, and not just about the Queen. I had not been sleeping, and every night I thought of Will. Should I try to repair our relationship? But then, what if he rejected me again? I knew Sir Thomas would be a trustworthy person to confide in. Maybe I even thought that he might beg me to stay. Would I like to be his mistress? Well, yes. His kindness to me had salved my wounds after the break with Will. But it was a dangerous path to take, putting myself so much into one man's power.

He took me to his chamber, and I remembered the night we had spent together.

"Sit, Kat," he said. "Have some wine with me." He poured two goblets of wine and handed me one. I took a sip, watching his handsome face. He was always beautifully dressed. His black doublet and hose emphasised his spare, muscular physique, and the white linen shift that showed at his wrists was edged with lace. I loved his hands and shivered to remember how they had touched me.

"So, the Queen is in the depths of despair," he said. "The King has not been again to see her. Her mother nags her, and her father shouts at her. It gives me pain to think of her."

"I haven't seen her, not really, since the miscarriage."

"Nor I," he said, "but Margaret tells me what is happening. I wish she would admit me. She needs her friends around her now." I looked at him, talking so earnestly, and took a risk.

"Do you still love her?" I asked, already knowing what the answer would be. He smiled sadly,

"I will always love her, Kat, you know that. But she is not for me, and life goes on. I would die for her, but I know I cannot live with her, in this life or the next."

"So, what will you do? You cannot spend your life as a single man."

"You know that I am married, Kat. I cannot change that."

He looked at me thoughtfully and took another sip of his wine.

"So, what is the future for you Tom? Will you take a lover?"

"Like you, Kat, my marriage is broken. Maybe I should take a lover." He looked into my eyes. "Is that what you want Kat? Should we become lovers?" He took my hand and kissed it, very softly, looking into my eyes.

I was so tempted. He was a handsome man, a kind man and easy to get along with. But something stopped me. I knew I had to give Will one more chance. Of course, Tom and I had been intimate, but only once. That was survivable. Being Tom's mistress, on the other hand, would end things with Will forever. I gently removed my hand,

"I was going to say yes, Tom. That's what I wanted just an hour ago. Your attention to me has been entirely welcome, and I love you dearly. But I must try again with Will." He looked at me with sad eyes, but then smiled.

"I know Kat. Like me, you have a longer lasting love. But, unlike me, you may be able to rekindle it again. And life with me, as a mistress, would be very difficult for you. You could not take part with me in my duties, or in court functions. Oh, I would look after you. I'd set you up in a house and hire some servants. But you would be on the sidelines." He laughed gently.

"And, Kat, I do not see you on the sidelines. Not ever." I smiled regretfully at him.

"I must be mad, turning you down." He nodded emphatically.

"Yes indeed."

"That night we had together was so perfect. I will never forget it."

"You will not be able to, as I will write poems about it, which will outlive me for certain."

"But I will not tell Will they are about me." He took my hand and grasped it tightly.

"That would not be wise, Kat. Go to him when you can and mend your hearts."

I left and resolved to seek Will out as soon as I had a few hours spare. But I knew I would always remember Tom. And I see myself in some of his poems that were handed around at court, although I never copied them. There was one verse, though, that I haven't forgotten:

"My lute awake! Perform the last
Labour that thou and I shall waste
And end that I have now begun:
For when this song is sung and past,
My lute, be still, for I have done."

CHAPTER 11

It was a cold, wet February, and I didn't feel well. I spent a lot of time resting in the maids' dormitory. Queen Anne didn't notice. She was morose and told me she was not in the mood for music. What I didn't realise until later was that Will Smeaton was worming his way into her chamber. That happened later when things came to a head and Tom told me that the musician had fallen in love with the Queen, and the trouble was, like me, he was an outsider and didn't know the rules of the game.

Lent crept on for ages. Not that I missed the meat and eggs. My illness dragged on and I had no appetite. The very thought of roasted meat made me retch. At last Easter came, towards the end of April, and I decided to go and seek out Will. It took me a while to decide that this was what I wanted. After all, it had been Will who rejected me. I still smarted when I remembered the last things he'd said to me. His accusations had hurt, and I was devastated that he hadn't understood my need to say goodbye to my mother, Katherine of Aragon.

But Will and I had so much history together. And he knew more about me than anyone else alive. I still loved him, I had to admit that. And I had to find out if he still loved me, and whether we could rebuild our future together.

Now that Master Cromwell was so important, his offices were close to the King, and he no longer worked in the administrative block. When I went over there, a busy clerk told me that Will wasn't working there anymore.

"He's not been here for months, mistress," he said sniffily. He turned away from me and started stacking files in a pile on the table. I coughed apologetically.

"Do you know where I might find him?" I asked, hoping that he would be nearby.

"No idea, try Austin Friars – Master Cromwell has part of his team there now."

My heart sank. The last place I wanted to go was Austin Friars. It was full of memories for me, our courtship, our life as a married couple, good company where all were accepted. It would be hard to return and be reminded of everything I'd lost. But then, if I didn't go, I might never regain the happiness that we had shared.

I had the afternoon off, so I decided to take a boat into London, and make my way to Austin Friars. As Cromwell's importance had grown, so had Austin Friars. It was now an extensive group of buildings, with gardens and orchards going down to the river. I walked up from the landing stage, loving the feel of the sun on my face. The apple trees were in bloom, and the air was full of the song of the birds. I felt my heart lift. I was determined to get Will back. I would apologise, and promise that from now on, my focus would be on him.

I entered through the great hall and decided to go to the kitchen, where I hoped I would find someone I knew. But as I was rushing out of the hall, I felt a hard tap on my shoulder. I wheeled round and saw Thomas Cromwell. He had always been an imposing figure but now he exuded power and a faint sense of threat.

"Kat! What are you doing here? My good wishes to you on Easter Day!" He beamed cheerily, and I wondered if he'd forgotten that night when he'd threatened me. Had he forgotten

I'd visited Queen Katherine as she was dying. I couldn't help it, but I shivered at the thought.

"I'm looking for Will. I was told he might be here," I said.

"That is good news," he said genially. "Now Katherine is dead, we can look to the future again, and you can reunite with your husband. It will lighten his mood to have you around the house." I let out a sigh of relief. It seemed that, as far as Cromwell was concerned, my birth to Katherine of Aragon was no longer an issue.

"I hope so. But I need to talk to him. Can I see him now?" Cromwell laughed; his eyes twinkled at me.

"You will have to wait, Mistress Kat! He isn't here."

"So where is he?" I asked. Cromwell paused for a moment, wrinkling up his face in thought.

"I guess, given the date, he is deep into Lincolnshire, or it could be Yorkshire."

"What is he doing?"

"He's with a team of mine. I've sent people out all over England. They're tidying up the monasteries. Checking they've all taken the oath of Supremacy, making an audit of their assets, that kind of thing. I need to know exactly where we stand before we start to close them down. It's a long job. He'll be back by Michaelmas. I don't expect him before then." My heart sank. How could I wait until September to see Will? It had taken me so long to screw up my courage to find him. But to find now that he was away was a terrible blow. My face fell. Cromwell noticed, and gave me a wry smile.

"Missing him, are you? Is that why you're so white-faced? I regret this, but I cannot spare him just now. But if you write to him here, I will make sure it is forwarded along with all the other letters." With that, he took hold of my shoulders and planted a firm kiss on my forehead.

"Don't worry Kat. Everything is under control." Daughter, I can tell you honestly, that did not reassure me. Cromwell's geniality was real, and he was a good master to those who served him. But I had seen the menace that he occasionally showed when he needed to. He was not a cruel man, in the sense that he did not delight in destroying others for the sake of it. But he was absolutely capable of carrying out terrible deeds if he deemed them necessary. I knew now to be careful when I was around him.

"I will write to him and send it here," I said. "Thank you, Master Cromwell." I curtseyed to him and turned back to go through the hall.

"You are welcome here, Kat!" he called out. "Call again and see Joan and the others."

"I will!" I hurried to the door. Forgetting me, he had already turned to go on his business. I made my way back to Greenwich and resolved to write a letter to Will that week. I would have to be careful, as Cromwell's men would probably read it. But I could assure Will of my love and wish to reunite. I sat up late on Friday night, turning the phrases over in my head, thinking them, but then rejecting them, re-writing them, then going back to what I had said before. In the end, daughter, this was what I wrote.

28th April in the year of our lord 1536

My dear husband,

I understand from Master Cromwell that you are working in the north of the country. I would that I had seen you before you departed, as I miss you. I hope that we may speak together when you are returned to London.

Your loving wife,

Kat Cooke

I could not write more. But I hoped that this would be enough to convince him that I wanted a reconciliation. I folded it and put it away in my pouch, resolving to take it to Austin Friars when I was next able to go. It wouldn't be that weekend, though. And somehow, with all that happened over the next few days, I forgot about it.

Queen Anne was in a snappish, irritable mood, and she decided she wanted me to play to her all day long.

"You are a better musician than Mark Smeaton," she said, "and poor boy, he is mad with love for me. It is so wearing!" I smiled inwardly. I was sure Mark would be recalled soon by the Queen. Although relations with the King were frosty, she took some comfort in the adoration of the men that surrounded her. But, daughter, I must tell you this. There was never anything sinful about it. I knew Queen Anne, and I knew she was one of the most principled women at court. She would no more be unfaithful than she would convert to Rome. But, poor lady, it warmed her heart to hear the adoration of the gallants that surrounded her and read Tom Wyatt's lovesick poetry.

That day she was teasing Sir Henry Norris, a middle-aged widower, close to both her and the King.

"So, when are you going to get married, Sir Henry?" she teased. This was all a game. The idea was that the gentleman concerned would protest he loved only the queen, there would be laughter, and that would be that. In due course, he would get married anyway, but would continue to express his undying love for the remote, unattainable queen-goddess that he worshipped.

But this time, Queen Anne didn't play by the rules. Sir Henry Norris was laying out all the courtly love sentiments, almost polishing them for the Queen to look at. But she didn't listen. She shushed him, and turned, looking at all of us who surrounded her. She rapped out,

"But you have been offered a good match with my cousin, Madge Shelton. Why do you delay sir? You have been single for nearly five years now." Maybe sensing danger, George Boleyn took his sister's arm and tried to lead her away from the group.

"Come, sister, let us walk. It is sunny and warm outside."

She shook his hand off and turned her blazing eyes on Henry Norris,

"It is because you look for dead man's shoes, isn't it? If ought happened to the King but good, you would look to have me!" Daughter, there was a gasp from everyone there. We all knew that it was treason to speak of the King's death, and even more dangerous to make plans of what might happen following it. Sir Henry Norris went white,

"Your Majesty, I have no such thoughts, I assure you. If such a thing would ever cross my mind, I would wish that my head would be cut off. I am a loyal servant to the King, and…" he paused, "and to yourself. I hope to serve you both for many years." Queen Anne's lips tightened in annoyance. Why was she doing this? She knew it was dangerous. I thought maybe she was so tired of the games that were being played that she wanted to call them out. She laughed contemptuously.

"Yes, you will serve the King, but not me. As I thought, this is all empty words!" George Boleyn put his arm around his sister.

"Come, sister, let us walk," he said firmly. He turned back to Sir Henry Norris, standing there frozen with shock.

"Sir Henry, let us cease this game. I shall walk with the Queen to take the air." He steered the Queen away and led her to the door. Sir Henry started to shake and put his face into his hands.

"What was she thinking of?" he moaned. "If the King hears of this, I shall be out of favour. Does she want to bring us all down?" Some of his friends came up to him and started talking to him in low voices. Gradually, the knot of people dispersed, and I was left alone. I was feeling a bit faint and decided I must make my way to the Queen's apartments. Swaying from side to side, I ran through the great door and sat down on one of the settles around the walls. Everything was going dark around me, and I put my head between my legs, feeling the room spinning around me.

Gradually, I started to feel a little steadier.

"Kat, what ails you?" I could make out a woman standing in front of me, her hand on my shoulder.

"I don't know. I felt dizzy. I had to come here to sit down." I looked at the woman. It was Lady Jane Seymour, her face bright with concern.

"Let me bring you some wine Kat. Rest there." A moment later, she was there with a goblet of Hippocras, the strong sweet wine that some said could revive the dead.

"There, is that better Kat?" I nodded. "That's good. I have something to tell you Kat, promise you won't say." I looked at her groggily.

"What are you talking about? Of course, I won't say. You are my friend." She sat beside me, and whispered in my ear,

"It's the King. He says he loves me!" Her face was pink, and her blue eyes were shining. I stared at her. Surely, it could not be happening all over again? Of course not, that would be completely improbable.

"Don't get your hopes up, my lady. He is married." She shook her head and almost bounced on the settle with excitement.

"He says he will find a way for us to marry. Maybe send Anne to a convent." I couldn't help but smile. Queen Anne, the scourge of the religious houses, in a convent! She would hardly be the most docile of nuns. I dismissed the very idea,

"She won't go to a convent, my lady. She would die rather than enter holy orders."

"Don't spoil things Kat," Lady Jane chided me. "The King has promised he will arrange it."

I didn't believe her. I liked her, she was a kind girl. But the idea that the King, who had married first Katherine of Aragon, and then Anne Boleyn, would be happy with a simpleton like Jane was laughable. I shrugged my shoulders and decided to let her dream. Nothing would come of it.

Princess Elizabeth would sometimes visit her mother,

and when she was at the palace, the great presence chamber became a playground. The toddler was walking now and putting everything she could find in her mouth. She was a headstrong little girl, like all the Tudor women, and if anyone tried to stop her, she would scream and stamp her tiny feet. On one occasion, she tried to grab my lute, and I pulled it back from her grasp. She was absolutely furious. It was as if the King's rages had taken over a small red-haired girl, leaving her shaking with the enormity of her emotions.

On this morning, though, she was sitting quietly enough beside her mother. Queen Anne tore off pieces of manchet bread, dipped them in a goblet of warm milk, and then fed them to Elizabeth. Like a little bird, she gobbled up each morsel. I was playing softly. Some of the ladies were reading, some sewing. In the April sunlight it was a tranquil scene.

The peace was broken by George Boleyn, who rushed in, ashen faced.

"Sister, the King is coming," he said. "He is very angry. You must talk with him." Anne pressed her lips together, then put the goblet of milk down and stood up. Elizabeth, sensing that her treat was coming to an end, let out a little wail. Anne shushed her and held her hand tightly.

The large doors were flung open, and the King strode in. We all curtseyed, even Elizabeth, who bobbed and nearly fell over. Anne scooped the child into her arms and stood upright, facing the King.

"And so, you wish me dead, Madam! Is that the action of a loving wife?" The King's face was red and distorted with anger.

"No, your Majesty, what do you mean? I wish you long life and happiness." Anne was brave, facing him without flinching.

"Plotting with Sir Henry Norris, talking about going into his bed once I am cold in my grave! Is that not high treason madam?" Anne held her head high.

"Your Majesty, it was not intended. There is no more loyal

subject to you than me, your wife."

"So why did you say what you did? Or will you deny that?" The King towered over her, and Princess Elizabeth started to cry.

"Your Majesty, it was a stupid comment, and Sir Henry misunderstood what I meant. I can only say I am sorry for such foolishness." She tried to comfort the little girl, who squirmed and wriggled in her arms.

"Foolishness? It was treason, and you know it." The King was not convinced, although his voice quietened a little.

"Your Majesty. Look at our daughter, Elizabeth, made from our love. I would not do anything to imperil her, or you, my beloved husband. Why should I want you dead when I love you above all things?" She started to cry, and Elizabeth became inconsolable.

"See, your Majesty, how much she loves you. I beg of you, do not separate her and me from your love. It is our life!" He looked her up and down, and then reached out a hand and stroked Elizabeth's head as she lay in her mother's arms. Queen Anne, sensing that he was softening, lay her own hand on the King's arm.

"By next year, there will be another child in the nursery to love you. But this time, it will be a boy." However much she tried to hide it, I could feel the desperation in her voice.

"Hmm. So, you won't lose the next one?"

"No, your Majesty. I will go to bed and rest for all of my time. And if I do not get any more unpleasant shocks, we will get our boy." The King stiffened. We all knew she was talking about his serious accident during the joust, and his fondness for Jane Seymour. He was very unwilling to give up either. But then, if Anne was in bed, she wouldn't know, would she?

"Very well. I forgive you. But you must learn to mind your tongue, wife. Such ill-judged jesting is not fitting for a queen."

"No, indeed, your Majesty." She swept him a deep curtsey, then rose and took Elizabeth's hand.

"I will bring Elizabeth to sit with me at the joust on Monday," she said. "She is learning to be a Tudor princess." King Henry looked troubled, and then shook his head.

"No, don't bring her. She's too young, and she will distract me." Anne's face fell. She knew that Henry loved his daughter, and she needed to keep reminding him that a son would follow. Elizabeth's presence was therefore an advantage. King Henry noticed her face, and then added hurriedly,

"Well, bring her if you must. But, er, she will need to go to her governess if anything happens." I don't know if anyone else did, but I picked up a sense of foreboding from his words. What might happen? Fortunately, Anne understood him to mean childish bad behaviour,

"Nothing will happen, your Majesty. I will rap her on the knuckles if she misbehaves." Henry laughed uneasily and patted his daughter on the head.

"Very well, very well. I shall see you both tomorrow." Anne came close to him, leaving Elizabeth behind.

"Unless you wish to see me tonight, your Majesty?" she said softly. Henry cleared his throat,

"I have many matters to attend to, wife. Another time." He blew a kiss to Elizabeth, who responded,

"Daddada," and waved her small hand at him. He then turned and walked out of the room without a backward glance. I looked at Anne. Her face was full of disappointment. She had hoped she would be able to win the King back this Spring and be carrying a prince by September. Anne being Anne, though, she gave a small, forced smile and said to the company,

"I shall await his Majesty's presence patiently, and I am sure I shall be rewarded." I could tell she was unhappy. This great love they had shared had fizzled into the ashes, or so it seemed. But I do not think she was frightened. Not at that point. She knew that she needed to win Henry back to conceive again. But she was certain that she would be able to do that.

The next morning, we were all preparing for the joust. The dressing of the Queen was a lengthy affair, and she insisted that every task was performed exactly right. She stood there in the centre of her bedchamber, completely naked, but still a queen.

First, she was rubbed all over with violet and rose oil, maids using linen cloths to massage her body until it was glossy with a faint sheen. Then a fine cambric shift, thin and soft as mist, with small seed pearls sewn all around the neck. She was laced into a kirtle of deep blue damask, and then a gown of imperial purple, heavy with precious stones. Sleeves edged with ermine, the sapphire and diamond earrings the King had given her, a heavy golden necklace with amethysts and white sapphires. The Queen, when she was ready, was a human work of art. Like the King, she carried the treasury of the nation on her back. She chafed at it.

"Kat, can you not play something more cheerful?" I had been playing softly in the background, as instructed. "Where is Mark? Fetch me Mark, he will know what to play." One of the ladies said,

"He is not here today, your Majesty." Anne was annoyed.

"So where is he? You musicians are always vanishing! We may as well have no musicians for the amount of time you spend here." She aimed this at me in the absence of Mark Smeaton. I had seen him last night, leaving the hall with Thomas Cromwell. I wondered if he had drunk too much at Cromwell's table and was sleeping it off. I was sure he would reappear soon, complaining about a sore head. Fortunately, Anne forgot about the music when Elizabeth's governess brought her in to join her mother. She too was dressed magnificently in cloth of gold, although she had already started to dribble down it. Seeing Anne, she toddled precariously towards her.

"My sweetheart!" the Queen cried. "Come with me and we will sit with Papa at the joust!" And so, after much fussing and discussion of who was going to sit where, the procession lined up to leave the chamber.

I was glad when they left. I was feeling very tired and thought I might lie down for a little while. But the door opened again, and Lady Jane Seymour appeared.

"Queen Anne sent me for some linens to wipe the Princess's chin," she said. "She is always sending me away!" I would normally say something sympathetic, but this time my feelings overcame me.

"I don't care! I have my own concerns," I said, starting to weep. Lady Jane looked surprised, and then put her hand on mine.

"Kat, whatever is the matter? I have never seen you so distressed."

"I cannot tell you, for the disgrace, I cannot even admit it to myself," I howled. Jane took one of the linens intended for Princess Elizabeth and handed it to me to wipe my face.

"You can tell me Kat; we've been friends for years. Whatever it is, I won't tell anyone." Tears streaming from my face, I at last told her what I had been thinking for the last two months,

"I am with child Jane. I have missed four of my courses, and my breasts and belly are swelling. I don't know what to do. Will and I are separated. I am on my own, and I don't know what to do." I didn't tell her what I most feared, that the baby, if I was indeed carrying one, was Sir Thomas Wyatt's baby and not Will's. Jane beamed at me.

"Oh Kat, is that all? You are blessed to become a mother."

"But Will is not in London," I said. "When I get to full term, who will look after me?" Jane shook her head.

"Kat, I will! I will be Queen by then, and I will make sure you are well looked after." I stared at her, disbelievingly.

"Do you really think that?" I asked.

"I know that. I have so much to look forward to Kat! But you mustn't worry. You can go and stay with Mistress Mead until you have the baby. Then we can find Will." I smiled, remembering Mistress Ashdown, whose nickname was Mistress Mead because she was sweet like honey. Her cottage, in the grounds of Wolf Hall, would be a safe place to have my child, I knew. And afterwards, maybe, Will and I could find each other again.

Queen Anne swept in, with Princess Elizabeth grizzling in her wake.

"Lady Bryan, put her to bed, she is tired," she said to the governess, who took Elizabeth in her arms and carried her to the door, speaking soothingly to the little girl.

"Kat! I want music! God only knows where Mark has gone." I started to play a traditional dance, "My Lady Carey's Dompe," but she was not calmed. She fidgeted and tweaked at her earrings. She started to talk, almost as if to herself,

"Why did the King walk out? He enjoys the joust, enjoys the attention. So why did he leave, and so suddenly?" Lady Jane Seymour told me later that he'd left with a small number of men to ride back to London. But why? What had been so urgent? It had unsettled the Queen. She could not sit still but paced up and down her chamber as if she were in a cage. Once or twice, she picked up a book to read, but she couldn't concentrate and threw it back on the table. She gestured impatiently at me to stop, and then called her women to help her undress. I heard her ordering one of them to read a passage from the Bible to her, in English. Before I left, I glanced into her chamber, and saw her, on her knees, praying. Her husband was not present, and so she entreated Lord Jesu to watch over her. It was the last time I ever saw her.

The next morning, some of the gentlemen were playing tennis. The Queen had gone to watch them, so I had little to occupy myself with. It was a sunny, warm day and the window was open to let the warm air into the chamber. I could hear the sound of the ball being hit from one side of the court to the other, and the clapping of the assembled crowd. Suddenly, it stopped. There was the sound of men's voices and a woman's protest. I can still hear that cry now. Queen Anne's farewell to freedom, and to her life. It will haunt me for the rest of my days.

I learnt later she had been summoned to the privy council, where she was accused of committing adultery. Two men had been named: Sir Henry Norris and Mark Smeaton. And although she had objected, telling the council that she had always been a faithful wife, she was to be sent to the Tower. If the Queen was to be found guilty, the penalty was death. I remember looking out of that open window and seeing a slender figure getting into a barge, flanked by nobles, soldiers and guards. For the second time in my life, I saw one woman ranged against many powerful men. She had no chance.

"It was her uncle, the Duke of Norfolk, who told her," Tom Wyatt said. "Her uncle! Do not expect loyalty or compassion in this court." He was angry but afraid to speak in public. We were closeted together in his chambers, whispering in case we were overheard. "I am afraid Kat. There are more arrests to come. Keep away from me, I do not want you implicated."

"Implicated in what? She has done nothing wrong!" Tom Wyatt took my hand and pressed it to his heart.

"You know, and I know, that this is a wicked plot against her. But because I love her, I may be charged too. And because we are friends, it might be said that you had become involved."

"This is ridiculous. It is so silly!" I said. I could not believe it.

"Silly, yes. But deadly dangerous too. Kat, go to the maids' dormitory. Play dumb. Stick close to Lady Jane. She is the favoured one now. Under her patronage you will be safe."

"But what about you?" I could not bear to think of this man, my friend, being caught up in the dance of death that was threatened.

"I will go to the country," he said. "I'll leave tonight and keep out of the way for a while." His voice caught, and he hugged me suddenly.

"To think of her.... Such a blazing star, and such a cruel fate. It cuts me to the heart." He kissed me on the forehead and then pushed me out of the door.

"Goodbye, Kat. May God protect you," he muttered,

"Goodbye, Tom, I shall never forget you," and turned and ran down the steep steps away from his chamber, through the many spaces of the palace, the tears wet on my face.

CHAPTER 12

After Queen Anne had been taken to the Tower of London, her household became listless and miserable. What were we to do? The woman we had served was a prisoner. There was no other lady who could take charge. So, we drank, we played cards, we gathered every bit of information that we could. I could feel my belly swelling, but so far it didn't show when I was dressed. My sickness had decreased, and I found myself eating well again. In all the chaos, I held on to Lady Jane's promise that when my time was near, I could go and stay with Mistress Mead at Wolf Hall.

Lady Jane Seymour was one of the few people in the household who was excited. Her face was pink and almost pretty. She was wearing a pale pink gown, shimmering with pearls, with an apple green kirtle. For her, Spring had arrived.

"It won't be long now Kat," she said. "He will get the marriage annulled and send her away. We will be married by June." She took me to her chamber and showed me the bolts of cloth the King had sent her to make her wedding dress. Lying on the bed was a heavy roll of scarlet velvet, embossed in gold with her emblem, the phoenix rising, and the Tudor rose. There was another roll of golden tissue, shot through with tiny diamonds, and one of silver tissue blazing with rubies. Jane was delighted with them.

"His Majesty is sending his tailor and seamstresses to me today, to make up the gown. They have assured him they can finish it in a fortnight." I must have looked dubious because she added defensively,

"It will all be done by then Kat, and we will have a June wedding. He has promised me the Queen's jewels, and preferment for my family. He is so kind, Kat; you must realise that." I shook my head. It wasn't politic to disagree too fervently with Jane, as she, after all, may soon be Queen. But I wasn't convinced by her account of how things would go.

"It may be more difficult than that," I said. "Remember how long it took with Queen Katherine?" Jane crossed herself and nodded.

"I understand that. God bless her. But she was the rightful Queen, and everybody loved her. That was why it took so long! Anne Boleyn is not our rightful Queen; she is a usurper. I don't like to say what they call her on the streets. What is it? Goggle-eyed whore!" she said triumphantly. "When she departs, the nation will celebrate, I know that. Hey Kat, will you play at our wedding?" I smiled. She was such an innocent. It was not up to me to disillusion her, not now.

"Yes, if the King wishes me to do so, I will," I said, thinking that by the time anything happened, if it did, I would be down in Wiltshire, nursing a new baby. That morning I had felt the baby for the first time. Daughter, that was you. You felt as if you were blowing a bubble that burst on the inside of my belly. Of course, it was your tiny foot that made that almost insensible impact. You were already claiming me as your mother. And I was starting to talk to you in my thoughts as my child, my future.

"I'm here, my love, nothing will hurt you. God will watch over you, and your mother's love will be always there."

To be honest, it was you daughter, that kept me going during that terrible time. The news got worse and worse. I heard from Ned, another musician, that Mark Smeaton had indeed gone to Thomas Cromwell's house, but what had happened there was not a drinking session, but prolonged torture. The thought of that happening in the house where I had been so happy with Will made me shudder. Had Mark Smeaton cried out for mercy in the very chambers where we had known love? I remembered Cromwell's wife, his lovely daughters. He had been a devoted husband and father. Why had he soiled their memories by conducting such a despicable action at their family house? I had known for some time Cromwell was dangerous. But it was only at that time I realised that he was completely without scruple. He had dragged a tale of Queen Anne's adultery out of Mark Smeaton through fear and pain, by knotting and tightening a rope around his neck until he could barely breathe. What is more, I was convinced he knew that it was all lies.

Each day we heard of a different man who had been arrested: Sir William Brereton, Sir Francis Weston, Sir Richard Page. Then the shocking news that George Boleyn, Queen Anne's brother, was in the Tower. I had never liked George. I could not forget the time he had tried to rape me by tricking me to come to Anne's chamber. But he was charged with incest, with being intimate with his sister. I knew, and all the court knew, that this was nonsense. They were very close, they loved each other dearly. But he had never bedded Anne.

What was even worse were the rumours being spread in every alehouse and marketplace in London. The King was impotent, and so Queen Anne had looked to conceive by having sex with other men. Even her own brother! Who spread these rumours? It could not be the King's men, for he would have not allowed such a tale to go out. I came to the conclusion that it must have been Cromwell's agents that did so. I thanked God that Will was safely in Yorkshire and could not have been asked to do this. I knew that if he had been in London, he would have had to obey Cromwell's orders, and that would have driven another rift between us. But I guessed that if Anne Boleyn was no longer in favour, Will might be less concerned about my links with Queen Katherine. I still dreamt of him almost every night and prayed for a reconciliation. But I was starting to realise that if he and I were to reunite, we would have to have some distance from Cromwell. I could not bear the thought of being under the patronage of a man who had been so friendly but was in reality a killer. I still had the letter to Will that I had been going to send to Austin Friars. But how could I send it now? I did not want it to go through his hands, to be defiled by him. It stayed in my pouch, knocking gently against the baby in my belly.

Tom Wyatt was taken the following Monday. He had been right. He was a target because of his well-known affection for the Queen. He was imprisoned in the Tower, along with the other men. It seemed to me that Queen Anne's accusers must have expected her to have spent her entire waking life committing adultery. Five men were charged. Five men! If this had been true, where did the Queen find time to visit monasteries, hunt, debate theology, dance, sleep with the King? It was unbelievable. Only one of the men, Mark Smeaton, had admitted to adultery with her, and everyone knew it had been tortured out of him. All the others protested their, and her, innocence. I looked at the names on the charge sheet, Sir Henry Norris, Sir William Brereton, Sir Francis Weston, Mark Smeaton, and George Boleyn, Lord Rochford.

"Tom's not on here," I said out loud.

"No Kat. Just give it a few days!" Ned said. But I couldn't help but hope that this was a good sign. Tom was getting a rap over the knuckles, no more. There were other men in the Tower, too. All of them waiting to hear if they too would be charged.

For a few days I existed in a state of disbelief. This could not be happening. It was all a mistake. I prayed that Queen Anne would agree to an annulment of her marriage to the King. Then the way would be clear for her to go to a convent, and the men involved to be exiled for a few years. That is what I, and many at court, believed would happen.

But then it was announced that the men would go on trial, and following them, the Queen and her brother. The speed of it was what was so disorientating. Only two weeks before, the Queen had been magnificently presiding over a May Day joust, and only four months before, she had been pregnant with the King's child. All the systems and protocols of the court seemed to be dissolving before my eyes. The King, closeted alone, said to be impotent, the Queen imprisoned, the Queen's brother accused of incest and treason. Only Lady Jane continued serene, updating me on the state of readiness of her wedding gown and debating what jewels she might wear.

By the end of the week the men were put on trial. Not George Boleyn, he would be tried with his sister. But all the others, Norris, Brereton, Weston, and Smeaton. The charges were adultery and treason. All of them pleaded not guilty to treason, and only Smeaton admitted adultery. They all stood their ground in court, but to no avail. The word came out that they were all found guilty, sentenced to death by being hung, drawn and quartered. It was to be Anne and George's trials on Monday. The court was deathly quiet, everyone going about their business almost stealthily, the only sound the hushed buzz of the latest gossip. I could barely stand being there. But I had nowhere else to go, so there was no choice.

I went to church on Sunday, as we were required to do, and then decided to spend the rest of the day walking around the countryside park that surrounded Greenwich Palace. I remembered so many hunting parties, so many games and disguises, so many maydays. But now, although the weather was sunny and springlike, the park was deserted. I walked, breathing in the scent of the grass, and praying to the wind,

"Dear Jesu Christ, have mercy on the Queen, and the men with her. Let the King be merciful, I beg. Please God, keep Tom safe. Of all of them, he is the best. But they are all innocent." I made a mad kind of bargain in my head with God. If Queen Anne and the others escaped with their lives, I would go back to Will. I would become submissive and pleasing to him and live under Cromwell's patronage, however much I hated it. I would do everything I could to forward Will's career and live a contented life as a lawyer's wife. There would be no more dreams of queens and royal ancestry.

I got back late, when the night was just tipping over the sky, and went straight to bed. The next day was one of the longest I have ever experienced. All the servants, the ladies, and the courtiers who were not involved were just waiting for news from the Tower, where the trials were to be held. I imagined Queen Anne. The gossip was that she had wept and screamed in her imprisonment, but in public she would be magnificent. She would know that the charges against her were trumped up, and she would be able to prove that. Inside my head, I reminded God of the bargain I had made with him,

"Let them go, let them go, please God," my internal voice kept saying. Maybe if I prayed hard enough that would work. As I walked around the court, all I could do was to continue my dialogue with God. I tried to join in a card game. But my head was full of superstitious incantations that were more to do with witchcraft than religion. I kept on telling myself, "If I turn up a Queen, she will be released, but if I turn up a King, she will die." But I lasted about half an hour, until the other players ended the game, saying we were all too distracted.

Late that afternoon, the news came out. The Queen had made a good defence, but she had been found guilty of treason and adultery. The punishment given was either burning or beheading, the King in his mercy to decide. In his mercy! What mercy was this? The sentence had been pronounced by Anne's uncle, the Duke of Norfolk. Her father was on the jury.

So powerful men repay the women who brought them that power.

All around the great hall, people were talking. Some were laughing, others looked grim. Servants mingled with nobles. There was no structure to our existence on that day.

I made for the chapel, brushing past the crowds. I could not talk to anyone. Tom, my only friend, was still in prison. Queen Anne, my patron, was sentenced to death. The worst I could imagine was happening. I knelt down, and I am ashamed to admit it, I berated God.

"How can this happen? I've seen it once with Katherine, now with Anne. They are good women, religious women. And the men that bring them down are evil! Lord Jesu, why do you allow this?" I felt the tears pouring down my cheeks, and I bowed my head so that no one could see. There were only a couple of elderly ladies in there, and they were both lost in prayer.

The silence was broken, a woman rushing through the gloom.

"Kat, come! I must talk with you!" It was Lady Jane Seymour, looking white and afraid. Her hood was askew, and her nails bitten to the quick.

"What are you doing here? I would have thought you would be with the King, preparing for your wedding." A note of anger had crept into my voice, but she didn't notice it.

"I can't, I can't! Kat, come to my chamber! I need to talk." I got up off my knees and followed her. I wasn't feeling well inclined to her at that moment, but she probably knew more than me about what was going on, and I might learn something.

We hurried to her chamber, guarded now by one of the King's men. She brushed past him and ushered me in. In the corner of the room was a large oak chest. The table was piled high with perfumes, creams and syrups, and her bed hangings were now blue velvet and gold. She shut the door and immediately clung to me.

"Kat, what am I to do? He is going to kill her and marry me on the morrow! I didn't think it would be like this, Kat. He told me he'd send her to a nunnery. But now, now, she is to die. He will kill her." She clasped at the crucifix hanging around her neck.

"Did you not think that this would happen?" I asked her. There was a chance that she hadn't. She was such a naive girl. "The King wants them all out of the way, he doesn't want to ever see them or think of them again. It will be as if she had never been, and you will become his Queen."

"Kat, I'm scared, I'm so scared. I don't want to go through with it. If he can execute Anne, then he can execute me. What if I displease him? What if I don't give him a son?" I felt like telling her she should have thought of that earlier, but I was kinder than that.

"My lady, we know what Queen Anne is like. She disputes with the King; she shouts at him. He got tired of it. But you, you will never say a word that makes him angry. That is what he wants, some peace and quiet." I thought to myself that she would be a change after Henry had spent so many years with women who were more intelligent than he was.

"But what if I don't give him a son?" she wailed. I was forced to concede that this might be a problem. But I told her comfortingly that in that case, he would simply send her to a nunnery. There was no way he could find anything to bring her to the scaffold.

"They say she might burn," Lady Jane whispered. "I'm so scared Kat. I don't want to do it now. But if I say no, my father will force me to obey. I have no choice Kat." Tears were flowing down her cheeks. She started to shake uncontrollably. Then she took a deep breath, trying to control herself. She took a key from her pouch and went over and unlocked the chest.

"Come, Kat, look at these," she said. I gasped when I saw what was inside. It was dark, but within it was a mass of gold, diamonds and other jewels, twinkling in the candlelight. A Queen's crown, so ablaze with jewels that you could scarcely see the gold they were set into. Many, many linen bags. She pulled one out of the chest and retrieved its contents. A gold chain set with pearls so large they were like quail's eggs, each one mounted in its own nest of diamonds.

"The Queen's jewels," she said flatly. "He sent them to me. Two weeks ago, Anne was wearing this." I nodded.

"Yes, and Queen Katherine before her. They are very beautiful, my lady." She held the chain around her neck and started to wail,

"They are chains, Kat, made for queens! They will imprison me!" I had never seen her like this, hysterical with fear. I took her into my arms to try to calm her.

"Don't worry, my lady. You will not suffer Anne's fate; I am sure of it. And once I have had my babe, I will come back to look after you, I promise." She looked at me as a drowning women might when thrown a life raft.

"Will you Kat? I need someone. I can't do this on my own." I soothed her as if she were a little child,

"You will be safe, my lady. You need not worry. You will be a great queen, and the King will love you." I put the certainty into my voice that I did not feel. Slowly, her sobs ceased.

The next day, Lady Jane was no longer at court. I guessed she had gone to join the King, wherever he was. It was as if the pair of them had vanished, unwilling to take part in the macabre events that were unfolding inexorably in London. I heard from Ned that the King had exercised his prerogative for mercy.

"Mercy? So, they are not to die?" Maybe God had listened to my prayers after all. But Ned cut short my hopes,

"Oh, they will all die right enough. But they are not to be hung, drawn and quartered. Instead, they will be executed on Tower Hill. It is mercy enough Kat. Their end will be swift, so long as the axeman knows his business."

"And what about Queen Anne?" Ned allowed himself a little smile.

"The King has given her the greatest mercy. She is not to be burned, but to be executed."

Burning would have been a terrible fate. I was glad at least she would not have to go through that. But I imagined a heavy, blunt axe on her slender neck, and shuddered.

"Poor lady, she does not deserve this. The King loved her so much, I cannot understand why he has changed so much. Surely, he could send her to a nunnery?" Ned, though, shook his head. He looked around and then whispered,

"She was promised that, I heard, in return for agreeing to an annulment of their marriage," he said. "But they went back on their word. The King says he is chivalrous and merciful, as instead of an English axeman, he has engaged a swordsman from Calais whose sword is so sharp she will barely feel it." I felt my stomach lurch at this, and I almost vomited. But my fellow musician Ned hadn't finished,

"Kat, they sent for the swordsman before she was tried. You know what that means? It means the whole thing was decided before she was pronounced guilty, maybe before she was even charged!" So the King and Cromwell had had it all planned weeks ago. And because they'd had to concoct a story that Queen Anne was unfaithful, in order to justify her execution, the very lies about her adultery had hardened his cruelty against her. And all of this because he was tired of her! Thank heavens that no other man in the kingdom has that power, or else the executioners would never cease cutting off women's heads! Although the King was my father, I had never hated him more than I did when I heard that. All the time, he pretended that he was a good and pious man, but in fact, he was evil. I turned away from Ned and retched.

"Are you alright, Mistress Kat? Do you need to sit down?" I didn't know Ned well, but these times of chaos made us all into one-day allies.

"No, I'm fine. It's just hard to understand. One day she is wearing the crown, two weeks later, she is mounting the block. I am glad I am just an ordinary person." Ned nodded.

"We are much safer Kat, so long as we are not dismissed and starve to death."

All we did was wait. Like Katherine, Anne was no longer considered the Queen. So, we had no Queen to obey, no dancing, no dainty embroideries or merry madrigals. We heard that all five men had been executed on the Wednesday. All of them had uttered pious words about being sinners, but that was expected on the block. And they wouldn't dare go against the King. They all had families who might suffer otherwise. But only Mark Smeaton ever said that he'd had sex with Queen Anne. He, poor man, had had it tortured out of him, and was too scared to retract his confession. They were all executed on the same block, which became more and more bloody with each soul that perished on it. It seemed so wrong to me, daughter, to be killing men in a fit of pique. Men whose mothers had carried them as babies, who had been loved. I knew that love was in my body, with my baby. And I knew that it was completely opposed to the death that was all around me. That was you, daughter, and it was you who gave me the hope to continue through those terrible days.

Anne was meant to die on the following day. At Greenwich, we all held our breath for news. But it was postponed. The Tower had been full of foreign dignitaries, gathering to watch the day's entertainment. And Cromwell had decided at the last minute that they shouldn't see it. Letters to all the capitals of Europe giving the bloody details of the beheading of a queen were maybe not the best way to encourage alliances.

And so, it was Friday that she was killed. On that day I don't think many of us ate. Of course, it was a fast day, and we didn't usually eat meat. Instead, there would be fish, rabbit and chicken. But none of us had an appetite that day. We hadn't loved the Queen as Queen Katherine had been loved.

But although we didn't say it, we didn't think she had deserved what was happening. And then, what would become of us? There would be no Queen. That was, unless King Henry married Jane Seymour within hours. And surely, he wouldn't do that?

It was around half past nine that we heard the distant canons rumble, and we knew that the deed had been done. In the crowd watching was Master Cromwell. I wondered if he had felt proud of the success of his plan. She and he had been on the same side for many years. But they had disagreed towards the end. Her allegiance to France threatened his aim to build stronger links with the Holy Roman Empire. And, most importantly, in the end, King Henry got tired of her. A second divorce would be too messy. Thankfully Anne had no friends who might threaten war if she was executed. And so, she was eliminated. The whole process took less than three weeks.

Also watching was her uncle, the Duke of Norfolk, the King's illegitimate son, Henry Fitzroy, Duke of Richmond, and the Mayor and Aldermen of London. I wondered how she had felt, seeing all of her one-time friends ranged against her. I heard she spoke well, was dignified and queen-like to the end. But no dignity after that, when her body was bundled into an old arrow chest, as no one had thought to obtain a coffin.

Strange to think, daughter, that she was the mother of our current great Queen Elizabeth. She had ended her days in disgrace, unable to provide an heir. But her despised daughter is now our Queen, and a wiser monarch there never has been.

Less than two weeks after Anne's death, I heard that King Henry had married Jane Seymour privately at Whitehall. There was to be no large wedding, no feasts or celebrations. I guess even he had decided that this might be in bad taste. But as the news leaked out, the dancing started. It was all presided over by King Henry and Queen Jane, sitting under the canopy of royal estate, both magnificently dressed, but Jane looking as if she would rather be reading a theological book than be at the centre of this brilliant court.

We were told that most of the household was being retained. Some of the ladies-in-waiting would go, but others would stay. And all of the servants were allowed to remain. We were not important enough to be excluded. None the less, I must admit I was relieved, daughter. I needed my wages, and I feared what was going to happen when I had to go to the country to give birth.

I need not have worried. Queen Jane rapidly sent for me and told me that when my time came, she would give me leave of absence. I curtseyed deeply in gratitude to her. Then she looked at all the courtiers standing around her. I think I caught a small look of panic in her eyes. But she collected herself.

"My lords and ladies, I have a slight headache. I wish to retire for a short time. Mistress Kat Cooke, you may accompany me, to play me soothing music. The rest of you may take the afternoon for yourselves." The courtiers dispersed, talking and joking loudly. Strange how quickly life returned to normal. Jane led me into her bedchamber, pulled her heavy hood off, and lay down on the bed.

"What would you like me to play, your Majesty?" I asked. She waved her arm, as if to wave away a fly.

"No, I don't want music. I want to talk with someone I trust," she said. I laid down my lute and stood there waiting. She sat up on the bed and patted the space beside her.

"Come Kat. Sit here. I'm still scared Kat. He is not always kind, you know." I was not surprised. "If I say anything that he doesn't like, he accuses me of disobedience. So, I end up not saying anything! And married life. I didn't know it would be such an unpleasant duty." I didn't tell her that it was King Henry that made it unpleasant. My experience of lovemaking with Will, and with Tom Wyatt, had been delightful.

"It can be a shock the first time," I said. "But I am sure you will get used to it." Jane looked unconvinced.

"But he is so heavy, I can't breathe Kat. And he dribbles over me. I feel dirty afterwards, all I want to do is to wash and then have some wine to help me forget." Suddenly she started, as if she'd remembered something, "Kat, you won't tell anyone, will you? I am scared of him, honestly."

"I won't tell anyone," I assured her. And I did not. Of course, I am telling you now, daughter, but they are all long dead. But the truth was that they were not the perfect couple that they were portrayed as. Although Henry said he loved her, she became more and more terrified of him, fearing that she too would be sent to the scaffold. And to be honest, daughter, if things hadn't worked out differently, she might have trodden in Anne Boleyn's footsteps. Was she lucky? You can judge daughter, when you ask yourself if you would have considered yourself lucky to be in her position. And despite all the fine clothes and magnificent surroundings, despite the manors that Henry gave Jane, and the jewels he lavished on her, she lived with a golden sword positioned above her neck, and she knew it.

CHAPTER 13

The court was preparing to go to Windsor. It was early September, and the plague was threatening London. I always tried to avoid all the work that went into moving the many hundreds of people, horses, tapestries, chairs, paintings and goblets to another of the King's castles. Luckily, all I was responsible for was my two lutes and my personal belongings. I remembered how Anne had given me both instruments and felt grief for her tear inside my heart. She was a difficult woman, I knew. But she was honest, and in the end, she had been good to me. In the court, it was as if she had never been. Anything with her initial on, or her emblem of a falcon, was erased. The King ordered all portraits of her to be burned. This dark, striking and intelligent woman was wiped from history relentlessly. Her brother had been executed, her child made a bastard, and her family had retreated to the country. The Boleyn influence, once so powerful, had withered and died within a few weeks.

The King was not in a state of newly wed bliss. His illegitimate son, Henry Fitzroy, the Duke of Richmond, had died in July. I remembered how Henry had celebrated his birth, much to the distress of Queen Katherine. I knew that Henry had considered making him heir to the throne but had hesitated. What he had wanted was a legitimate son, born in wedlock, who could ascend to the throne with no dispute. Henry Fitzroy wasn't quite good enough.

He was given titles and offices of state. Maybe the King had thought to keep him in reserve in case his other plans didn't work out. Be that as it may, when Fitzroy developed a cough and a wasting sickness, the King was distraught. When he died, aged seventeen, King Henry was overwhelmed by grief. This was the time when he and Queen Jane were meant to be celebrating their union, enjoying the fruits of love. But for many weeks he withdrew from her, and everyone around him.

Gradually, the vivacity of the court returned. The King became once more a loving bridegroom. Queen Jane did not confide in me again after her outburst. She looked happier, as the horror of Anne's death receded, and, like a little girl dressing up, she enjoyed the many rich gowns and wonderful jewels she had been given. I remember her in white cloth of gold, with a silver tissue front piece and ermine-lined sleeves. Her little, plain face was beaming, and she looked as near to an angel as an earthly woman can. Only the bulky gable hood that she wore took away from her ethereal gown. Of course, all the ladies at court no longer wore the French hood. Too much linked to Anne Boleyn, too sexy, too sophisticated. But Jane was popular enough. On occasions when she and King Henry showed themselves to the people, she was greeted with friendly, if lukewarm, responses. She was not Anne, and so she was bearable. That seemed to be it. She showed no signs of being pregnant, but it was only months since her marriage.

On the other hand, I was finding it more and more difficult to hide my condition. My belly was large and protruded under my kirtle. I tried to position my lute so that it concealed the bump, but that was very uncomfortable. I asked Queen Jane when I could go to Mistress Mead at Wolf Hall, and she told me once the court had settled at Windsor, I could take to the road and go down to Wiltshire.

It didn't take long to settle back into Windsor Castle. It was an ancient castle going back hundreds of years. But King Henry had made improvements. His name was over the gatehouse's great arch. He'd completed the beautiful chapel of St George, where he planned to be buried. But at the moment it was hunting that was on his mind and romancing his new wife. And he wanted to show her the fine living to which she could now become accustomed.

Within a few hours, the servants had made the castle comfortable. They servants worked overnight to put up the tapestries and move in some of the King's most precious furniture, including a large carved oak bed. I tried not to imagine Queen Jane in that bed, lying there gasping for breath, under the bulk of the King. Instead, I concentrated on what was going into the kitchens. I was feeling very hungry now. Daughter, you were telling me you needed nourishment. And so daughter, I was pleased to see the hams and the cheeses being taken in, the fresh herbs and vegetables, the meat that had been slaughtered all over the county. I enjoyed eating in the kitchen. The cooks knew me and were happy to let me eat with them. I avoided the formal dinner in the great hall. There was no joy in it now, although we could hear the forced laughter sounding up from the feasting courtiers. I was happier sitting at one of the big weather-beaten tables with the kitchen staff, eating the leftovers from the hall, many of the dishes barely touched. I particularly liked the custards, the dried sweet fruits and the trout cooked in cream.

I was present, though, at the King and Queen's first audience in their Great Hall, presenting themselves for all the courtiers, servants and local dignitaries. As always, there were people with matters to be resolved, petty disputes to settle and new arrivals to introduce themselves. I stood towards the back. I wasn't part of the King's official musicians. They were playing stately, majestic music to mark the King's entrance. But my role had always been more informal, playing for the women in private settings. I felt very tired and was holding on to the edge of one of the great tables for support. The morning was already hot, and I was feeling a little unsteady. These events were usually monotonous and sleep-inducing. One after another, people were welcomed, their arguments sorted out, and their instructions given. I felt my eyelids start to droop and kept pinching my cheek to keep awake.

"Your Majesties, Sir Thomas Wyatt," I was jerked out of my drowsiness. There, bowing to the King and Queen, was Tom, looking thinner and older. But unmistakably Tom. I looked at him, and my heart flipped. How had he managed to leave the Tower? He had escaped the terrible trial of Queen Anne and her so-called lovers, but I thought he was still incarcerated. Now, seeing him again, back at court already, I could barely believe it.

I felt a rush of relief washing over me. So, Tom was safe, and what's more, back in the King's favour! I had no idea how he had managed it, but I was so happy to see him. The King got off his throne and went to meet him, clasping him in both arms. He hugged him, then stepped back, and threw back his head.

"Sir Thomas, welcome!" he cried out. "You have been a very foolish man, but you are forgiven!" Tom bowed his head and kissed the King's hand.

"Thank you, your Majesty. I am indeed fortunate to have had your mercy extended to me." I don't know how he did it. He who had always seen the King with a cynical eye, and now I guessed he must hate him. But he couldn't afford to do that, and so he was playing the courtier now, with great conviction.

"I have a diplomatic mission for you, Sir Thomas. You worked well in your post at Calais. Now I want you to go to the French court and foster our alliance." That was necessary, I thought, for the French would not be best pleased that their foremost ally, Queen Anne, had been so brutally killed. "Come and meet with me and Cromwell after dinner. We will talk about it fully then. Meanwhile, welcome! Take a few days to see old friends. Write a poem for my beautiful Jane!" Henry glanced towards his wife, listening obediently. "Tell her to make ready for her prince, who surely must come soon." Jane flushed. Henry had started referring to her delay in conceiving, often in public. I saw her hand shaking as she held it out and allowed Tom to kiss it. I could not think that he was keen to celebrate the King's bloodstained nuptials, but who knows? In this court, you could not be yourself, it was too dangerous. Tom bowed again and left the great hall.

The audience continued. I looked to find where Tom had gone, but I couldn't see him. Would I manage to get some time alone with him? I remembered that he had told me to keep away from him, for my own safety. Was that still the case? Would he welcome me as an old friend? Or maybe now he was back in the King's favour, he would not want to associate with me. I couldn't concentrate on the audience. Should I try to see him, and should I tell him what was becoming very clear, that I was pregnant and near my time? Suddenly, I started to feel very strange. I put out my hand, trying to catch hold of someone. But it was too late. I felt the room spinning, and blackness closed in on me.

"She's fainted, give her some air." Servants gathered around me, putting a goblet of wine to my lips, helping me up from the floor. I noticed the audience was still going on, most courtiers oblivious to what was happening at the back of the hall.

"She needs to rest, in her condition," one woman said. Was it that obvious? She took my arm and walked me back to the maids' dormitory. She looked severe, with her hair completely covered, and a frown on her face.

"Does the Queen know about this?" she asked, "because you had better tell her pretty quickly. "

"She knows," I said. "She is going to help me." The woman looked dubious, as if she doubted that very much. But she relented, and her voice became kinder,

"Now rest. I'll send up some dinner for you."

I slept deeply, so tired that I had no choice. The dormitory was a peaceful place at that time of day. All the maids were busy, and I was the only occupant. It was a bare room, with many pallet beds covering the floor. But the sunlight streamed in through the windows, and there was a clean smell of lavender coming from the fresh rushes. I woke after an hour or so to a gentle tapping at the door. Startled, I sat up straight and called out,

"Who is there?" The door opened a crack, and I heard a hoarse whisper,

"It's Tom. Are you there Kat?"

"Tom! What are you doing here? This is for the maids only." I heard a quiet snigger.

"That's why I want you to come out, Kat. Come and talk with me." Shaking the sleep from my body, I pushed myself upwards to my feet and made for the door. He was standing there, grey-faced and sad. He was so much thinner, and his body trembled at my touch. But yes, it was Tom. I hugged him, overjoyed.

"Come with me, Kat, to my chamber. We won't be disturbed there." He must have noticed my belly, but he didn't say anything as he hustled me past the passing courtiers and up to his small chamber. We got there, and he gestured to me to sit on the bed. Then he shut the door and started to weep. I cried out to him,

"Tom, Tom, I'm so sorry. How are you? I thought I would never see you again." I got up off the bed and put my arms around him. He sobbed on my shoulder as if he was a little child. I guided him to the bed and gently pushed him down. We sat there, me with my arm around him while he cried and cried. At last, after what seemed like many minutes, he quietened and started to speak.

"I saw her die, Kat. Did you know that? I saw my love go to her death. The little girl I adored, from when we were very young. Do you know Kat, what it feels like to see someone you love put to death? I was put into a cell that overlooked the execution. I don't know if they meant to do that. I think that they did. It was a warning, you see, for all those suspected but not charged. This is what will follow if you ever fall foul of the King again. I was lucky, you know. Thomas Cromwell knows my father, and he made sure I wasn't named. I was told it was because I was needed in the diplomatic service. But that wasn't it. They knew the whole thing was false. So long as they had their guilty men, it didn't matter who they were. It was a complete lie, Kat, the whole thing! She was innocent. The only thing she was guilty of was holding the King to account. She was too brave and too clever for her own good, poor lady."

"What happened Tom? What could you see?" I wanted to know how her death had been. It was a topic that was not allowed at court. All we were allowed to know was that treason had occurred and the traitors had been punished. Tom turned to me, tears again running down his face.

"This must go on record Kat, so that her innocence is known, and her courage recognised. My sister Margaret was one of her ladies those last two days, and she told me much of what happened. The execution was meant to happen the day before, and my love, she was ready. But it was delayed. She had prayed, made her peace with God, distributed her small possessions amongst her ladies, and suddenly she had another night to get through. I heard it was that Cromwell didn't want foreign dignitaries watching, but someone else told me the executioner was delayed. Whatever it was, Margaret told me it caused her so much suffering. She didn't sleep, how could she? Instead, she prayed over and over again for her daughter Elizabeth, for her safety and wellbeing. Poor little child, without her mother! Then she prayed that her soul would go swiftly to Paradise. I tell you Kat, she was not a sinful woman. She was intense, passionate, and she made enemies. But she was not evil. Margaret showed me the poem that Anne wrote that night. It makes me weep whenever I read it." He pulled a document out of his pouch,

> "Oh Death, rock me asleep,
> Bring me to quiet rest,
> Let me pass my weary guiltless ghost.
> Out of my careful breast.
> Toll on, thou passing bell,
> Ring out my doleful knell
> Let thy sound my death tell.
> Death doth draw nigh;
> There is no remedy."

He stuffed it back in his doublet, twisted by emotion.

"She did not deserve this; she was destroyed for no fault of her own! You know, she swore twice on the holy sacrament that she was innocent? You knew Anne, she would not risk her soul through all eternity for a temporal lie." His face crumpled. Overcome by grief and guilt, he let out a groan of agonising pain that could not be healed. I rocked him in my arms, letting him cry. He had probably not been able to express his grief since he had been released from the Tower. Everywhere, there would be people watching. The slightest sign of grief was very dangerous.

"Margaret told me she wore a red kirtle underneath her black gown. She was a martyr, and she knew it. But she was a queen too, and she wore ermine around her mantle, and a regal English hood. You know she laughed when she was told she would die? She put her hands round her neck and laughed. She said she'd heard the executioner was good at his job, and, as if to make it easier, she said she had a little neck! I tell you Kat, she went to her execution composed and ready. From what I saw, she was so beautiful. All the anxiety and fear had gone from her face. She had great faith in God, and she knew she was going to an eternal kingdom. I had never loved her so much as I did in that instance. She spoke to the crowd, but she would say nothing that would threaten her daughter. So, she praised the King who killed her. She said he had always been to her a good and gentle sovereign lord. Good and gentle! How much it must have cost her to call him that, but those we love make liars of us all. Then she asked everyone to pray for her, and she knelt down. I saw a moment of panic cross her face. Oh, Kat, how much I longed to go and rescue her! I wished that she had become my mistress, with all the disgrace that would have brought, she would have still been alive, and safe. We would have lived in Norfolk, with a stable full of horses and a herb garden." He knew, and I knew, that this life would never have suited Anne. But better to be discontented and alive, we both thought at that moment. His voice lowered to a whisper,

Margaret heard her say very quietly, "Oh Christ, receive my spirit," and then it was done. One moment, to turn life to death. It was terrible, seeing such beauty bloodied and defiled. The ladies were all weeping and hurrying to cover her up, to collect her head – her head Kat! – and wrapped it in linen. Such is goodness destroyed, it was terrible, terrible. Two days before they made me watch the executions of George, William, Mark and Francis. So much blood, so much terror. I cannot get these pictures out of my mind Kat. They will stay with me as long as I live."

I felt anger mounting inside me.

"So, they made you watch it all?" I asked.

"Yes, as a warning. It is a common enough thing. There were probably others they forced to stand at the windows." He sighed deeply. "Kat, I'm writing something for her, and for them. It's in my head. I can't write it down yet. But listen a little, please."

Of course, I listened as he spoke, with the tears pouring down his face,

"These bloody days have broken my heart,

My luck, my youth, did them depart,

And blind desire of estate,

Who hastes to climb seeks to revert,

Of truth, circa Regna tonat."

He saw that I did not follow the Latin. "It means, around the kingdom, thunder. But Kat, I cannot finish it. I want to speak of her innocence, to tell the world of her courageous spirit. But I can't, Kat. It must remain in my head only." He fixed me with an intense stare.

"What think you Kat? You will not betray me, will you?" I hastened to reassure him.

"No Tom, I will not. I will keep silent. It is the safest thing." He gave me a wry smile.

"Yes Kat. And you must keep safe. I shall be in France for the next few months, and so far away from danger." Then he looked me up and down, and for the first time took in my changed figure.

"You are sturdier than before, Kat," he ventured. I smiled and nodded.

"Yes, indeed I am. I have been growing since May." I patted my belly.

"Kat, are you... are you... with child?" He knew, but he couldn't quite believe it. He had been so surrounded by death that ordinary life seemed of no consequence to him.

"I am." I smoothed my skirts over my swollen belly.

"How far?"

"I am due next month, in October," I replied. I could see him counting back, calculating when I was likely to have conceived.

"So, was it me?" he asked.

"I think so. I cannot be sure, but the dates fit." His face looked troubled.

"Why didn't you tell me Kat? Why didn't you ask for help?" I pointed out that this had been difficult,

"As far as I knew, you were still in the Tower. That meant I was on my own. Don't worry, I have made preparations. Queen Jane is sending me to her old nurse to give birth, and then I am returning to court." I got up to leave his chamber, but he pulled me back.

"Don't go like this! I cannot marry you, you know that, as my wife is still living. But I can look after you. I can find you a little house on my father's estate, and I can visit you whenever I am in the country." I shook my head.

"No Tom. You know, and I know, that the one woman you loved was Anne Boleyn. No one can take her place, and I don't wish to."

"You don't wish to?" He sounded offended. Tom was a good man, but he had his share of vanity. I smiled to myself.

"Tom, I have realised that I love Will above all others. He is away from court, but I do hope to see him soon." This was the first time in many months I had set out my desire to be with Will, and suddenly it seemed like the only thing to do. Tom looked doubtful,

"But he would not wish to take on another man's child," he said. "Very few men would do that."

"I know that," I answered, "but I must try. And there is the slightest possibility it is his. That might make it easier." Tom laughed out loud.

"You are ever the optimist, Kat. I love that about you. Look, I won't give you a house, and I won't bother you with visits. But I cannot leave you without resources." He walked over to the chest at the far side of the room, opened it, and took out a cloth bag.

"Here, take this. If you need more, you will need to send a message to me. But this should help for the next year." I opened the bag. Nestling inside it were several gold coins. More money than I had ever seen in my life. I looked at him appraisingly, considering.

Then I thought, well, why not? He most probably had made this child, and his gift would make our lives very much easier.

"Will you take it?" He was afraid that I might turn him down.

"Yes, Tom. Thank you. That will mean I do not have to hurry back to court. I will know once the babe is born. It will have a look of you, I think." He smiled and looked down at the floor. I realised that the tears were back in his eyes.

"Maybe one day, maybe, I might see the babe," he whispered, "but I will pray God watches over you both." He held me in his arms and kissed me tenderly. I responded warmly to him, knowing that he was the only person that I could trust at court. Now he was going to France, to resume his career as a diplomat. I would miss him, but I knew that he would be safer in Paris than in London.

I didn't know then that a year later, he would fall in love with Elizabeth Darrell and set up a home with her. I often wondered, daughter, what would have happened if it had been me. Would I have been satisfied with what he could offer me? And would he have got bored with me? We thought alike, him and I. I might have held him back. He was always a highflyer. He never knew the secret of my birth. But as it had to be kept secret, it wouldn't have made any difference anyway. In the end, though, it was Elizabeth Darrell who was his mistress for the rest of his life. They lived together when they could, and they had children together. I didn't begrudge them their love. He had suffered, and would never be the same teasing, handsome man that he once was. We were all trying to build our lives back again in the midst of some terrible wreckage. Nothing would ever be perfect again. But we were human, and we all needed love.

I knew though, that he would never be free of Anne. Late at night, there was only one woman who haunted him. She appeared in his dreams, sometimes joyous, sometimes crying out for revenge. Sometimes he dreamt of kissing her, whole and beautiful. Sometimes she was horribly bloodied, and mangled. Then during daylight hours, he would think he had seen her running into the next chamber, but when he went there, she was gone. She was always just around the corner. While everyone else had conveniently forgotten her, she was burned into Tom Wyatt's heart, and his poetry.

> "In mourning wise since daily I increase,
> Thus, should I cloak the cause of all my grief;
> So pensive mind with tongue to hold his peace
> My reason safety there can be no relief:
> Wherefore give ear, I humbly you require,
> The affect to know that thus doth make me moan.
> The cause is great of all my doleful cheer
> For those that were, and now be dead and gone."

CHAPTER 14

I didn't stop hoping that Will would come back, but he was nowhere to be seen. He didn't seem to be at court. I passed my letter on to his father, Tom. At least he would be able to give it to Will once he'd returned to London. I knew my time was near, and still Queen Jane hadn't said anything. So, I decided to ask her early one morning as she was being dressed. It was normal for me to play for her, but I usually didn't ask her anything. This time though, I took a deep breath and put down my lute.

"Your Majesty, may I ask you a favour?" The ladies that were dressing her breathed in and looked down their noses at me. Times had changed so much from when I worked for Queen Katherine, and even for Queen Anne. Gone were the times of midnight confidences, shared prayers and secrets. I had to know my place now.

Queen Jane looked at me vaguely. Then she gave a gesture of recognition.

"Kat, I remember. You must go to Wolf Hall!" She saw my swelling belly, and her face looked unutterably sad.

"I am near my time, your Majesty. I need to depart within the week." She was thoughtful, sad.

"I cannot spare you until the end of this month, Kat." I wondered why, but I didn't have time to ask. The great door swung open, and the King swept into her chamber, scattering ladies who retreated from him as he came. I turned to look at him, just for an instant, before I curtseyed. He was getting very weighty now, and he limped due to a long-standing injury to his leg. His face was almost square, lined by a close-clipped beard. His cheeks were red, but not the rosy red of his youth, more an unhealthy flush. But he was dressed magnificently, and no one could doubt that he was the King. He was angry, I could see. He pointed his finger in Queen Jane's face, jabbing it towards her eyes. My father. I hated him.

Queen Jane flinched for an instant, then tried to compose herself. She was standing there in her shift, her state gown put aside by her dressers, who had vanished. Uncomfortably, she gave a small curtsey, narrowly avoiding the King's finger as she dipped her head.

"Tell me Madam," he roared, "tell me now. I hear you have your courses again. That is four months since we wed. God send that you are not barren!" Queen Jane hung her head.

"I am sorry, your Majesty. I know it must be disappointing," she whispered. The King's face swelled with rage, and he exploded at her,

"Disappointing Madam? Disappointing? You speak as if there is no mutton for dinner. This is not a disappointment; this is a crisis. I need an heir, you know that. God has taken Henry Fitzroy. All I have are two bastard daughters, Elizabeth and Mary. Which one would ruin the kingdom quicker? We need a boy. So why are you not with child? Tell me that Madam, why are you not with child?"

"I... I don't know, your Majesty." I backed towards the door, embarrassed for her and wanting to get out of the way.

"You don't know! You had better find out, Madam, and quickly!" He turned on his heel and stormed out of the room. Tears started to roll down Jane's face.

"Don't go, Kat," she said quickly. "I need a moment to compose myself. Sit with me." I poured her a goblet of wine.

"Here you are, your Majesty," I said. I could not say more, because if I did, I would give vent to my feelings about the King. He must understand that it was not Queen Jane's fault if she had not yet conceived. But he had always blamed women, first Katharine and then Anne. Jane would be no different. But while the other two queens had vigorously contested Henry's attempts to blame them, Jane was very different.

"It is my fault, Kat. I missed my prayers last week. And I did not rest after... after... we were intimate. His Majesty is right to be angry with me. I must strive to do his will."

I couldn't help it; I reached out and touched her on the shoulder. It was fragile, like a bird's. I could feel her bones underneath her shift.

"We have no control over whether we conceive, your Majesty," I murmured, trying to reassure her.

"But you conceived Kat," she said. "You conceived and I did not." I smiled cynically.

"It would have been better if it was the other way around, your Majesty," I said.

"Indeed, it would Kat. So what am I doing wrong? I have prayed and fasted and listened to the midwife's advice. But nothing!" She looked me straight in the face, and asked directly,

"Do you think I will conceive Kat? You know more than me about these matters." I could not tell her that I didn't know. Instead, I lied,

"Your Majesty, I know the look of fertile women. There is a look, a fullness about the skin. You have that look, your Majesty. You will conceive very soon." She shook her head sadly,

"It had better be soon, or the King will have no use for me." Her words were chilling. She accepted that if she didn't soon carry a child in her belly, she would be replaced. After what King Henry had said, I knew she was right.

"No, no, your Majesty," I said unconvincingly. She waved me away.

"No more of this Kat. You may go to Wolf Hall. I will find a manservant and a maid to accompany you. Now fetch my ladies. It is nearly time for the Mass, and I am not dressed!" I curtseyed and left her, praying inwardly that if she was replaced, it would be by an annulment, not an execution.

I travelled down to Wolf Hall three days later, with an irritable manservant and his teenage daughter. He started the journey by being curious, a nasty leer on his face,

"So, if you're married, as you say you are Mistress, why is your husband not looking after you?" He leered at me, and I knew that he thought I was a maid who had got into trouble and was being helped by the Queen. He was probably right, I thought. But I wasn't going to give him the satisfaction.

"My husband is away on business for Thomas Cromwell," I replied icily. "He will be returning before All Souls Day." That silenced him, and I had no more insolent comments. But it made me think. Will might be back in London now. If the Court hadn't gone to Windsor, I might have seen him. But it was nine months since our argument, and I hadn't heard a word from him. There had been no reply to the letter I'd given to Tom. And once I was with child by another man, it hadn't seemed right to contact him. But now I knew that I still loved him. Tom Wyatt had been fun, and a good friend. But it was Will that I wanted. Should I tell him my child was his? There was an outside possibility. But then, that would mean lying, and I had never lied to Will. What I wanted was to tell him the whole truth and ask for his forgiveness. I also wanted him to ask for my forgiveness, as it was he who had, after all, made me leave. But would he want to do that? Maybe he had found someone else in the wilds of Lincolnshire and was even now setting up home with her. I still hoped that he missed me, though, and resolved once my baby was born to try to find him.

It took us nearly a week to reach Wolf Hall. I could not ride far, due to my pregnancy, we stopped frequently to rest. Fortunately, the autumn was mild, and I was able to stop whenever I needed to. Eventually, we got to Wolf Hall and rode along to Mistress Ashdown's cottage. As we trotted up, her door opened, and she ran out to meet us.

"Mistress Kat, it is good to see you. Welcome to my home!" She waved irritably at the manservant. "Help her down you! When did you ever see a lady in her condition, left perching on the top of her horse?" The manservant swore under his breath but went to lift me down. Mistress Ashdown hugged me and led me into her cottage. The two servants departed for the main house, where they would stay the night in the servants' quarters.

The cottage was as warm and welcoming as I remembered it, with a cheery fire burning in the hearth and the table set with plates and tankards.

"Sit down, Mistress Kat, sit down," Mistress Ashdown told me. "You are here to rest now. You must not lift a finger!" I sat in the rush-bottomed chair beside the table.

"Thank you, Mistress Ashdown, but I am not ill. I can still help you in the house," I insisted.

"Call me Mistress Mead," she said, "better still, Meady! That's what Jane used to call me when she was little. 'Give me my dolly, Meady,' she would say. 'Pour me some mead, Meady.' Of course, I gave her a little. She loved it and grew bonny on it. What a strong little girl she was."

So, I called her Meady from that day onwards. And so, I rested, and ate rabbit stew, and drank goblets of mead, fresh creamy milk, and small ale for breakfast. Dear Alice, my daughter, you have a sunny disposition and a calm temperament. That is all down to Meady, who looked after me. I, who had looked after so many others, was at last being cared for. Meady did everything. She washed my shifts, baked bread, and cooked every day. At night, she would make up the fire and tell me to sit beside it. After a few goblets of mead, I would go to sleep in her wooden bed, made up with lavender-scented sheets. Despite my protests, she slept on a pallet bed, saying that I needed the big bed to spread out and be comfortable. Every morning she would be up before dawn. I would lie there in the bed, hearing her bustling about, and feel as if I was a little girl once again, with Joan baking bread for my breakfast.

Meady told me stories of Jane when she was a little girl,

"She was such a good little girl. Not like her brothers! They were always fighting, but she never joined in. I can see her now, around three years old she was. Her dolly was her baby. She would go nowhere without that dolly. Going to Mass, picnics, walks in the garden. Always Dolly was with her, tucked under her arm. She liked to watch me at my work, and she always wanted to join in. She loved gathering herbs with me, putting the sprigs into her own small basket. With the lavender, she would do what I did; squeeze a head between her two chubby fingers and then bring them up to her nose to smell the scent." Meady looked wistful when she remembered the times past.

"She wasn't one for her books, she preferred to copy the maids as they went around their tasks. And she loved animals! She had a little dog once, when she was about eleven. A tiny spaniel, the runt of the litter, but she loved him. He was called Faithful, I remember that. She would wash him, dress him in ribbons, and feed him titbits from the table." Meady shook her head. "he was killed by one of her father's horses. He got into the stables, I don't know how, and Sir John's stallion kicked him to death. Poor Jane, she cried and cried!"

"Did she get another dog?" I asked. I had never seen Lady Jane with a dog, although many of the court ladies had them.

"No, she said that no other dog would replace Faithful.

That's her, you see. Once she loves something, or someone, she commits herself to them utterly." I nodded.

"We were friends from when she first came to court," I said, "but even though she is now so grand, she hasn't forgotten me." Meady nodded her agreement.

"That is my Jane. She wrote to me about you. I was surprised to get the letter, I thought that she was too busy to write now she is Queen. But no, she asked after me. She checked that my pension was sufficient and then asked me to take you in for your confinement. It was the least I could do!" Meady looked curiously at me.

"Tell me this, Kat, why couldn't your husband look after you?" Her face was concerned rather than condemnatory. I couldn't tell her everything, that would involve giving away the secret of my birth. So, I muttered,

"We had an argument. I couldn't live with him anymore." Meady was up in arms,

"And so he won't take responsibility for his child? No argument justifies that!" I looked down at the stone floor.

"He doesn't know," I confessed.

"Kat, you must tell him! Let me ask his Lordship to send him a message for you." But any message would have to go to Austin Friars, and I did not want to be involved with Thomas Cromwell anymore.

"Meady, it is... difficult. I will tell him once I am back at court. I need to speak privately with him, and I do not wish to put it all into a letter." She sat back, shaking her head.

"You've chosen a difficult path, girl, but I will look after you, I swear. I told Queen Jane that you would be safe here, and you will. When your time comes, we will send for the village midwife, and she will deliver your baby for you."

And so, the days passed. It was October now, and there was a chill in the air. Meady and I ambled into the forests around Wolf Hall to pick sloes, late blackberries, and elderberries. Sometimes she would collect honey from the hives around the main house and return with it to start the brewing of her famous mead. It was a calm and happy time, so far away from the dangers and excitement of the court, that I found myself relaxing after many months of feeling like I was living on the edge.

One morning, unusually, I woke before Meady. I was feeling nervy and uncomfortable. I got out of bed and went to the kitchen, thinking I would sit beside the fire that had been banked up the previous night. But before I got there, I felt a rush of warm liquid flooding down my legs, as if I had urinated on myself. I stood there in the puddle for a moment, wondering what was happening. Then I looked around to find a rag to clean up the mess on the floor. Meady came in when I was on my knees, cleaning the cold stone floor.

"What are you doing? Get up Kat. You shouldn't be cleaning floors in your condition." I saw the concern on her face, and it released something in me that I had kept firmly buried. I started to cry, tears streaming down my face. As I cried, I felt my belly contract, with a shooting pain worse than anything I had ever felt before.

"Hey, Kat, Kat. What is the matter? Here, come and sit down. Let me fetch you some small ale." She bustled to the table and returned with a tankard.

"Why are you crying, sweeting?" Her use of the word 'sweeting' only made me cry more. I hadn't been called that since I was a child. And now I was having a child myself, bringing you, my daughter, into a future that was uncertain, maybe even dangerous. I vowed then that I would always protect you, always love you, until the end of my life.

"I can feel pain, Meady, oh, here it comes again!" I slammed the tankard down on the table and held my breath as another agonising spasm swept over me.

"It's your time child. Your babe is on its way. Let me get you back to bed, and then I will go and fetch the midwife." She helped me back into the bedroom and then dressed quickly, throwing on a cloak and pulling on her boots before she turned to me.

"Kat, I will be gone no more than an hour. When I come back, I will bring the midwife with me. Don't move, stay warm in bed."

"What if the baby comes?" I cried, panicking at her leaving me. She smiled and laid her hand on my face.

"You have hours to go yet, sweeting. Don't worry, I will be back with the midwife well before then." She withdrew her hand and crept downstairs into the dawn.

Left alone, I talked to you, daughter. Every time the pain swept through me, I felt that you were knocking at the door of life.

"Let me be born, Mother. I am eager to see the world." And, in my head I was telling you,

"Beware, baby, the world is a dangerous place, and there are many evil people out to destroy you." You didn't like me saying that daughter. Another pain, even worse than the last, gripped me. I hastened to reassure you,

"Nothing can hurt you, my love. I will always love you. While I live, I will protect you." In a quiet moment, between contractions, I felt you flutter inside me, as if you had understood what I'd promised you. But those quiet moments soon ceased. I was no longer talking to you. Instead, we were in a battle, fighting to bring you into the world. The pains were coming all the time now, and I was afraid I could not bear it. I got up and tried to pace up and down, but the pains took my breath away, and I was not able to continue.

Daughter, giving birth is women's battlefield. Some of us do not survive. We suffer uncertainty, immense pain, and fear. More of us die on this battlefield than do men on theirs. It takes courage to be a warrior, courage and indomitable hope. We are said to be weak, but we are as strong as the soldiers who fought in France and the midlands of England. The difference is that our battle is to give life, whereas theirs is to take it. We are the warriors of life, us women.

I was screaming out now. I couldn't hold it in. Where was Meady? How had I allowed myself to conceive this baby anyway? Never again, never, never again.

I heard the door open and footsteps rushing up the stairs. Meady burst into the room.

"I heard you from the lane. Are you near the end now?" She stripped off her cloak and stood over me. She was on her own.

"Where is the midwife?" I cried out. "I need help, so much pain, I can't bear it!"

"The midwife is with another woman. I went to find her and then was directed to the woman's house." I was mad with pain.

"So why isn't she here?" I wailed. "I can't do this without her."

"The other woman is very close to delivery. The midwife will stay with her until the babe is safely arrived. Once the birth is over, she will hasten to you. She will be here within two hours, Kat. Don't fear." I was getting desperate.

"She has no business to do that, she should be with me." Daughter, I was unreasonable. But that is how labour makes you. You are fighting for your life, and your babe's life. You are not polite, not pleasant. You are in it to the death.

Meady tried to reassure me,

"She will be here soon. And I have some experience of birth, so I can help you. Let me go and fetch some towels." She bustled out of the room, leaving me crying almost continuously. Returning swiftly, she made me lie on the bed.

"Spread your legs out, Kat. That's a good girl. When the pain comes, just breathe in and out. Just breathe through it."

"But the pain never goes!" There was no relief now, no rest from the agony. I was hysterical, thrashing about on the bed. I was so afraid; I could not control it. The panic was rising in me, and I was screaming uncontrollably.

Meady leant over and slapped me across the face. For a moment, I stopped, surprised.

"Kat, you must calm down. Your baby is depending on you. This is the most important work you will ever do. You must concentrate." I stopped for a moment, trying to catch my breath,

"It's so hard, Meady, I can't do it."

"Yes, you can Kat. It won't be long now. Let me look at you, maybe I can see the baby's head." Gently, she pushed me down and parted my legs. It was the middle of the day now, and she could see clearly.

"Kat, I can see your baby's head! A little redhead, like you. It is just ready to come now." I groaned, not able to believe it.

"Within the hour, you will be holding your baby, Kat, I promise!" It didn't encourage me. I was in too much pain to care.

"Where is the midwife? I want the midwife!"

"Kat, she has been delayed. So, it is you and me. We must do this together. Now, when I tell you, you must push down with all your might, as if you were passing a stool." Briefly, I remembered Lady Boleyn, many years ago, telling me this. Times past, times past.

I tried to push, straining down with all my might.

"Meady, I can't. I can't do it!"

"Yes, you can Kat. You must."

"But it hurts so much!"

"You must be brave, Kat, think of your baby and push!" I pushed as hard as I could, feeling the agony increase as I did.

"Well done, sweeting. It's coming now, I can see it coming!" I pushed again, screaming as I did so. But then Meady stopped, looked, and spoke urgently to me.

"Kat, you must stop pushing. There is a problem. If you push more, you will damage yourself and your baby."

"Help me, Meady, what shall I do?"

"We must wait for the midwife. Your baby is stuck in the birth canal."

Stuck? I was in despair. Was this how it was going to end, with me dying in childbirth and taking my baby with me? Mistress Mead was looking very worried. She had experience of normal childbirth, but not of emergencies. I started to pray. I prayed for you, daughter, and for me.

"You must baptise it, even if it is barely here," I gasped. If we were going to die, I was not going to send you to limbo, where unbaptised babies went. Mistress Mead nodded and fetched a basin of water. She wet her finger and reached up between my legs to the baby's head.

"Innocent soul, I baptise you in the name of the Father, Son and Holy Ghost." For a moment, the terrible pain stopped. But then the world went black, and I was on my way to my maker.

CHAPTER 15

I surfaced into consciousness, barely aware that another figure was standing in front of me, in a plain kirtle with her arms bare. I was so hazy and couldn't see anything properly. But I felt the baby straining inside me, pulling so hard it felt as if my insides were being ripped out. Then a voice said to me,

"Now, Kat, you must push. You must push with every bit of strength that you have."

"I can't, I can't," I mumbled, "too much pain." I felt someone pulling me upright and shaking me by the shoulders. I blinked, surely it wasn't. Surely not? But yes, it was. There was Maria de Salinas, Lady Willoughby, holding me and staring into my face. Behind her, Meady hovered, looking worried.

"Kat, listen," Maria said calmly. "I know of these things. It happened to me once. Now Kat, we must get your baby out. Mistress Ashdown's hands are too big to reach inside. She cannot help you. But I have small hands." She held them up for me and Meady to see. She was right, they were tiny. Meady looked regretfully at her large, reddened hands, swollen by hard work.

"Get me some water, and a towel," Maria demanded. Meady gestured her to the pile of towels and the bowl of water from the well. Swiftly, Maria rinsed her hands in the water, and dried them. She bent down to me and took my face in her hands.

"Kat, I can hold the baby's head and ease it through. But you must push. If you want your baby to live, you must push now, and do as I say." I couldn't think clearly, my mind was drowned in a sea of pain. But I trusted Maria, and I knew I had to do what she said. She let me lie back and positioned herself between my legs.

"Put your knees up, like this," she told me. "Now push, push, push!" I pushed and panted out,

"It hurts, please, it hurts." I was crying now, but Maria spoke to me calmly.

"You're doing well," she told me, "baby is starting to move now. I'm turning the head round. Now push!" I arched my back and pushed down as hard as I could. I had never known pain like it.

"That's good, keep pushing! It won't be long till baby's here." I could feel her hands moving the baby, turning it like a screw, and at last, with one long agonising scream, I pushed the baby out.

"Kat, you have a little girl," Maria said, "and she is a beauty." She held the baby up for me to see. It was you daughter, of course, and I fell in love with you from that moment onwards. You were a big baby, very red and angry. You cried as soon as you entered the world, and all three of us women laughed. It was as if we were all thinking, "Just wait, it can only get worse from now on!" Maria took the scissors that Meady gave her and cut the cord. Then she handed you over to be cleaned up. Meady washed you and wrapped you in linen, then handed you back to me.

Oh, my daughter, you were so beautiful! You had tufts of red hair and dark grey eyes. I couldn't stop touching your hands and feet. So tiny, and so soft. Your fingers already curled around my finger, and I could see the insteps on your feet.

I felt such tenderness for them. They were not hardened by life, by many hours of walking and wearing strong shoes. New-minted, a miracle. You started pushing against me, your mouth open, like a baby bird.

"Loosen your shift. Let the baby come to the breast," said Meady, and I held out my nipple for you to fix on. You sucked the first milk from me, while I looked down at you and marvelled. After you had sucked your fill, I lay you down in a large basket that had been brought up from the kitchen, lined with soft towels. You closed your eyes and slept, that deep, deep sleep that babies have at first.

Meady cleaned me up, while Maria pulled her long robe on back over her. Fortunately, it had been a travelling robe, and was fairly loose. She went down to the kitchen and returned a few minutes later with a cup of warm milk with honey for me.

"Here, drink this Kat." I struggled to sit up and took up the cup. I focused on Maria. She looked a little dishevelled, her hair had strayed out from under her hood, and her robe was muddy. But there was no doubt it was Maria. So, what was she doing here, in Wiltshire? How had she found me?

"How did you get here?" I asked blearily. Her face creased up in a smile.

"I wouldn't leave you alone, Kat, with a baby to bring up," she said. "I've been going back into court a little since the concubine was killed." I knew there was no point in trying to argue with her that Anne wasn't a concubine.

"And so, have you seen Queen Jane?" I asked. I knew that when they were both Queen Katherine's ladies, they had liked each other, and shared a loyalty to the Queen. Maria nodded briskly.

"Yes, I have, briefly. It is a great relief to be able to visit the court now, and she is a lovely girl. She told me that you were with child a couple of weeks back. I knew that I owed it to Queen Katherine to be with you." Meady looked a bit puzzled, and Maria made an excuse to send her out of the room.

"Mistress Ashdown, after our travails, I would welcome a cup of your famous mead! The Queen herself told me how good it was. Would you mind bringing us all some? And I think I should like it mulled, with a little cinnamon if you have it."

"Yes, of course, my lady." Meady looked pleased and hurried off down the stairs. Maria waited a minute and then started to whisper,

"You are Queen Katherine's daughter, and I owe you allegiance, just as I did her. When I heard about your pregnancy, I had to come to you. You were her daughter, and now you are my daughter. I arrived just as you blacked out. Fortunately, I have had much experience of childbed, and I knew what to do. And now, praise Jesu, you are both safe." I felt the tears gather in my eyes. I had felt so lost and alone during the last few months, and her kindness moved me deeply.

"But Kat, where is Will?" Maria asked. "He is your husband; he should be supporting you." I wondered what to tell her. But I trusted her enough to give her some of the details,

"You remember when we went to my mother, Queen Katherine, on her deathbed?" I asked.

"Sweet Jesu, how could I forget?" she cried out.

"When I came back, I told Will, and he was very angry with me. You know that he works for Master Cromwell. He didn't want me to go to the Queen, it might have caused problems for him." Maria looked crossly at me.

"Cause problems? You visiting your mother? That is not a kind thing to say." I made excuses for him,

"Cromwell can be very hard, Maria. And if Will falls out of favour, he will be lost. We do not have money, or a title." Maria nodded, conceding that in this matter she had been protected by both.

"So, you argued. But why are you down here on your own? Surely Will wants to see his child? Provide for her, take care of her?" Maria was still asking questions, unsatisfied with what she had learnt so far. I took a deep breath,

"He told me to leave, Maria. We were living at Thomas Cromwell's house, and he told me to leave." I could see the anger in Maria's face, so I hurried on,

"He doesn't know about the baby," I said, "he has been away on some work involving the monasteries."

"Well, my dear, you must tell him!" Maria was unequivocal on this. Will was being denied his rights as a father, and his responsibilities.

"It's not that easy. You see, I think the baby is Thomas Wyatt's." I managed to get it out, just. A moment later, Maria's anger and concern descended on me in a crescendo of Spanish. I understood enough to pick out swear words, cries to God, and prayers for the innocent babe. I waited for a moment to let her calm down.

"We were friends, and he comforted me. That was all there was to it. But now it means I cannot go back to Will. Don't you see? I would like to, but I don't think he would accept me." Maria became a stern Catholic matriarch,

"I am disappointed in you Kat. You have sinned grievously, consorting with a man with whom you are not married. What were you thinking of? Have you made confession?" I said quietly,

"Yes, I have, and received absolution." I didn't normally go to confession, but I had been desperate in those months I was with child. Maria snorted.

"That, at least, is good. But what of the child? Have you thought of that? Who will support her?" At least I could answer that easily,

"Tom Wyatt has given me some money for the first year. I am to contact him when I need more."

"And what of the shame, Kat? What of the bad blood that will taint this child forever? Will you have her adopted?"

"No!" I found myself shouting at her. "She is mine, and I will not give her up, not for anyone!" To my surprise, Maria's face softened.

"Maybe you are right. And maybe I should help you. She is the Queen's granddaughter, just as you are her daughter. She would want me to keep you both close." She sighed,

"You have committed a mortal sin, Kat. But thankfully, the priest has given you absolution. So, let us put it behind us. We will work something out." We heard Meady's footsteps on the stairs, and a moment later she came in with a tray of three tankards of steaming mead.

"Here you are, my ladies," she said. "Best mead in the West Country, or so I'm told." I breathed in the scent of honey as I sipped some of the sweet liquid, and I felt comforted. I was sure that Meady and Maria would work out what to do next. I wasn't that concerned, all I wanted to do was to hold you, touch my finger gently to your little smudgy nose, and stroke your fragile pulsing head. You were alive, you were well, and that was enough for me.

Maria, Lady Willoughby, didn't stay for long. But she left me with instructions that when I returned to court, I must at first live with her. But that was months off. I would stay with Meady until you were weaned and then leave you in her care. I wasn't going to find a wet nurse and hand you over straight-away to another woman. I wanted that special time with you, that time when a mother and baby are as one. Safe in this warm cottage with Meady, I didn't want anything to spoil our time together.

You were a bonny baby; not like I was. I had been scrawny, on the edge of death, but you were always plump and pretty. I delighted in every gummy smile you gave me, every gurgling laugh, every blissful snore. I called you Alice. I knew, because Tom Wyatt had told me, that Alice meant noble. And you are noble, my dear girl. Your name is a secret clue to your real identity. I smiled every time I called you by that name. My noble little daughter.

There was no immediate need for a christening, as Meady had baptised you. But after a few months we had a small service in the nearby parish church. I wrote to the man I had known as my father, Tom Cooke, telling him I'd had a child, and asking him to come down and act as your godfather. I didn't tell him that you might not be Will's child. I just let him assume that you were. I hoped that when we met, I could pass a message to Will through Tom. Meady was your godmother. I didn't know who else to ask, but Meady surprised me by saying that Lady Maria had told her she would stand as the other godparent. She sent a rather sniffy young woman called Isabel to act as her proxy, who made the promises on her behalf. So, during the Advent season, you were christened in the church, Alice Kate Cooke. Your middle name is for me and your Spanish grandmother, Queen Katherine. But nobody at the service knew that. It was our secret.

After the service we all went back to Meady's cottage to drink her ambrosial mead. I was glad of the chance to speak to Will's father, Tom. I didn't know if Will knew about you, Alice. But at last, I had a chance to find out.

"So where is Will?" asked Tom. "I thought he must be working in the West Country, but he isn't here."

"I was told he was working on the dissolution of the monasteries," I said. "But I don't know how to get hold of him to tell him about Alice. Have you not seen him?"

"Not for nearly a year now," Tom said. "I know he is a busy man, but I wish he would return to London."

"He must come back soon, surely," I said. "Tom... father... have you still got my letter for him? if you see him before I do, will you tell him I would like to see him?" Tom looked puzzled, but he nodded.

"Of course, Kat, and I'll give him your letter. But surely, he will see you before me?"

"I have written to him, but every time it seems I miss him, as he's moved on." Not true. How could I explain to Will through a letter? I knew I had to see him face to face. Tom, knowing nothing, told me that as soon as he saw Will, he would pass my message on.

"And if you see him first, Kat, tell him that his father wishes to see him!" I laughed and agreed enthusiastically, although I didn't think that was likely. For now, though, my life was you, Alice. My bonny, red-haired and dark-eyed daughter.

I knew that come next Spring; I would have to leave you behind. But I didn't like to think about that. It was too painful to consider it, although I knew that if I wanted to go back to court, it would have to happen. Why didn't I just stay with you? I asked myself this many times. But I knew if ever I was to reconcile with Will, I would have to go back to London. And if ever I was to progress with my music, I would have to be back at court. Tom Wyatt had given me enough to live on for now. But I would need more. And those people who would help me, him, the Queen, and Lady Maria were all at court. I had to face the fact that life would take me from you daughter. Although, I swore, it would not be for long.

Come April and you were sitting up, eating bread and milk from a spoon. Meady looked at me and said,

"I have a cow in the back field, giving good milk. Alice can drink from her. And she is eating well now." I smiled.

"She has teeth too!" I said, feeling the soreness around one of my nipples where you'd had a tiny nip.

"Time for her to be weaned," Meady said. "You can go back to London, Kat. She will be safe with me." I knew she was right. Tom Wyatt had left enough money for her to be well looked after, and Meady would be the best of nurses. She adored you, Alice, and treated you as a grandchild. With her, you would have plenty of love, fresh country air and good food. I would miss you terribly, but I could not return to London with you. I knew no one in London that I could trust to take care of you, whereas here, at Wolf Hall, I was sure you would be happy. It was such a hard decision, and it tore me apart. I couldn't bear to be away from you. The last night I was with you, I took you into my bed and slept with your little, pudgy body beside me.

Only I didn't sleep. I kept looking at you, watching you, listening to you breathe. I tried to store up these memories in my head, to sustain me once I had left. I can tell you the truth, Alice, I have never loved anyone as I have loved you.

Next morning, I left with a manservant and maidservant of Lady Maria's who had been sent to accompany me to London. I was determined not to cry. I hugged you and kissed you and told you to be good. Then I hugged Meady and told her I would be back before the end of the year. I thanked her for her immense kindness to me, for caring for me and looking after me so well. Then I mounted my horse and started the long journey back. I must admit that the tears came just after my last sight of you, before I turned the corner. You were there, in Meady's arms, waving your little plump hand at me. I swore to myself that we would be together soon, whatever it cost me. Then I cried soundlessly, the tears streaming down my face. The maidservant looked at me sympathetically.

"I had to leave my little one mistress," she said. "Hardest day of my life. But I had no choice. My husband died of the sweating sickness." I looked at her sympathetically, and immediately felt that my lot wasn't too bad. I had a profession, I had the promise of support from Tom Wyatt, and, I hoped, the prospect of a reconciliation with Will. I stopped crying and asked the woman her name.

"Jane, my lady," she said. I was shocked. No one had ever called me 'my lady' before. I wanted to tell her not to use that term, but I realised that if I was to be frank, I would need to give her details of my life story, and I didn't want to do that.

Lady Maria Willoughby's London house was on the Barbican. It was a well-appointed half-timbered building with gardens to its front. As we rode through the tradesmen and street sellers who crowded the streets nearby, I felt my anxiety rise. I had always liked Lady Maria. She had been kind to me when I was a simple foundling, so much despised by the other ladies. And now she knew Queen Katherine was my mother, she would always be loyal to me. But still, I wondered how I would be received. If she treated me as an aristocratic lady, then rumours would swiftly go around London and the court. But if she treated me as a servant, that would make a mockery of the deep friendship that had grown between us.

Lady Willoughby had solved that problem by taking me back to our times together with Queen Katherine. She told her household that I had been Queen Katherine's musician. I had served the Queen loyally for many years and had become a friend. Lady Maria insisted that I be respected as the Queen's friend. And that was that. For the first time in my life, I was a milady. It was strangely unsettling, but Lady Maria made me so welcome that I felt comfortable in my new position. Jane, the maidservant, was assigned to look after me, and we got on well. We talked of our babies and how we missed them. Later, I told Maria, and we arranged for Jane to have a day off to go and see her son. She was so grateful when I told her, crying and laughing all at the same time. I took her in my arms and kissed her. At first, she was surprised, but then she responded by kissing the tips of my fingers.

"Thank you, my lady, I will not forget you," she said, and indeed, for the rest of my stay, she made sure I got the best of everything: the freshest bread, the sweetest dried fruits. I settled in well, sleeping in the same chamber as Lady Maria, practising my new compositions, and getting measured for two new gowns.

There was another side to Lady Maria. She had married into one of the richest and most powerful families in England, the Willoughbys. King Henry had even named a ship after her, the HMS Mary Willoughby. Although she was now a widow, she remained in control of large estates and houses in Lincolnshire, which yielded her a sizeable income. She had one daughter, Catherine, who was newly married to the Duke of Suffolk, King Henry's lifelong friend. And now, with Queen Anne gone, Lady Willoughby was once more in favour at court.

I was in no hurry to return. Life was comfortable with Lady Maria, and as she sang the Spanish songs she taught me, it was as if I was back with Queen Katherine. At first, I was a little unsteady on my lute, but my facility soon returned. Maria taught me to play Spanish cancióneros, the secular songs of the people. She would often sing with me, her voice a deep, passionate counterpoint to my more ethereal tones. I modified some of my own compositions, introducing Andalusian and Moorish phrases. There was the haunting vibration of the voice, or sometimes an almost martial rhythm, where I would hit the case of the lute to give a thumping, repetitive beat.

My new gowns arrived from the tailor. One was a sober black velvet, very much a gown of wealth and propriety. The other, by contrast, was made of buttercup yellow silk, with its sleeves slashed to show a lining of deepest red. I tried them on in front of Lady Maria.

She looked me up and down critically.

"Is that too tight?" She touched my bodice. My breasts were much larger now I was a mother, and the gown almost paraded them for inspection. "Come, Kat, let us lace you more loosely." She came up behind me and started unlacing the yellow gown at the back. She allowed me a little more space, and then relaced the gown. I felt my breathing become easier.

"That's better," Maria said, nodding her approval. "That will be good for court." She looked sharply at me, "I do not wish it, but you should return to court now."

"I know. I must make myself known again. But I wish I could just stay with you." Although I knew it was important for me to renew my contacts, I dreaded returning to the hothouse atmosphere around the King and Queen.

"It can't be done, my dear. The Queen has asked for you. She heard from Wolf Hall that you had returned to London, and she was annoyed. 'Why, pray, has she not come to me, her Queen?' She ordered that you come to her at once." Maria laughed. "Such a mild-mannered girl she was. But being Queen has made her much grander."

"Why can't she wait for a while?" I grumbled. "I have barely kissed Alice goodbye." Lady Maria looked mysterious and leaned forward to me.

"Kat, my belief is that she has something important to tell you, and that the time she has is limited. You must go, my dear. The Queen needs you."

CHAPTER 16

I arrived back in the middle of May. The court was at Greenwich, and the orchards were in full green leaf. I made my way to the Queen's Presence Chamber, feeling very alone. Sir Thomas Wyatt was now ambassador to the Holy Roman Emperor, Lady Willoughby only an occasional visitor, and Will was far away, both in distance and his heart. As I approached the chamber, I was halted by a small procession making its way across my path. At its head was a young woman, followed by a child and a number of gentlewomen. I paused and curtseyed, aware that these were important people.

"Why Mistress Kat! I have not seen you in several years. What are you doing at court? Have you been employed as a chambermaid?" I recognised her voice instantly. And her tone, intentionally insulting, could only come from one woman. It was Princess Mary. Only now I knew she was called Lady Mary.

I rose from my curtsey and answered calmly,

"No, my lady. Her Majesty has ordered me to return as her musician. I am just about to be presented to her." Mary glowered at me. I realised suddenly that she had been jealous of my close relationship with her mother. Our mother, only she didn't know that, nor ever would.

"So, I will see you often. You must know that I attend on the Queen daily," she said, looking at me as if I was the dirt on her shoe. Her scorn wasn't shared, though, by the little girl behind her, who came running up to me,

"Hello," she said, peering up at my face, "will you play with me?" The Lady Elizabeth, now nearly four years old, bright and chubby. I was about to tell her that I would play whatever games she wanted, when I was free, when I was interrupted by Lady Mary.

"Elizabeth, we do not mix with servants! Do not demean yourself, sister. You may be a bastard, but you are of royal blood." Elizabeth made a face but went back to stand behind her sister. I smiled inwardly, knowing that royal blood ran as much through my veins as theirs. Mary turned her face away from me and continued to lead the procession. I noticed, as they passed, that Elizabeth had stuck her tongue out at her, and some of the gentlewomen were giggling. Unaware of this, Mary went through the door, moving solemnly towards the presence chamber.

I waited a moment outside the door. I was to be met by the Queen's chamberlain and presented by him. When he arrived, he told me,

"Lady Mary and Lady Elizabeth are with the Queen now. We will need to wait outside until I get the signal." I curtseyed my acknowledgement, and then said,

"How long have they been back at court?" The chamberlain was effusive,

"Queen Jane begged the King, on her knees, to allow them back. And once Mary had signed the Act of Succession, declaring herself to be illegitimate, and the Act of Supremacy, acknowledging that the King was now head of the church, he was pleased to allow her back to court, along with her small sister."

I wondered how she had brought herself to submit to her

father. I knew both acts went against everything her mother had taught her. A proud woman, she must have been brought low in order to put her name to them. I didn't like her, but I could understand why she was so unpleasant. Her beloved mother put to one side, now almost forgotten. Her status as heir to the throne snatched from her.

But the King still did not have an heir. So, the Lady Mary's position was more powerful than it had been for a long time,

"The Queen has been very kind to Lady Mary," observed the chamberlain, who had come to join me, "and the King sits beside her at supper. It is good to see her back at court." What he didn't say (and who could?) was that if Queen Jane was unable to produce a son, then the Lady Mary would have to be reinstated as the King's successor.

"Come with me," the chamberlain said, and brought me through the heavy oak doors into the Queen's Presence Chamber. It was as magnificent as I remembered, with the bosses of the ceiling all Tudor roses, with each one having the Queen's phoenix rising out of it. Queen Jane sat underneath a canopy of state, embossed with red and gold, and the royal arms of England. She wore a heavy English hood, blazing with rubies, the white cambric of her coif just showing underneath. Her gown was cloth of gold, covered with a tissue of silver, as if she was surrounded by a lustrous mist. Massed behind her were around twenty ladies, the representatives of the most powerful houses in England. I noticed Maria Willoughby's daughter, the Duchess of Suffolk, was amongst them. Also, Anne Seymour, Jane's sister-in-law, Lady Rutland, and the Countess of Sussex. They were like jewels in a box, each one more dazzling than the last. At the very front of the group was the Lady Mary in a gown of green velvet and gold. Beside her stood a gentlewoman, trying to control the young Lady Elizabeth, who was getting bored.

I looked at Jane in the middle of all of this. She looked like a little girl caught dressing in her mother's clothes. Her face hadn't changed. She looked pale, almost overcome by her grandeur. She sat very stiffly, but I knew that this was because it was hard to move in the state gowns she had to wear, so heavy were they with precious stones. I approached her and curtseyed deeply.

"Mistress Kat!" she beamed. "I have missed you! Now, you must come with me afterwards, and tell me all the news from Wolf Hall. Have you brought your lute?" I smiled and told her,

"Yes, your Majesty. I have it." One of my lutes was with my belongings in the maids' dormitory. The other one was with Mistress Meady for safe keeping.

"Well, you must start practising immediately," she ordered. I remembered that Maria had said that she had become more confident in playing the Queen's role. She was used to giving orders now. She beckoned me towards her and then gave me a secret smile. "I will have need of you very soon Kat. I'll speak with you later."

I watched as she welcomed ambassadors, returning courtiers, and turned her head occasionally to smile at the King's daughters. She did it well enough, but she didn't have the presence of Katherine or the intelligence of Anne. And when they bowed, it seemed like the noblemen were not bowing to her, but to her queenly dress. I realised at that moment that the golden dress had once been Anne's. Yes, I remembered her wearing it well enough, when she went to Calais, I think. I thought of Anne wearing the gown, at the height of her radiance and power. Did Jane not shiver at the thought that Anne had touched, gathered, inhabited the same gown? It might still have traces of the violet perfume she had worn, maybe at the neckline. But I was being silly and sentimental. It was common practice for clothes to be passed on to other family members. And the Queen's clothes were as valuable as her jewels. But it was one thing, wearing a gown from your mother, or your sister. Quite another to wear the golden bridal gown of a woman barely cold in her grave. I thought Anne would have smiled that wry smile of hers, and laughed at the thought of the ungainly Jane Seymour in the glamorous cloth of gold.

"I wore it better than she did Kat, you must admit." For a moment I felt very sad, but I knew I must banish all thoughts of Henry's previous Queens. I would see them, maybe, as ghosts, every now and then, but their time had gone.

When Queen Jane got back to her privy chamber, she was in high spirits. She tapped her foot impatiently as her ladies lifted the heavy gown carefully over her head. Then Anne Seymour handed her a pink velvet loose gown, lined with ermine, which she wrapped around herself. She sat down on the settle beside the fire and beckoned for me to join her. I saw a look of distaste pass through the assembled ladies like a fast-flowing stream. But Jane didn't notice. She was happy to see me and sent them all away. They gathered up Jane's clothes and made their way out, muttering in hushed tones. Jane took my hands in hers.

"They keep telling me what to do," she whispered. "They don't like me having friends outside the circle. But I had to see you Kat. You remind me of what it was like when I was just a girl. Do you remember when we got drunk on mead together?" I laughed but pointed out,

"And then the King gave you a lift home on his horse, do you remember that?" Jane nodded.

"I just thought it was fun back then. Do you know Kat, I had never had anyone telling me I was beautiful before the King did? I was the plain one, always. My brothers wouldn't dance with me, unless my father forced them to do it. I was always the one standing at the edge of the dancing. I'd try to move back so people wouldn't notice me." She was on the edge of tears now. "I never thought I'd marry, Kat. And, truthfully, I was quite glad. I even thought about being a nun." I teased her a little,

"You wouldn't be drinking mead if you were a nun! That

is if you had a convent to live in nowadays." Slowly, over several years, the convents and monasteries were being closed down. Every item of property held by them was recorded, prior to the King taking possession. This was the work that was taking Will away from London so often. I remember that Queen Anne had wanted the money raised from this to go towards education. But the King, with Cromwell's help, simply took it all. Some lands were given to favourites, some sold. But the money that poured into the treasury was subsidising the King's lavish lifestyle, not establishing colleges for the poor.

"That is so sad," Jane said quietly, "those poor holy men and women, told to leave the only place they have ever known as home. Some who resisted were even put to death. I tried to raise it with the King, but he was very angry with me." She paused for a minute. "He slapped my face, Kat. I was so frightened. I won't meddle in politics ever again."

"That is a good idea, Jane," I said, quite forgetting her position. She stiffened a moment, and then relaxed and laughed.

"It's alright when we are together to use my name, but don't forget to address me as the Queen in public. My ladies would be angry."

"Yes, and I might get accused of treason!" I said, only half joking. She smiled at me.

"Dear Kat, it is so good to have you around. You make me feel like a girl again. Kat, I have something to tell you, but you mustn't tell anyone. Promise you won't, not even Will!"

"I haven't seen Will yet. We are still living separately, your Majesty," I couldn't stop the sadness creeping into my voice. "But I won't tell him, even if we do make peace between ourselves."

"Kat, I am with child! I felt it quicken in my womb three days ago, and then I knew. I've missed my courses, I think, February, March and April. But that has happened before, and nothing came of it. So, when I felt my baby move, Kat, I was so happy! Everything will be alright. I will have a baby, and maybe two or three more, and I will be safe." I hadn't noticed before, but in the loose wrap I saw that her belly was indeed swollen, although it was still very small.

"Jane, congratulations! I am so pleased for you. How have you been? Have you been sick? Ginger is good for sickness; I can fetch you some if you want." I babbled on for some minutes, asking her for all her symptoms and telling her about mine. I didn't mention my painful labour, though. When you have been through that, you only share it with those who know. You protected any young or inexperienced women from the terrifying reality of what lay ahead of them.

Jane was too relieved at having a well-established pregnancy to be worrying about her confinement just yet. She confirmed that she was feeling well and eating far more than normal. She hadn't been sick, except a couple of times near the beginning. She had a longing for quail pies and had been sending down to the kitchens for them every day.

"Have you told the King?" She shook her head.

"I wanted to be sure. I was scared of his disappointment if it turned out that I didn't have a baby after all. I will tell him tonight." She clapped her hands together, "Oh, he will be so happy!"

"There will be no quails left in London," I said drily, "for the King will commandeer them all for you. What a celebration there will be!" Jane looked worried for a moment. She didn't like these big occasions. I took her in my arms and hugged her.

"And everyone will want to dance with you, your Majesty!"

Of course, I wasn't there when she told the King, but his whoops of joy could be heard all over the court. He organised a three-day festival of food, dancing and music to honour his Queen. Bonfires were lit across the nation, and subjects gathered around them to drink their Queen's health. A Te Deum was sung at St Paul's Cathedral, with the Lord Mayor and all the Aldermen present. Prayers were offered in every church for the safe delivery of an heir.

In the middle of all of this, Jane stood, lost and a little bewildered. Apart from her bump, she was very thin and pale. But throughout it all she was smiling. At last, she was not a disappointment. Her family was smiling. Power was shifting their way, and if an heir was produced, they would be without rival at court.

The King found it hard to leave Jane alone during her pregnancy. He hovered over her ladies, passing on recipes for herbal infusions, telling them what she should be eating, what (limited) exercise she should take, and how much rest she should be taking. He even told me off for playing some music that was too spirited, too arousing for a woman with a very precious child in her belly. He stood over me, his bulk blocking out the light.

"Leave that din! Can you not play something more soothing, girl?" As he spoke, a drop of his spittle landed on my face. I lowered my eyes and started on a softer melody. Inside myself, I was saying, "I hate you. You have no idea how much I hate you." Fortunately, my choice of music was acceptable, and he turned his attention back to Jane,

"Are you eating enough, my love? You are making a son. You must make him strong and lively." Jane, who loved quail pies but felt queasy at the greasy smell of roast boar, shuddered imperceptibly. He ignored her and spoke to her sister-in-law, Anne Seymour.

"Make sure her Majesty eats a good portion of chicken at every meal. And she should not eat sweets. Don't let her forget!" Anne Seymour said,

"I will, your Majesty. She will not evade me!" Anne Seymour was not Jane's favourite person. She used her marriage to Edward Seymour as a means of controlling the Queen. And the Queen was too frightened to object. I felt sorry for her. Neither Katherine nor Anne had allowed other people to dictate to them. But Jane was a very different person.

The King dismissed us all to allow him to spend some time alone with Queen Jane. I rushed outside, desperate for the calming fresh air. I needed some time on my own, away from the gossips of the court. But as I ran into the knot garden, I could still hear King Henry through the open window. He was booming at Jane,

"Wife, I was told you were seen playing cup and ball yesterday. How can that be? You know that vigorous exercise is dangerous." I couldn't hear what Jane was saying, but I knew that she encouraged the Lady Elizabeth to play with her and guessed they had been chasing each other around the Queen's chamber. Whatever she had said, it didn't pacify the King,

"Madam, have a care! If you lose this baby, I will hold you responsible! Hear my warning, I will take any careless behaviour on your part as an assault on a royal prince. I have no time for a woman who will not do her utmost to protect my heir. Beware, Madam, of wilful disobedience!" I heard a small cry, probably from Jane. Had he hit her?

Something inside me exploded. I had for years hidden my hatred for my father deep inside. But hearing the way he was treating poor, helpless Jane made my anger boil over. I stood facing the window and shouted as loudly as I ever have,

"For pity's sake, leave her alone! You are a bully and a coward! You are killing this woman. You're not content with driving Katherine and Anne to their graves, she will join them soon. I hope they haunt you in your dreams!" A furious roar came from inside the palace, and I saw his portly figure approaching the window. I turned round, ducked my head down and ran. He saw me as I fled.

"Who is that? Guards, catch the girl! Treason!" I got away from the open garden, towards the maze. I was swift on my feet and managed to dive into it before they had reached the knot garden. Panting, my heart thumping, I burrowed under a hedge near the centre of the maze.

What had I done? Why had I been so foolish? Had anyone

seen me? I don't think the King had come to the window in time to see my face. But had anyone else been walking in the gardens nearby? More than anything I had ever done, I had put myself in danger, and for what? Just to relieve the furious anger that raged inside me.

I curled up into a ball and made myself as small as I could. My breathing was fast and panicky. I tried to slow it, to concentrate on a ladybird crawling along a leaf nearby. I heard men's voices,

"Where has she gone?"

"I saw a woman over there, making for the orchards. She was wearing a dirty brown gown."

"A street woman, no doubt. How did she get in here? She's vanished. She must have got away. You go to the orchards, and we will search the park!" I heard them run past the maze without venturing into it. In truth, they probably didn't want to get stuck for hours. The maze was treacherous. One could spend a whole day in it, fruitlessly going round and round.

I lay quietly for what seemed like a long time but was probably only a few minutes. I stiffened when I heard footsteps hurrying along, separated from me by only a hedge. Who was it? Had the guards decided to brave the maze?

"Kat! I thought it was you. What were you doing, my love?" It was Will, holding out his hand to me to pull me up. I stood up and brushed the leaves from my skirt.

"Did you see what happened?" I asked.

"No, but I heard it. I was walking towards the palace, and I heard the commotion. I would know your voice anywhere, Kat. What possessed you?" I couldn't afford to get angry with him, so I admitted I'd made a mistake.

"He's mistreating Queen Jane, and I couldn't bear it after everything he did to the others." Will sighed deeply.

"Kat, when will you understand that we ordinary people cannot challenge the rich and powerful? You don't seem to realise how much danger you put yourself in. You could have been killed." I felt stupid.

Everything he said was right,

"I felt that I had a right to confront him, he is my father!"

"You had a right to confront him?" Will said incredulously. "So, you were going to join Cardinal Wolsey, Thomas More, Queen Katherine, Queen Anne? Your confidence amazes me Kat."

"I'm not confident now," I confessed. "I'm very scared. What should I do?" Will took pity on me,

"You should come with me into the court. We have been for a stroll along the river, man and wife. I am sure they didn't see you properly. They said they were looking for a street woman in a brown dress." I felt some relief.

"Why do they blame the street people? The courtiers are much more dangerous." Will laughed.

"That's better. Come on Kat. I will say you have been with me for the last hour. But now we must return. Come!" He put his arm around me and guided me out of the maze.

"How did you find your way out so quickly?" I asked. He smiled.

"Put it down to a love of puzzles. I studied the plans for the maze one afternoon, I was interested to find out how to beat it." Will was well suited to being a lawyer, I thought. He had a love of detail, which I found tedious. I squeezed his hand.

"I guess, for once, it's been useful. Thanks for rescuing me." He brought my hand to his lips and kissed it.

"We must talk, Kat," he said. "But for now, let's parade ourselves." He took me into the great hall of the palace. There was no royal presence, but people were milling around, talking excitedly. My fellow musician, Ned, saw me and waved, beckoning me to him. Will and I walked towards him, Will greeting a few people that he knew, every time introducing me as his wife.

"Kat, where have you been? You've missed all the excitement!" I smiled at Ned and replied,

"I've been walking by the river with my husband. Have you met him?" I introduced the two men. Will said,

"So, what's been happening? Why is everyone so jumpy?" Ned was always ready for a gossip,

"A witch broke into the palace grounds. A filthy, wild woman, I've heard. And then she called out treasonous attacks on the King. He is so angry that she was allowed through he has dismissed the guards on duty." I felt sorry for the guards, but relieved that the focus of enquiry seemed to be a wild witchy woman.

"What of the Queen?" I asked.

"She has gone to her bed. She was so distressed, the King ordered her to rest." I nodded, feeling some relief that Jane was absent from all this trouble.

"They won't catch the woman now," Ned said conversationally, "she'll be back in London by now."

"Let us pray that they do manage to bring her to justice," Will said smoothly and led me on to another group of his friends. Punctiliously, precisely, he was introducing me to everyone he knew, and telling them all of our walk. I loved him for that. He was establishing my alibi, and I told myself that if he hadn't cared for me, he wouldn't have bothered.

After about an hour, when we had heard the story many times, Will guided me out of the hall.

"You just saved my life," I said. "I can't ever repay you." Will's face looked stern.

"Maybe you can't," he said, "but we must talk. Let us now take that walk by the river." It was early summer, and the trees were in full fresh leaf. Skiffs went up and down the Thames, but the walkway we were on was quiet. We didn't speak for a while, until Will took my hand.

"Kat, I am so sorry I told you to leave. I have regretted it for many months. I should have sorted things out with you, not ordered you to go." His eyes rested on me warmly. "Will you forgive me?"

"Why did you do that to me, Will? I thought you would never let me go. What changed with you?"

"I was angry, Kat, because you had gone off without telling me, to put yourself and me, at risk."

"But she was my mother, Will! Queen Katherine was my mother! I know it was dangerous, but she was dying, I had to see her!" Will looked down at the ground.

"Kat, I was jealous. I'm sorry, but I was so jealous."

"Jealous of my mother?" I was very surprised. "But she was just an old woman, Will, she was no threat."

"It wasn't her. It was what she represented. Your royal blood, your lineage. When you chose to visit her, even though you knew it would be dangerous, I thought you didn't want me anymore. I could see that you were regretting marrying me. All those arguments."

"Will, I don't regret marrying you. I love you. I chose to live with you. I didn't try and live with her. But when I heard she was dying, I had to go. Will, if it had been Joan, you would have gone." Suddenly he started to cry.

"I never said goodbye. That stays with me. At least you were with Joan, and later with Katherine. I envied you that."

"Was I lucky, to be at two deathbeds? It didn't feel like that at the time." He nodded slowly.

"I've been stupid. I know that. Do you really not regret marrying me?"

"Never!" I said emphatically.

"So, will you forgive me? I am truly sorry Kat."

"Will, of course I will. But there is something I must tell you." He held up his hand.

"I know Kat. Tom told me. You have a girl, a little girl." Then it was my turn to cry. I missed you so much, daughter.

"Yes, she is being well cared for. Her name is Alice." He looked thoughtful.

"And so, when did you give birth?" he asked. I remembered he had an eye for detail.

"In September," I said, not giving the exact date. Will looked at me questioningly.

"Kat, there is something I must ask you. Please do not be offended. Is the baby mine? I don't want to blame you, but I must know." We sat down on a bank which was covered in daisies and buttercups. I had a sudden stab of memory, of Joan gathering sweet meadow flowers with me and Will so many years ago. I picked a daisy and started pulling the petals from it. He waited. At last, I said,

"Will, I don't know."

"So, she could be someone else's?" A spasm of pain crossed his face.

"Or she could be yours. I don't know Will. I am so sorry." He made a strange sound, and I realised he was starting to cry.

"How could you do that to me?" he said. "I have been faithful, but you, you took up with a man just after we parted! Who is he?"

"I will tell you sometime, but not now." I was afraid Will might go to find Thomas Wyatt and try to pick a fight with him, and thus ruin all our lives. "He thinks Alice is his, and he is paying for her upkeep." Will screwed up his eyes.

"I could have helped you! Why didn't I do that Kat? I cast you away, and now it is all spoilt."

I threw the bare remnants of the daisy to the ground.

"It isn't all spoilt Will," I said. "We could try again, build a life together again." Will shook his head.

"I don't think I could do it Kat, bring up another man's child. You won't even tell me who it is. How could we live together with that secret hanging over us?"

"I didn't tell you because I didn't want you to do anything, not because I wanted to keep it a secret." Will laughed.

"Kat, you are the one who 'does' things. Not me! I am the careful one. You think if I found out which man fathered your child..."

"It could be ours," I interrupted.

"But you don't think it is," Will snapped. "Do you think I would assault the man and get myself into trouble?"

"No, I don't really," I said, realising that I wasn't being fair to Will.

"Well, who is it then?" he demanded.

"Will it make a difference to your decision?" Will looked coldly at me.

"It might do, but I doubt it. So tell me!" I took a deep breath and took his hand.

"Will, it was one night..."

"Yes?"

"It wasn't important, Will. One night with Tom Wyatt. That's all."

CHAPTER 17

"Tom Wyatt? You mean Sir Thomas, the poet?" Will almost screamed it at me. He dropped my hand like it was burning. I held it and nursed it against my chin, as if to protect it. He paced up and down as if he couldn't bear to be still.

"Yes. He was kind," I shouted, "not like you. I was broken-hearted, Will. I couldn't eat, couldn't sleep. You don't know how much you hurt me, Will. He was there for me, he listened to me, and he made me laugh."

"But Thomas Wyatt? What is it about you, Kat? You could have had a nice little affair with a squire or something. But no, Sir Thomas Wyatt! He was lucky he didn't lose his head over Anne Boleyn, the way he kept mooning over her. Why are you attracted to trouble? Is it a death wish that you have inherited from your mother?" I felt this was deeply unfair. Queen Katherine had never sought trouble, just tried to defend her position. I flared up at him,

"Don't insult her. She had no death wish, she had a wish to live and to be a wife! She was far better than me, and you know it."

"At least she didn't throw herself at other men to revenge herself on her husband!" He was almost spitting with rage. I tried to reply calmly,

"That's not fair Will. I'm sorry, but try to understand. I didn't fling myself at him. It was never meant to happen. We were friends. He loved Anne Boleyn, I loved you. We consoled each other. It was just one night, and we were drunk…"

"That makes it worse," Will fumed. "If you had fallen in love with someone, then it would mean something! But if you just fall into bed with a man because you are drunk, then you could do it again!"

"Don't shout at me," I cried out, "it was you; you threw me out. You don't know how much you hurt me by doing that. If you hadn't done it, this never would have happened."

Will lent over and seized me in his arms and covered my face with kisses, pulling my coif off and loosening my hair. I responded to him, feeling the need I had covered up for so long. I remembered his scent of clean skin and rosemary soap. I wrapped my arms around him and clung to him. I never wanted him to release me. He spoke to me hoarsely,

"God help me, Kat, I love you! I made a mistake, I accept that. And you made a mistake too. That should make us even. But I don't know if I can trust you again. What if Tom comes back to you? Would you leave me for him?" He was calmer now, and he spoke in between kisses.

"Will, I promise you can trust me. I wouldn't go back to Tom Wyatt, and I think you know that. He's abroad now anyway, and I hear he has a mistress."

"If he didn't have a mistress?" Will asked, kissing me again.

"I still wouldn't want him, Will. I want you. I love you; don't you know that?" I wrapped my arms around him and held him as if I never wanted to let him go.

"I know that, " he acknowledged softly. "And I love you so much. I cannot tell you how much I missed you. I want to take you and leave this damned court with you. But I don't know if I can live with another man's child. I just don't know."

Daughter, I felt that as a blow to my stomach. I could no

more give you up than I could cease breathing. But If Will couldn't live with you, then I couldn't live with him.

"I can't live without seeing my daughter," I said, "even if she were to have the best care in the world, I could not give her up, ever." He stiffened, and we pulled apart from each other. He started back to the court, and I followed, both walking silently. As we approached the main courtyard, I said quietly,

"I guess that's it then, Will, isn't it?" He looked into my eyes, both of us crying. He waited a minute, to see if I would change my mind, but I didn't speak.

"I guess that's it," he repeated. He bowed and left me at the gate.

I cried myself to sleep that night and had to reread the letter from Meady to take my mind off Will. She told me that you were growing well, and that you had started to try to walk. Oh, I was so proud of you! But it made me sad to hear that your first word was "Meady". It should have been "Mama". I resolved that I must come to see you so that you didn't quite forget me.

But first I had to face the court. The household was buzzing that morning, with gossip about the bent old witch who had cursed the King yesterday. Apparently, she was toothless, ragged, and without hair. I was relieved to hear this. The description of the culprit had never been much like me, but now it was so different that no one could imagine I was the guilty party. I went quickly to the Queen's chambers, where Anne Seymour again told me the story. This time though, the witch was French. I smiled to myself and hurried off to get my lute.

The orders were that I should only play religious music from now on. The King did not want the Queen to get unduly aroused by popular songs. And, of course, sacred music would clothe the Queen in an aura of sanctity, which would no doubt protect her precious child.

The household moved to Hampton Court in the summer, where the Queen started to settle in to have her child. It was the grandest of the King's palaces. Newly built for Cardinal Wolsey, it had five courtyards at the front, each one surrounded by grand buildings. It had the look of a Roman Forum to it, with the marble statues of eminent men lining one of the courts. Of course, the Cardinal had given it to Henry. Near the end of his time, when he was desperately trying to buy his way back into the King's favour, he had gifted this most magnificent of palaces to Henry. He realised I think that it was unwise to own anything that was larger, grander and more imposing than what the King possessed. And so now, Hampton Court also had a large Tudor rose in the gatehouse, inscribed with the words, "Dieu et Mon Droit". The King liked the palace, and the Queen liked whatever the King liked. She had her own suite of rooms, where she started to withdraw, to await her baby. She was getting quite large now and unwilling to move around much. She took a fancy for some mead. Mead from Wolf Hall, which would help her relax in the final months of pregnancy.

"I have such heartburn, Kat. My son is making me suffer! I need to soothe the pain. Will you fetch me some mead? You could go to Wolf Hall. I'll get a couple of manservants to accompany you. It is a chance for you to see your Alice." She looked so pleased at her little surprise. She loved to make people happy.

"Yes, of course I will go your Majesty," I said, "thank you for thinking of me."

"You can't stay for long!" she told me. "I shall need you when my time comes. Just two days mind." She dug into her pouch. "Here, take this for Alice." It was a tiny gold bracelet fit only for a toddler's wrist. "It was mine when I was little, Kat." I refused to take it.

"But, your Majesty, surely you will want to pass it on to your babe?" She shook her head.

"This is better on a girl, and I am not having a girl. All the soothsayers are predicting he will be a boy. So, I must give this away, and who better than you?"

I took the bracelet and put it safely in my pouch. I left the next morning with two cheerful painters, who were excited to have a few weeks away. They were employed almost constantly to decorate the royal palaces, and they had many tales to tell.

"Took us a year to get rid of the Hs and As," one said, referring to the initials of Henry and Anne Boleyn, that had taken pride of place in the palace. "Now, we're well on with the Js. But it never stops, mistress! And if the Queen has a son, no doubt there'll be another initial to put somewhere. And the cost of it! You wouldn't believe how much that gold paint is."

We spent a happy few days riding down to the West Country. At each inn, we would eat, and then the painters would stay up late every night drinking. I didn't join them. I was fortunate enough to be housed in the female dormitories at each inn. I was eager to see you, Alice, and all I wanted to think about was you.

At last, we arrived at Wolf Hall. While the painters were entertained in the servants' quarters of the main house, I went straight to see Meady and you, my daughter. As soon as I arrived, I took out the bracelet that Queen Jane had given me and fastened it onto your wrist. Meady gasped when she saw it.

"That was Jane's when she was small," she said. "I remember the day she was given it. It would be New Year, when she was about two. She was so proud of it!" Then she turned to me.

"So why has she given it to you for Alice? It meant so much to her." For a moment, I wondered if Meady suspected me of stealing it. She saw the expression on my face and put her hand on my arm.

"I know she has given it to you, Kat, in her great generosity. What I wonder is why she decided not to keep it." I knew what she meant.

"It made me uncomfortable too. But I think she wants a boy so much that she is reluctant to do anything to risk that. To keep the bracelet might mean she expects a girl to pass it on to. And that is not something she wishes to consider." Meady looked serious.

"Such pressure, to produce a boy. It cannot be good for her. I know all men want a boy, but this baby is the first of many. Surely it isn't that important?"

"It is for her," I said, "if she wants to stay in favour with the King." Meady shook her head.

"So difficult to see a baby you've loved suffering. I pray God will give her a boy." She wiped tears away from her eyes with a handkerchief, and said,

"But what am I doing? I haven't welcomed you properly yet Kat, and after such a long journey!" She then proceeded to rain kisses on me and pour me copious draughts of mead. But although she was very kind, my attention was all for you, my daughter.

You were nearing the anniversary of your birth, and you were walking, lurching from one bench to another, toppling over into Meady's arms. You hid your face in her skirts when I tried to take your hand.

"She doesn't remember me," I said to Meady, flatly.

"Don't trouble yourself," she said. "Give her a few hours, and the memory will return to her. She has you deep in her soul, I know." And she was right, daughter. I spent all afternoon playing with you, rocking you on my lap when you were tired, singing to you in your cot. And yes, you did respond to me, as if you realised I was your mother. You giggled when I played peep bo, you held your hands up to me, wanting to sit on my lap, and you even kissed me, a wet baby's kiss, right on my lips.

That night, I slept with you beside me. I knew I only had the next day with you before I would have to return to court, together with the painters and a cart full of mead. But I decided I would concentrate on nothing but you, drink you in, so that I had memories to sustain me over the next months.

I rose with you and made you some warm bread and milk to break your fast. I helped to spoon it into your mouth, but you were impatient and kept grabbing at the spoon. So then I let you have the spoon to feed yourself. Meady laughed as I did so.

"She will spill it all over herself," she warned, and so you did. But I brought out some clothes I had made for you from my pouch, changed you, and promised Meady that I would wash the milk out of your wet baby's gown.

Suddenly, a putrid smell filled the air. Meady sat up.

"Quick, take her to the pot." Fortunately, I was in time, and you did not dirty yourself. Meady wiped you and re-dressed you while I took the pot outside. For one day, I wanted to do everything for you, even the unpleasant bits. Afterwards I had you on my lap and sang a lullaby to you. It was the one Queen Anne had sung,

> "Lullaby, lullow, lullay lully,
> Beway bewy, lullaby lullow
> Lullay, lully
> Baw me bairne, sleep softly now...".

Your eyelids started to droop as I rocked, and you made little snuffling sounds as you buried yourself into my breasts. It was the nearest I could ever come to heaven on this earth. I sat there, feeling drowsy myself, and utterly content. Meady had gone to the big house to fetch some smoked venison that she had been promised. I could hear nothing but the sound of your breathing, gentle, safe.

I started awake when I heard the front door open, and then footsteps. Meady must be back. But as I looked up, it wasn't Meady that I saw. It was Will.

He looked very large in Meady's small cottage. I was sure

he'd had to duck his head to get through the door. He gazed over at me and you, daughter. I could hardly bear his look, it was full of love and pain. He and I had hurt each other so badly, and however much we loved each other, that hurt could not be banished.

He took his hat off and put it on the table. Without a word, he came up to me, dropped to his knees and started stroking your head.

"See, she has nothing that is ugly, or unkind. She is beautiful," I said to him. He nodded.

"She is perfect, her fingers, her little nose, her eyelashes!" he whispered. Your eyes were closed, and your eyelashes showed up golden against your cheeks. "She takes after you," he said. "She is lovely."

I turned to him and said quietly,

"Why are you here Will?" He took one of your hands in his and kissed your little pudgy fingers.

"I wanted to see her. I heard you were coming down here, so I followed you."

"But why?" I did not remind him, although I was sure that he had not forgotten, that he was unlikely to be your father.

"I love you Kat, and I wanted to see if I could love her. I had to see her. Do you understand?" I nodded.

"Yes, I do. But what will you do now, Will? Does this mean that we can start again?" He hesitated.

"I don't know Kat. Yes, she is beautiful. But she isn't mine. I don't know if I can get over that." I felt the tears gathering in my eyes.

"So why did you come, if you weren't sure? You have raised my hopes, and then dashed them again!" He sighed and took my face in his hands, looking at me as if he was seeing me for the first time.

"I had to see her Kat. I had to meet this little person who came from you. Your daughter. And now, I must decide what to do. Give me some time. Let me pray and talk it over. I'm not ready yet, but just give me time!" With that, he kissed me hard on the lips, took up his hat, and walked to the door. He turned for a moment and gazed at me, before he turned and left, without saying anymore.

He left me with a small hope that he might come to accept you daughter. But he also left me with many doubts and fears. He still believed that he couldn't bring up another man's child, that was clear. He loved you when he saw you, but then his doubts overcame him. I didn't know whether to laugh or cry.

Meady returned, and at the sound of her closing the door, you stirred in my lap and started to cry. I hushed you, and tried to smile at Meady, but she could tell that something was wrong. Tears started to well up, and I couldn't meet her eyes.

"Why what's the matter? I saw a man leaving here. I thought he was up to no good. What has happened to upset you?" Your cries got louder, and you wouldn't be pacified.

I told Meady the truth, that my husband had visited. She chuckled excitedly and scooped you into her arms.

"And did he fall in love with Alice? How could he help himself?" But then, when she saw my face, she stopped abruptly. "But why didn't he wait to return with you tomorrow? Coming all this way from London just for a few moments."

"Things are not good between us, Meady," I confessed. She didn't know the truth, so she was forthright in blaming Will,

"And him with such a beautiful baby," she mused angrily. "I'll warrant he has someone else, Kat. Just you make sure that he gives you money for Alice." I sighed. I couldn't explain to her that the money came from Sir Thomas Wyatt, because you, Alice, came from Sir Thomas Wyatt.

"He's a good man," was all I was able to say. "We may be able to reconcile, sometime in the future." Meady snorted,

"Men! It all goes their way, doesn't it? Now don't cry Kat. Put Alice to bed, and we will sit by the fire and drink mead. We can tell stories and sing songs together. Be brave, my dear."

So that night we sat together, drinking her good mead.

Queen Jane was right, it would soothe not only the most irritated of stomachs, but also the most unhappy of souls. That night I slept with you beside me. You were a real little person then, not a baby. I watched your eyelids flutter, and your mouth making silent words as you dreamt. What were you dreaming of? The blackbirds that you loved to watch, or maybe the shabby little doll that you loved above all things. I knew, daughter, that I could never let you go. I had to go back to court, but my plan now was to bring you to London. I had some money left from Thomas Wyatt, and there was still my small pension from Queen Katherine. If I could persuade Queen Jane to pay me more, I would be able to employ a girl of good character to be a nursemaid for you. Having resolved that, it made the parting with you a little easier. But still I cried when the time came.

"I hate to say goodbye," I sobbed, "I feel I am deserting her!" Meady was kind, but brisk. She took you from me and held you up for me to kiss.

"Now then, you can see she is fine. I promise to take good care of her, until you can bring her to London."

"Bye bye, little one. I'll see you soon. Maybe we can be a real family. Wouldn't that be lovely?" You giggled and cooed at me while Meady helped you to wave your hand.

"That would be the best all round," she said, "your husband needs to have a good talking to!" I got up onto my horse and joined the painters who were accompanying me.

"Goodbye, Meady. I can never thank you enough for what you are doing!" I called out. She stood there, rosy-cheeked, stout and as kind as any human could be.

"Don't thank me, I love your little daughter as my own! Now go and find that husband of yours. If he was anything like a good man, he wouldn't let you go! I will pray he sees sense and realises what a diamond he has for a wife!"

CHAPTER 18

I was subdued on the way back to London, but the two painters didn't notice. For them, our trip had been a few days off, with plenty of stops in inns and alehouses. They were in a holiday mood, with plenty of jokes and singing. But they were pleasant enough, and left me to ride just behind, absorbed in my own thoughts.

We spent our last night at an inn in the village of Wimbledon, leaving just a morning's ride between us and Hampton Court. I woke early and went to the door to breathe in the cool autumn air. We were still far enough away from London for it to be sweet smelling. I composed myself for my return, knowing that by the evening I would be playing for Queen Jane. I wondered how she was now and looked forward to appearing with her longed-for mead.

I was impatient to start, but my two companions were still abed. I felt a suppressed excitement, barely able to wait until I saw the Queen. It was as if my world was about to be turned over on its head. I became aware of something different happening around me, and for a while I couldn't identify what it was. Then I made out a very faint sound in the distance, a melodic sound, like birdsong. I wondered whether it was church bells, but they were so very far away it was hard to tell. Then, with a peal so loud it startled me, the small church in the village started to ring its bells. I could hear now other churches joining in, one by one, as the sound surrounded me, with different peals coming from every direction. I saw the inn-keeper's wife running along the street from the church, clutching her coif in one hand so that it didn't blow off.

She reached me, and for a moment was out of breath,

"Mistress, good news!" she panted, her chest heaving up and down.

"What? What is it?" I cried. The sound of bells was all around us now.

"The Queen! She's had a son!" the woman gasped. "The priest told me at the church. All the bells in London and round about are ringing to mark his birth!" She hurried off to tell her husband and the other customers of the inn.

My first thought was, ridiculously, that Jane would not need the mead anymore, as her pregnancy-caused heartburn would have stopped. But I was being silly. The mead mattered little. What was important was that the Queen was well, and her baby son was healthy. The insistent cacophony of bells told me that this must be true. I rejoiced for Jane and was impatient to get on the road. I wanted to see her and the new prince. I realised with a jolt that he was my half-brother. But that secret was never going to come out. Now King Henry had a son, his daughters were of little importance.

The painters were slow to rise, and then celebrated the royal birth with some strong ale before they saddled up and we left.

"Born on the eve of Saint Edward's Day," one remarked.

"I'll warrant it will be 'e's' and the Prince of Wales feathers," the other one said. He turned to me and smiled.

"Our job, it never stops, Mistress. But thank God, it keeps us in work."

We made slow progress, as the painters stopped at every

inn. People were spilling into the streets, drinking and dancing for joy, and my escorts were determined not to miss a moment. As we approached the outskirts of the city, we heard a rumble that seemed to make all the houses shake. Again and again we heard it, and our horses stamped and shied at the fearful noise.

"It's the guns at the Tower of London," the older man said, nodding towards the distant city. "England has an heir, they always mark it like that." We moved forward slowly, trying to keep the horses calm.

As we got further into the villages around the city, the streets were busy with wild parties. There were butts of wine and beer at each street, with people free to drink all day long. Children ran freely, dodging our horses, stealing sweetmeats and roast sausages. Huge fires blazed dangerously close to the wooden houses. We saw actors declaiming in praise of the King, musicians playing for the Queen. I had never seen people so joyful.

"We're safe now! We have a boy, God be praised!" one man called out, staggering towards us and then falling in a heap on the street. A little boy bent over him, searching to see if he had any valuables, but my escorts shouted at him and scared him off. He scuttled back to an alehouse, where he would at least have free food and wine all day.

We reached Hampton Court by mid-afternoon. The royal standard was flying, and flags were everywhere: the King's arms, the Queen's arms, the flag of England. I parted from my companions, who delivered the mead to the royal cellars before they went back to work.

"It won't stop now," one of them remarked, "no time off till Christmas!" Fortunately, the bells had stopped by now. I had a headache and was feeling very tired. But I knew I had to see the Queen before I did anything. I hurried to her apartments, desperate to share in her joy. She would be feeling so much happier now, and so long as the prince was healthy, her position would be secure.

I found Jane lying in the great state bed, eating sweet-meats. Her face was serene, and she almost looked beautiful. Beside her stood a vast cradle, embossed with precious stones, where a baby lay, dwarfed by its magnificence.

"Kat!" Jane called out. "You missed it! But I'm so glad to see you now. Have you brought some mead?"

"Yes, your Majesty. It is in the royal cellars now," I assured her.

"Go, go and get it," she cried. "I cannot wait! I have such an appetite for sweet things." I went to the door.

"Very well, I will go."

"No, not you Kat. Tell one of the maids to go. You stay here and talk!" So, a maid scurried off to collect a large flagon of mead and two goblets, while I sat on the edge of Jane's bed. She leaned forward and whispered to me,

"You didn't tell me it was so bad, Kat. Two days and three nights! I was in so much pain, I thought I would die!" I smiled at her, deeply relieved that she had come through it.

"But you didn't die, and now you will have the joy of watching your son grow up and become a King of England." We both looked at the baby in the crib. He was asleep, bonny and pink-cheeked.

"He has been crying for hours," Jane told me. "The wet-nurse is exhausted. How do ordinary women do it, Kat? Go through all that agony and then be kept awake night after night?" I looked gently at her, feeling sorry that she would miss the wonderful first months with her baby.

"It isn't hard, your Majesty, not when you love them." Jane nodded, then told me to go over to the table,

"There are some quail pies there Kat, bring me one." At this moment, the maid reappeared with the mead and placed it on the table.

"Let me drink, Kat, and you have one as well. How was your baby? Is she good? Does she know you?" I smiled.

"I think so, but it is hard to tell." Jane took a large gulp of her mead.

"My son will know me," she said. "I know he has a wet-nurse, but I am going to spend every day in the nursery! The King will have to tear me away!" She giggled. Sadly, I knew that the King would tear her away. Not just for ceremonial duties but to make another baby. Once produced, a King's children can be looked after by servants. What is important is that the Queen is ready as soon as possible to conceive again.

"You know they have sung a Te Deum in St Paul's Cathedral? All the Mayor and the Alderman were there, and most of the bishops. And did you hear the bells, Kat? They quite disturbed me! But I was excited, especially when I heard the gun salute. Only for an heir, the King told me. I am so happy, and I feel so well. He is to be christened on Monday, and I am determined to go! The King tells me I must rest, but that I can go in a litter if I want to watch the procession. Kat, will you be of my party? I need someone nice to talk to, who won't tell me to rest. Please say you will! Everyone else will be in the main party."

I smiled at Jane. I had never seen her so animated. Maybe this was all that she had needed, to be successful, and feted for her success.

"Yes, of course I will come," I said.

"And come back with us afterwards. We can have a celebration after the ceremony, you can play some galliards, and we will have quail pies and mead. And everyone will congratulate me!"

On the evening of 15th October, the Queen entertained the guests before the midnight ceremony. She was lying on a couch, and she had a cloth of gold loose gown on, with a red velvet wrap, lined with ermine. She was reclining on cushions, but she was able to watch everything. I stood beside her, with a small bottle of brandy in case of emergencies. She looked at me excitedly, as if she was a child awaiting the start of a play.

The King sat beside her, in an ornate chair, looking fondly at his wife, with her blonde hair spread loose on her shoulders. The favoured guests drank fine French wine and ate small pies and sweetmeats. The less favoured guests crowded at the door to watch the historic occasion. I noticed Queen Jane enjoying her share of the food and drink, with several pies and a large goblet of mead. She had recovered well from the birth, and her appetite was good.

After a couple of hours, the royal party moved to watch the start of the procession to the Chapel Royal. Jane was carried outside to see it as it started out. The King was standing some distance from her, watching intently. Jane beckoned for me to bend over her litter.

"Watch and see all the grand people," she whispered. "Everyone will be here." Slowly, the courtyard filled. First, two men with unlit torches, to be flamed once the prince was christened. Then the children and singers of the Chapel Choir, again not singing until after the baby was welcomed into the Christian Communion. Chaplains, abbots and bishops, all in cloth of gold vestments. Lords, knights, the Lord Chancellor, and Thomas Cromwell, the Lord Privy Seal. The leading aristocrats of the court, followed by the Lady Elizabeth, carrying the white chrisom cloth, ready for the baptism. She would have been dwarfed by all the powerful men around her, but fortunately she was carried by Viscount Beauchamp.

Jane shifted impatiently in her litter, she wanted to see her son.

"They are taking their time. What is delaying them?" she asked me. "Is he well? Has he the colic?" At last, he entered, carried by the lady marquis of Exeter and two nobles, under a canopy of estate. He was swaddled in linen, and then draped in a cloth of gold gown, with a silver tissue cap on his head. As if sensing the solemnity of the occasion, he was quiet, his eyes wide open and staring.

Lady Mary followed, as his godmother, her train born

by Lady Kingston. Two large men, in their broad-shouldered gowns of fur and velvet, the Dukes of Suffolk and Norfolk, and the Archbishop of Canterbury resplendent in his golden cape, were his godfathers. Jane and I watched as the procession formed and started to make its way to the Chapel Royal. Then a few of us retired with the Queen to her apartments to await the arrival of the newly minted prince. King Henry had been spirited to the Chapel Royal to watch the ceremony from behind a screen, so the Queen was able to rest a little. I played my lute softly to her, to help her relax. It was very late now, well past midnight.

After a couple of hours, the procession returned and tumbled noisily into the Queen's apartments. Lady Mary came up to the Queen, curtseyed, and embraced her. She was smiling and happy, and her position as godmother signalled that she was back in favour. She told the Queen,

"It all went well. Prince Edward was very good, he didn't cry once, except when the holy water was poured on his head. But that's a good sign, as you know, your Majesty. It means the devil has left the child." Jane smiled and murmured,

"That is a good omen. The devil will not threaten my son, or my family." Lady Mary's eyes filled with tears.

"Your Majesty, I am so happy for you, and for my family. I don't know how to thank you. Without you, I would not have been at court, not seen my father, nor been a godmother to our little prince." For Lady Mary, Edward's birth wasn't a bad thing. As a boy, he would always take precedence, and so the arguments about legitimacy had become less important. Maybe now she could marry a good Catholic prince and start her own life. Jane beamed at her.

"Mary, I am contented to have you at court. May I call you daughter?" Mary flushed with pleasure.

"Yes, of course." She curtseyed again and moved to the cradle to coo over her new brother. Jane turned to me.

"Kat, may I have some brandy? I am feeling tired now, and

a little faint." I found the flask I was carrying and passed it to her.

"Kat, look, Will is over there!" Queen Jane nodded towards the far edge of the crowd of guests. Will was standing there with Thomas Cromwell, both drinking wine and watching the crowd.

"Go Kat and talk with him. I am a little tired. Tell my ladies to come to me. I will ask them to help me to bed. Kat, go and make amends. I am so happy; I want everyone to be happy!"

I noticed that Will had seen me and was staring in my direction. I smiled at him, a wide, merry smile. To my relief, he smiled back, and started to walk towards me. I curtseyed to the Queen and gestured to her mother to fetch her ladies.

"Will!" I was surprised at how pleased I was to see him.

"Kat. Well met," he smiled down at me. "I was hoping to see you here. How are you?" I shrugged my shoulders.

"I am well thank you. Happy for the Queen."

"As we all are. At last, we are blessed with an heir. I hope that life at court will be less eventful from now on." I knew what Will meant. Now the King was married to gentle Jane, and they had a son, surely the conflicts and plots that had torn apart so many people, including us, would cease?

"I am meeting with my father tomorrow morning. Will you come with me?" I was eager to agree. I loved Tom, the man who had brought me up as my father.

"I will have to get consent from the Queen," I said, looking over towards her. There were now two women bending over her, and I knew she would soon be retiring.

"You will be back before she wakes," Will assured me. "Come and stay with me at an inn. I have a room I took earlier. Then we can get up and go early."

"Will, is that wise? Something might happen that we don't want. But what is it that you want?" Will looked at me a little cynically.

"Are you afraid you might drink too much and fall into my bed?" he asked.

"No! Well, yes. You say you can't bring up another man's child. But if we make love, we will want to be together again. And I can't leave my daughter." Will looked thoughtful, and then, to my surprise, he smiled.

"I understand. I promise Kat, I will not lay a finger on you. It is important to me that you meet with me and Tom. Please come." I paused for a moment and then agreed. I knew that I could trust Will to keep his promise. And I had to admit I felt so safe, so comfortable, in his company.

"Very well. Should I tell the Queen?"

"No, she is being cared for. Don't worry about her." I followed Will's glance over towards Queen Jane. Her mother was approaching, followed by a group of ladies. There were already two women beside her litter. I didn't know them, but then I thought that maybe I did. One was short and stout, dressed in dark red, and wearing a gable hood, the other was tall and slim in dark blue with a bejewelled French hood. No! It couldn't be! I rubbed my eyes. Queen Katherine and Queen Anne were hovering around Queen Jane's head. I saw Queen Katherine take her hand while Queen Anne leant over and kissed her on the cheek. They were tenderly taking care of her. I couldn't believe it.

"Will wait! Can you see those two women with the Queen?"

"Which ones? I see her mother and her ladies."

"No, it is Queen Katherine and Queen Anne," I said, almost afraid to say what I could see. I looked into Will's face. He was not in the slightest bit concerned but smiling at me.

"Kat, you are tired and imagining things. How could they be there? They are both long dead! I can't see them." I looked again, and they had vanished. My imagination. Will must be right. I shrugged my shoulders and turned back to Will.

"Let me get my things," I told him.

"I'll wait for you in the great hall," he told me, leading me out of the Queen's chambers. He went down the oak staircase while I got my cloak. I could still see those two queens bending over Jane in my mind. What did that mean? I stole back to the Queen's apartments and glanced inside. The Queen was being carried to her bedchamber, but there was no sign of the two dead queens. It must have been the light, and my imagination. I backed away and ran downstairs to meet Will.

"Don't worry about it Kat," he assured me. "You loved them both. It's quite natural that you should imagine that you see them. I've heard that these visions are quite common. But they are just dreams, not real." I told myself to believe him, I was very tired, and I had been seeing things that weren't there. I took his arm, and we walked together out of the palace, along the main street, and towards the small country inn that Cromwell used for his servants when the King was at Hampton Court Palace.

We went up two flights of stairs to Will's chamber. It was small and comfortable, with a dormer window overlooking the street. Will gestured to the bed.

"It is good to be sharing a room with you again Kat. It has been a long time." He smiled at me with a mixture of confidence and sadness.

"Yes, a long time. That makes me sad," I said honestly.

"It makes me sad too Kat. We must talk. But now it's late. Come to bed and let us sleep." Will took my hand and led me over to the bed. He sat down and started to pull his boots off. I took off my cloak and gown, leaving me in my linen shift. Hurriedly, I got into bed, and a few minutes later he slid in beside me.

True to his word, he did not try to touch me. We lay side by side in the dark, barely speaking. Just before I fell asleep, his hand strayed over to mine, and we touched. We stayed that way, fingers linked, until finally sleep came.

The next morning, Will saddled up two horses that belonged to Thomas Cromwell, and we rode into London. We met Tom at an inn near London Bridge. We embraced and then he ordered us some ale, refusing Will's offer to pay for the drinks.

"If I can't buy you both a drink, that would be a poor thing. You two are the people I love most in the world." Will bought us some mutton pies, and we were quiet as we ate. Tom was showing his age now. He had a slight stoop, and he was very thin. I wished I could offer him a comfortable retirement, but without a house, that was out of the question.

"So, we have a prince," Tom remarked eventually. "I'll warrant the court has been celebrating ever since last week." He looked at me as the person who knew the most about the court.

"Oh yes," I said, "the King is overjoyed, and everywhere people are celebrating. No one is sleeping, they stay up all night dancing."

"And the Queen, how is she?" Tom asked. Like me he had loved Katherine of Aragon more than her successors, but that did not mean he was not concerned for a mother who had just given birth.

"She is doing well, and was celebrating last night," I told him. "We will have a merry Christmas this year, I am sure!"

"So, you will be busy, Kat. Christmas is the season for music," Tom commented. "How is your little Alice? She will miss you both." He looked at me sadly. He didn't know about the uncertainty around your birth, daughter, and he assumed that Will was your father. "What a bonny little lass she is," he said. "Such a pretty little thing." I tried to dispel the feeling of guilt that swept over me.

"She is well-looked after," I said, "and after New Year, I will be able to visit her, I am sure." Tom's eyes misted over,

"I remember you as a little girl, Kat. You were so thin; we could never fatten you up! But you were as bright as a button. You and Will, you got up to some tricks together. Do you remember how you used to drive Joan crazy? Remember how you sneaked up to see Mistress Stabb? She was so angry with you both! But she loved you. You were her life."

"We were lucky, us two," Will remembered, "she loved us, and taught us our prayers. And we never went hungry. I have never tasted bread as good as hers."

"Did it make a difference to her that I wasn't hers?" I asked, afraid of what Tom might say. To my relief, he laughed heartily.

"Why do you say that Kat? She loved you both equally. She was afraid of what might happen if you found out you weren't ours. She didn't want to lose you."

"And me?" Will asked.

"You were our son, and we were so proud of you," Tom reassured him. "We were proud of both our children."

"But father, how was it for you, working to keep a child that wasn't yours?" Tom gave his son a puzzled look.

"You were both my children," he answered. "It didn't matter who was born to us, and who was given to us. You have a child in your house, and you delight in them. You tell each other about the words they learn, the first steps. You worry when they're ill and delight when they recover." He looked deeply into my eyes.

"Kat, I remember once you had a bad dream. You came to us crying that a wolf was chasing you. Joan was very tired, so I took you on my lap and held you close until you stopped crying. I wiped your face and kissed you on the top of your head. I stroked your red hair. You always had red hair, like a little carrot!" Will looked at his father, and there were tears in his eyes.

"So, you loved Kat as your own?"

"How could I not love her? She was a gift to us, as much as you were Will. We were blessed to have you both, blessed to watch you grow. When you love a child, you don't care about where they came from, you just love them."

CHAPTER 19

After our meal, Tom Cooke left to go to London Bridge, where he was working. I saw his figure disappearing down the lane, and again I wished that I could look after him, as he looked after me. But I didn't have time to think too much as I had to get back to Hampton Court. Will and I set off. Even with our good horses, it took several hours. As we approached the palace, Will said,

"I will see you again soon Kat, if you wish." I didn't know what he wanted. Did he mean that he was prepared to bring up you, my daughter?

"Yes, I would like that," I said. I wanted to say more, but a stablehand had come up to take the horses and was asking Will when they would be needed again.

"I must go to the Queen," I started to walk towards her apartments. Turning back, I saw Will heading in the opposite direction. For a moment he turned round, saw me, and waved. I waved back. What a handsome man he was, and how I loved him. I watched until he turned a corner and I could see him no more.

When I arrived at the Queen's apartments, all was unusually quiet. I could imagine that people had sore heads after the celebrations last night, but even the normally cheery chambermaids were subdued. I knew that there had been plans to move the royal household later in the day, but no one was packing. I went up to a group of ladies clustering around Anne Seymour, hoping to overhear something.

"It is nothing of concern," she was saying in an unnaturally calm voice.

"But she has not slept, my lady. She was up all night," said one small worried-looking woman.

"She has had the flux, nothing serious. And now, she is feeling better," said Lady Seymour. "The King has decided not to move his household today, simply to allow her time to get her strength back." She turned and saw me.

"You should not have given her that mead, Kat. She has been eating and drinking too many sweet things. It is no wonder that she has been sick." I bobbed a curtsey.

"I am sorry my lady. The Queen asked me to get it. She sent me to Wolf Hall for that reason." Lady Anne Seymour snorted,

"She has been indulged too much! How will she recover if she continues to drink such sickly stuff? Now go to her and play something quiet and soothing. She is awake, but weak." I curtseyed again and hurried into the Queen's bedchamber. She was lying in the great state bed, but she was no longer animated. Her eyes darted towards me, and then to the other ladies in the chamber. A tired little smile appeared on her face, and she tilted her head slightly, as if to invite me to her bedside. I walked towards her and curtseyed, and one of the women pointed at a chair where I was to sit. Not a word was spoken.

I played for several hours. At first, the Queen watched me intently with wakeful eyes. But as I continued, her eyelids drooped, and at last she fell into a deep sleep. She looked what she was, just an exhausted little girl. I finished and gently slipped out of the chamber. As I did, all but one of the ladies followed me. I looked back, and she was sitting in the chair that I had just left.

The next day, Jane was sitting up in bed, wearing a new loose gown of creamy silk. She called me over and asked me to play Tandernaken, a lively piece. I noticed she was again eating sweetmeats and smiled to myself. Jane may be a timid woman, but nothing would keep her from her marchpane and almonds. We spent a happy morning with her ladies bringing in and showing her the gifts that had been left for her. The King came in, in a hurry. He was due to go hunting but wanted to check on his wife.

"I am glad to see you well again, sweetheart," he said, planting a kiss on her forehead before he turned to the large cradle beside her.

"And how is our prince today?" he asked jovially, poking his large finger onto the baby's head. The infant woke and startled into a loud, piercing cry. The King withdrew his finger and laughed out loud.

"That's it boy, already giving orders what to do! You keep these women in line!" Elizabeth Seymour hurried forward and picked Prince Edward up.

"He needs a feed, your Majesty," she said, rocking the baby up and down, "shall I take him to the wet nurse?"

"Take him, take him," the King ordered, "and let him drink his fill."

"Bring him straight back when he has finished," the Queen called out. Everyone smiled. The Queen was a loving mother, and so much stronger than the day before. All was well.

The Queen was indeed an enchanted mother. The next two days she was often to be found with Prince Edward nestled in beside her on the great bed.

"Look at his toes," she exalted, "just so small and so well-formed!" I knew that wonder. That wonder of having made a child, fashioned him from your own body, and then looking at him and marvelling at his perfection. She popped her little finger into his rosebud mouth and let him suck at it.

"Eddy, Eddy my darling. You are mine, sweetheart. I made you, every inch of you. You and I will always be together. I will teach you your prayers, my little Eddy, and show you how to write your name." Prince Edward gurgled.

"I will choose a wife for you, and beat her if she is unkind to you," the Queen murmured. I was a little surprised at this. I could not imagine our Queen beating anyone. Although, poor girl, she had been beaten often by her own parents. Maybe she thought beatings were the way to learn? But for the moment, it was love that was on her mind. She sang to the baby, said prayers over his head, and kissed him on both cheeks. The wet nurse was only allowed to take him for feeds and changes. Apart from that, he was with the Queen, night and day.

I loved those days, although they also made me feel sad. I longed for you my daughter, while I was playing for a Queen's child. Prince Edward was a beautiful baby, with his fair hair and blue eyes. But he was nowhere near as beautiful as you, my darling little, brown-eyed flame girl. I had time, during those quiet moments, to think ahead, and plan how I might bring you to London. Once Queen Jane returned to her duties, I would ask her if I could be paid more and explain about you. I already had the small pension Queen Katherine had given me, and I knew that Thomas Wyatt would give me more money. But then could I afford a house on my own? I had a flash of inspiration. Maria, Lady Willoughby, had told me that she would always be there for me. Might she find an apartment somewhere, either in her grand house, or in one of the small houses she owned? I suddenly remembered Jane, Lady Willoughby's servant maid, who'd had to leave her own baby behind to work. Maybe I could employ her as a nursemaid, and she could look after you and her baby at the same time? It didn't seem an impossible dream. And where would Will fit in? He loved me, of that, I was sure. But he was a proud man, and he struggled with the idea of bringing up another man's baby. I wondered if he had decided against re-uniting with me. I hadn't seen him for a few days. He was, as always, busy on Cromwell's orders. I couldn't help but hope that he would find me, and everything would be alright again. But so far, nothing.

On Friday evening, Queen Jane said she felt unwell again. She was cold, and shivery, and her face was almost transparent. Lady Seymour told me to go,

"She needs rest Kat. Take tomorrow off." I was happy to do that. That Saturday was a crisp, clear October day, with golden sunshine gilding the leaves of the trees. I spent the day wandering in the park, making plans for the future. When you could walk, daughter, I would take you into these great parks, and show you the trees and the birds that sang. I would teach you their names, and the names of the different flowers that grew in the Spring. I wondered whether I should try to find Will, but I didn't know which palace he was working in at the moment, and it was probably easier to wait until we relocated to London.

On the Sunday morning I went to chapel, with the rest of the royal household. There were prayers for the Queen, but that was normal. We always prayed for the health of the King and Queen. Everyone in the chapel was in a good mood. We had a prince! Peace and prosperity beckoned. After the service ended, people trailed out, chatting and laughing, talking about the wonderful autumn weather we were having that year. I didn't see any of the Queen's immediate household, but again, that was normal. Since she had been with child, she had often attended services in her own apartments. I wondered if she was drinking wine with her chaplain, no doubt to the disapproval of Anne Seymour.

But when I arrived, the Queen's bedchamber door was shut. Anne Seymour came up to me.

"She is still unwell. But she has been asking for you. You may enter, and play, but it must be godly."

I tiptoed into the room. The curtains were drawn, and it

was dark. I could just make out the Queen, lying with her back to me. There were women in the room, but she paid them no attention. When she heard the door, she whispered,

"Is that Kat?"

"Yes, your Majesty."

"Play, Kat." She did not look at me as she spoke. This was the first time I feared for her. She had turned her back on everyone, even Prince Edward. But all I could do was to obey her. I played Laudes Deo, by Robert Johnson, although praising God was the last thing on my mind. She wasn't tossing and turning, she was just lying still, as if she no longer wished to look at anyone. Usually, my lute playing becomes a conversation between me, the audience, and God. But on that day, it felt like I was talking to no one. I left late that night, and lay on my pallet bed in the dormitory, praying for the Queen, imploring God to let her recover.

The next day, I was not allowed in her bedchamber. Prince Edward's cradle was now in the outer chamber,

"The Queen is too ill to see him," I was told, "he disturbs her." And so, the ladies took it in turns to rock him and sing to him as if all was well. I stayed with them, playing sometimes to lighten the atmosphere. In truth, without my lute and Prince Edward, the outer chamber would have been almost silent. No one knew what to say. All we could do was keep praying quietly,

"O Lord, deliver our Queen from danger, in the name of Jesu, do not let her die!"

The King came late that night. He looked haggard, as if he had not slept. He was accompanied by the Archbishop of Canterbury, who seemed to have been crying. They both went straight into the Queen's bedchamber without stopping to pet Prince Edward. The great door swung shut, leaving us outside, wondering what they were saying to her.

Was she able to hear them, I wondered? Anne Seymour had told me she was barely conscious now and was beyond speech. I heard the murmur of the archbishop's voice, and realised he was giving her the last rites. We all sat there outside her chamber, listening, and praying for her. Then the door opened, and the archbishop came out. He made the sign of the cross to us, bowed his head, and left. It was deathly silent, except for the infant snores of the prince. Every now and then, the candles would flicker, and we would all look up, as if someone was entering the chamber. And then we heard it.

It was a little wail, but it wasn't the baby's. It got louder, growing to become a howl, a scream of anguish. Then sobbing, sobbing as if his heart would break. Because, of course, it was the King who was crying over the bedside of his dying wife. Only a week ago, she had been entertaining guests at the royal christening, and he had been so happy. Now she was leaving him, the only woman who had ever given him what he wanted.

We waited, frozen, for at least an hour. We could not leave the chamber in case the Queen needed something. But it felt wrong to be there, overhearing the King's desperate grief. I would never forget it, that night when he showed himself to be human, but I would never want to live through it again. At last, he emerged, his face swollen and red. We all curtseyed, but he walked straight past us, without a look. Of course, we were nobodies, and it didn't really matter what we had heard. He opened the door and left without a backward glance.

Rising from my curtsey, I saw a lady going towards the Queen's door. She was an older woman, not one of the maids of honour, maybe even a maid going to sponge the Queen's face. But then she turned and looked at me. It was Katherine, I knew it. Her little round body, her old-fashioned hood, her dignity. Her blue eyes glanced at me fondly before she went into the room. I knew then she had come to fetch Queen Jane. She had loved Jane and been kind to her. She was going to help ease Jane's passage into the next world, just as she had eased Jane's passage into the Queen's household.

A moment later, someone sat beside me with a rustle of silk, and a breath of violets. Queen Anne turned to me, her black eyes shining,

"I hope she will sing better in Paradise!" she whispered, smiled her dazzling smile, and then disappeared. I looked at the space beside me. Nothing there, just a violet petal on the cushion. I pinched myself. I was imagining too much. I had known and lost two queens, and now a third. I suddenly felt unutterably burdened and bent my head to weep.

I realised that all the ladies were crying now, some saying prayers, some calling on God for mercy. On our knees, we were sisters, crying for a kind young woman, who had inexplicably got mixed up in power politics, given the King a son, and was about to pay for it with her life.

She died early the next morning. The death of a Queen. So different from the last two. I remembered Henry and Anne greeting Katherine's death by wearing yellow, almost dancing on her grave. And then Anne being murdered. This time, the King had not celebrated. He had not appeared at all. Instead, he had brought innocent little Jane Seymour into his trap, and married her.

It seemed though, that he did love her. He left Hampton Court that morning, and went to Esher Place, where he went into his chamber and did not emerge for several days. Everything around the court stopped. There were, of course, the embalmers that came and prepared Jane Seymour's body for the lying-in-state in the presence chamber. She wore a gown of gold tissue, and there was a small crown on her head. There were guests who came to pay their respects, who needed to be looked after, with wine and biscuits, and maybe a quiet place to weep. There was the baby to care for, but the wet nurse took over those duties with aplomb.

The truth was, there was very little for many of us to do. I was the Queen's musician, and now there was not a Queen, nor anyone in charge. Those of us in the Queen's household were grieving for her, but also anxious about our own positions. Now there was no Queen, what would happen to us? For the first time in his reign, the King was single, with no prospective spouse in view. A lot of us had worked for all three queens, and now we didn't know what was to happen to us.

We soon found out. Lady Mary was to be put in charge of the late Queen's household after the funeral, and she would be responsible for the staff. The King had told her to release most of us, retaining only the key ladies, who would move over to her. She would speak to us after the funeral to tell us what was going to happen. I didn't look forward to it.

The Queen's body was moved from Hampton Court on 8th November, processing over several days towards St George's Chapel in Windsor. Cromwell had found 200 poor men to walk after the hearse with torches, and they were followed by the chief mourner, Lady Mary, on a horse draped in black velvet. After her were twenty-nine noblewomen, one for each year of the Queen's life, then most of the nobles of the court. The only exception was the King. He did not attend funerals; the monarch never did. But I heard that he summoned Cromwell to him afterwards and asked him for every detail of what happened.

The night the hearse arrived at Windsor there was a vigil at St George's Chapel, with the Lady Mary silently presiding all night. I peeped in and saw her, very serious and yet composed in her black velvet, and black hood. She had loved Jane, I thought, but she must be relishing these ceremonials. For there she was, right back in the centre of the court, representing the King.

The next day, the ladies covered the Queen's coffin in black velvet, for the singing of the masses and laments. There was a wooden effigy of Jane, which was placed on top of the coffin. On 12th November, the Queen was finally laid to rest in a vault underneath the Garter Chapel. Her brothers were there, and Lords Norfolk and Suffolk, Thomas Cromwell, and all of those who had so recently been present at the christening of Prince Edward. Then there were the ambassadors, and the representatives of monarchs from all over Europe. I watched them enter the Chapel, along with many of the servants standing outside. Of course, we weren't allowed inside, we were not important enough.

Coming towards the end I saw a familiar figure. I hadn't seen him for some time, and didn't expect to see him now. His head was bowed, and he walked now without his usual swagger. But it was undeniably Sir Thomas Wyatt. He must have been visiting London to report to the King before all of this happened, and so had come to pay his respects. He caught sight of me as he walked past and gave me an imperceptible bow of the head. Later, he caught me as the congregation dispersed.

"Kat, it is good to see you, although on such a sad day. Are you well?"

"I am indeed," I answered, "but I need to speak with you. Do you have time?"

"For you, Kat, always," he said with a little of the old sparkle in his eyes.

"You said that I should approach you if I needed money."

"I did, indeed. What do you need?" I explained to him that I wished to be together with you again, Alice, but that I needed funds to be able to do that. I told him that I was afraid I would be dismissed by Lady Mary, who had never liked me anyway. He smiled his merry smile.

"She never liked me either. Best to leave the court, Kat. Bring up your baby. You need not worry about funds, ever." I was so overwhelmed by his generosity that I started to cry. Fortunately, there were many other people at this occasion with tears flowing down their faces, so it occasioned little comment, except from Tom Wyatt.

"Don't cry Kat. All will be well, I promise." He looked gently at me. "Are you alright? Are you on your own now?" I sniffled at him.

"Yes, I think so." Very quietly, he said,

"You know I have someone now. She is content to live in the background, and we make a good pair. So, although I will always support you, I cannot repeat my offer to live with you." He looked so contrite that it made me smile.

"No, Tom, I understand that. I am still hoping for Will. So even if you were to offer again, I couldn't accept you." He beamed at me.

"He is an idiot, that boy. I've a good mind to go and shake some sense into him." This was not what I wanted.

"Please, Tom, don't do that. He is a proud man. I believe if I give him time, I may win him back. But he must accept that if we are to live together, Alice is part of the bargain." Tom smiled and thumped me on the back.

"He will, he will! I will send my man to you tonight, with some money for the next year. And kiss my daughter for me, will you?" With that, he bowed his head again, and made his way back through the crowds to join the courtiers who were entering the palace for refreshments.

A week later, I was summoned to meet with Lady Mary. She was sitting in the audience chamber, in the chair that Jane had perched on. Small though Mary was, she inhabited that room with an enormous presence. All of those in the chamber listened respectfully to her, and there was no animated chatter, as there had been. I was called up to speak to her. I went quickly to her chair, and then curtseyed deeply. Rising from the curtsey, I saw that she was observing me closely with her sharp blue eyes.

"Kat," she said. "My mother loved you; I know." I felt tears springing into my eyes.

"Thank you, my lady. I loved her too." Mary clicked her fingers in irritation.

"It was not an appropriate relationship," she declared, "between a Queen and a servant. I never understood why she did it." I wanted to shout at her, to tell her that I was there for the Queen in the many lonely times when her family was not, that I had loved her truly, without any thought of advantage. If only she knew that I was, in fact, her sister! But that would only add to my problems. She had a streak of her father's ruthlessness, and she would have got rid of me if she'd known. As it was, she was getting rid of me anyway, but I would be free to go.

"I see from the accounts that you are receiving a pension that my mother authorised. I see no reason for that, as you went on to work for Anne Boleyn." She wasn't going to take away that small sum I received annually, was she? Although it wasn't much, without it I wouldn't have a chance to bring you, my daughter, to London. But her face softened.

"But, again, by virtue of the love you shared, however unnatural it was, I will continue those payments." I bobbed down.

"Thank you, my lady," I mumbled, my head bowed. Mary continued,

"However, Kat, we have no need for your services now. You have been employed as a private musician for the Queen, God rest her soul. But, as we have no Queen now, your post is redundant. Your duties were never really set out, maybe because of the attachment my dear mother had for you, followed by Queen Jane." I noticed she didn't mention Queen Anne, but she had never acknowledged her anyway. Mary's voice became harsh, "They certainly allowed you far too much freedom, consorting with courtiers far beyond your station." I bowed my head again. I couldn't look at Lady Mary, I was so angered by her words. I was the equal of all those courtiers and would have been whatever my parentage! I was their equal under God, and I knew that deep inside my heart.

"So, Kat, your position here has ended. The court no longer needs your services. You have one day to say your goodbyes and pack your things. I do not wish to see you from tomorrow."

CHAPTER 20

It didn't take long to gather my things together. I said good-bye to the few people I was still friendly with. Sir Thomas Wyatt was away again, the Seymour family was in mourning, and most of Anne Boleyn's party was dead. The musicians, chambermaids and cooks were kind, and I was slipped many small gifts of cake, sheet music and bunches of dried lavender. Most of the time I went through these goodbyes in a daze. I wondered what I was going to do. The first problem was where to go. Thankfully, I knew that Maria, Lady Willoughby, would always allow me to stay at her London house. I needed to tell Will what was happening, but I didn't know exactly where he was. I left a message at Thomas Cromwell's offices and hoped he would get it.

And so, after nearly twenty years, I walked out of the Queen's apartments for the last time. Looking back, I thought I could see Queen Katherine sitting there in all her splendour, reading an improving text. Or maybe across the room, Queen Anne singing, with her black eyes flashing. Maybe even poor Queen Jane, eating sweetmeats. Were they there? I don't know. I think in truth those three women had changed me so much that they would always be part of me. Did I see them because they were wishing me well from beyond the grave? Or was it that they had now become part of me, and would follow me everywhere I went? Such things are beyond our comprehension, daughter.

I told Maria, Lady Willoughby, about my visions. She smiled and nodded.

"I still see my darling Catalina, with her long red-gold hair and her blue boots. She was so pretty, and that is how I see her now! I know she is now at peace with Jesu, but she was ever loyal. Maybe she sends us a sign every now and then. Who knows? But it was her that told me you were on your way. She came, carrying a lute, and handed it to me. I knew she was signifying that you would come to me. She did not play the lute. No, the instrument represented you, dear Kat."

It felt so good to be with one of the four people on this earth who knew the secret of my birth. For the first two nights I stayed with Maria, we spent hours talking about my mother, Katherine of Aragon. How lovely she was, how learned, how her temper would splutter like an unwatched pot, and then just as quickly subside again. How brave, and how pious her life, and how many people had loved her. We wept, and then we laughed.

"The way she handled the King was impressive," said Maria, "no one since then has managed it." She would only refer to Anne Boleyn obliquely. She did not blame me for working for Katherine's rival, but she could never bring herself to directly acknowledge her. "It was dangerous to stand against the King, I know that, but that lady is one I cannot forgive."

Lady Willoughby was due to travel to her estates in Lincolnshire the following Spring, and she was determined to make sure I was settled by then. She told me not to worry,

"I will not let Catalina's daughter sleep on the streets!" I knew that she loved me because I was Katherine's daughter. I asked her once if she loved the Lady Mary in the same way.

She corrected me at once,

"Princess Mary, I will not deny her the title that is rightfully hers. Kat, I respect her and would serve her until death should she require it. But I do not know her the way I know you. Royal children grow up away from court. But for you, a foundling, there was no problem to stay with the Queen. I think maybe she did suspect something, because her love for you was so intense. But how could she have known? All we knew was that you had become dear to her, and to me. So, I cannot let you starve Kat, nor see you in destitution. Lady Mary will never need that kind of help, but you do."

She called in her Chamberlain, and had long discussions with him, which went on over several weeks. I planned to go and visit Wolf Hall and see you, my daughter, with Meady. But all journeys had to wait until the Spring. The weather was too bad for any but the most essential of travel.

Lady Willoughby's friends at court told us that Christmas had been overshadowed by the King's grief for Queen Jane. The court was still in mourning, and the merriment and flirting of previous years was absent. Lady Willoughby's household celebrated quietly. I talked to Lady Willoughby about Jane, the serving maid, and much to her delight, she was allowed two days off to go and see her son. On New Year's Day, we gave presents. I gave Maria, Lady Willoughby, a carved wooden jewellery box, which she placed immediately beside her bed. She gave me a small ivory comb, that she told me had belonged to Queen Katherine as a girl. I could have sworn that the scent of rose oil still clung to that comb.

"Will you play to me, Kat? Some of the Spanish songs she loved?" Maria asked me. I had not played for several weeks, but I took up my lute and started.

"Oh, that makes me remember when we were young together!" Maria cried. "Walking and laughing in the Alhambra gardens, picking oranges. We were so happy then." Her memories were interrupted by a manservant opening the door and approaching the two chairs where we sat beside the fire.

"My lady, there is a man downstairs who wishes to see Mistress Cooke. He says it is very important." I tensed up immediately. An insane hope rushed through me. Maybe, just maybe....

"What is his name?" asked Maria. "And what business has he, disturbing us in the middle of our New Year celebrations?"

"His name is Master Cooke," the servant said. "He works for Master Cromwell." Maria looked annoyed.

"I know he works for Master Cromwell," she said, "and that makes him no friend of mine." Then she saw my stricken face and relented.

"But he is Kat's husband, and so has a right to speak with her. Let him enter."

A moment later Will was ushered in, clasping his hat in his hands. He bowed to Lady Willoughby and then to me. She stood up.

"Fetch some wine for Master Cooke," she ordered. The manservant hurried off. "You are brave to come here, sir," she observed to Will, "to the house of the most loyal of Queen Katherine's supporters."

"I always admire loyalty," Will said gently. Lady Willoughby stiffened.

"But you never showed it to my Catalina!" she objected. "It was your master who brought in that woman to replace her." Will got down on one knee and bowed his head.

"My lady, I am sorry. I always respected Queen Katherine and would have been happy to serve her all my life. But I am an ordinary man, and my actions are dictated by the King. If I had disobeyed them, I would be in prison or under the ground somewhere. I would not be here asking to speak with my wife." Lady Maria Willoughby thought for a moment.

"Yes, I see. You are not protected as I am by my connections. Very well. Get up. Speak with your wife. I will go to my bed. I wish you both goodnight." She called to Jane, who was in the next room, and they both left together. I gestured towards the seat she had left.

"Sit down, husband." A big smile crossed Will's face as he heard the word. He crossed the room and sat down beside me.

"Thank you. I have brought you a New Year present," he told me. I looked at him. He was not carrying any package.

"So where is it then?" I asked.

"Just wait. You shall have it once you have heard me out," he told me. "Can you be patient?"

I lost my temper at this point.

"Will, I have been patient for many months! You say you love me, but you are unsure about Alice. You say you will be there for me, but then, when I need you, you are nowhere to be found. I think I have been patient enough!" He reached over to me and took my hand.

"You are quite right, Kat, and I appreciate that. I am sorry for all those months, but I had to be sure."

"And are you sure now?" Will's hand caressed mine and then raised it to his lips. He kissed it, and I felt his breath, wonderfully warm on my skin.

"Kat, when I went away, I went to Wolf Hall."

"Why did Cromwell send you there? There is nothing to be gained from a dead queen," I said bitterly.

"Cromwell didn't send me there. I went for my own business," he said. "You may not know this, Kat, but I am spending more and more time on my own practice. I am linked to Cromwell, yes, but I make my own choices." At this point a little flame of hope started to burn in my heart. Not much, but it was not the despair that had dogged me for so long.

"Kat, I went to see Alice." I was so shocked that I started to weep, and then fell on him, beating feebly against his chest.

"Why didn't you tell me? You had no right!" He held my hands and gently kissed me on my lips. Then he sat back, every inch a lawyer in his black velvet doublet and hose.

"I needed to be sure, Kat, before I came to you."

"And?" I demanded.

"And I am sure that what I want above all things is to live with you and our daughter. Kat, I want us to be a family again, to sleep together and love, and fight and do everything that families do!" I felt my heart lurch when he said, "our daughter", and started to cry.

"What about not wanting to bring up another man's child? I can never guarantee that Alice is yours." He looked long at me.

"It was my father, Tom, who convinced me in the end. He and Joan brought you up. They didn't know where you came from. But they saw a baby that needed love, and they gave it. They saw you, a girl who deserved every bit of kindness that they gave her. And you know, Tom still thinks of you as his daughter. That's why he went to Alice's christening. She's family. And she's my family too. I would be honoured to have her as my daughter, if you would consent to live with me as my wife. I know I am a long way below you Kat, but I love you more than any other." I threw myself into his arms.

"I have always loved you Will, always! I was false to you, and I am deeply sorry. Please forgive me." He stroked my face.

"That was because I ended it, Kat. You wouldn't have done it otherwise. At first, I was angry, and all I wanted to do was to hurt you. But then I realised that us, you and I, have been swept along by everything that's happened. We've worked for different people, and our loyalties have been divided. But from now on, Kat, my loyalties are just with you, and our family." I felt so happy that I could almost burst, but part of me still had questions.

"What about Thomas Cromwell? What about your loyalty to him?" Will answered honestly,

"I know you don't like this, but I will always have loyalty to him as a friend. However, I no longer work for him, and we will not live with him. He will not be asking me to harm people you love."

"So, we will have our own house?" I asked. "And I will not have to speak with him?" Will shook his head.

"Not if you don't wish it, Kat. Although you will, I hope, realise his life depends on the King, just as ours do. His actions are all dictated by that fact." I made a face and then decided that this was as good as it was going to get.

"Very well. Let us find a house as quickly as possible." Will chuckled.

"We can do that tomorrow! And then we can ride down to Wolf Hall and fetch Alice!"

We both stood, embracing each other, feeling each other's bodies again with delight and tenderness. To my dismay, after a minute he pulled back.

"Your present!" he said. "I left it with the servant. I will go and fetch it." I waited impatiently until he returned, carefully carrying a large linen bag. "Here, this is for you Kat." I went to the bag and pulled it open. There, gleaming against the plain white linen, was the sea green silk that Will had given me when we were newly married. Only now, it was made up into a gown, with separate sleeves slashed to reveal a yellow lining. I took the gown out and held it against myself. Underneath, there was also a buttercup yellow kirtle in the finest of wool.

I cried when I saw it all.

"You remembered, you had this made for me? I didn't deserve it!" He responded with mock anger,

"Of course, you deserved it. Now let us put it on and see how you look." We went up to my bedchamber and spent a giggly half hour untying my old gown and putting on the new one. Will was a little clumsy.

"I am unused to helping you dress Kat. I would be better at helping you undress." Indeed, my robing was interrupted many times by his kisses on my lips, my breasts, and even my thighs. At last, I was fully clothed, the silk swirling like waves around me. I looked in the mirror. The green showed off my eyes and my red-gold hair, and Will had somehow remembered my body and made sure that the gown fitted perfectly.

He sprawled back on the bed, his hungry eyes taking in every inch of me.

"Kat, you are magnificent! You are not a princess; you are a queen! Queen of my heart, my love, and you always will be."

And so, I was again disrobed, and the silk gown, the woollen kirtle, and the slashed sleeves were all laid over a chair. Will pulled off his clothes, with some help from me, and at last, we were both naked in my bed. We spent a long time stroking each other, kissing and licking every small part of our bodies. Somehow, we knew that this would be the best night of our lives, and we wanted to take it slowly. But we couldn't delay for too long, and eventually he lifted me onto a pillow, and with me clinging to him desperately, he reclaimed me as his wife.

Afterwards, we lay in each other's arms, unable to sleep, until the late winter sun dawned. There was no regret, only looking forwards.

Lady Maria Willoughby met with us after breakfast. She seemed to have forgiven him for his association with Cromwell and beamed when he told her that he was now working independently as a lawyer.

"So, you will need a house, Master Cooke, and as it happens, I have one!" She told us about a small house she owned in the City of London, which she proposed to give to me.

"I am old and ill now," she said, "and I must ensure that all those I love are provided for." Will looked at me and grinned.

"Thank you, my lady," he said, bowing his head.

"It belongs to Kat, you understand?" she said. "And if you try to take it from her, I will haunt you!"

"I would not dream of it, my lady," Will assured her.

"You will need a maid-servant," Maria said, "and I have just the person for you." She went to the door and called,

"Jane, come here!" Jane appeared, wiping her hands on her apron.

"I want you to work for Kat!" Lady Willoughby said imperiously. "Do you have any objections?"

"No, my lady, I would be pleased to, but in what capacity?" Jane looked at me. At once I knew what I must do.

"As a nursemaid," I said. "I will be bringing my daughter to live with us, and you may bring your son too. They may share a nursery. It is always good for children to have companions." Jane's face lit up.

"Oh, my lady, thank you so much! I will care for your Alice like my own, I promise you!" Lady Maria smiled.

"I should have done this months ago," she said, "but it takes a girl like you, Kat, to shake things up."

"That's my girl," said Will proudly, "a girl without compare."

We moved into our little house that spring. Almost at once it felt like we were at home. Will and I had a light-filled bedroom under the roof, while Jane slept next door with you and her small son Walter. Tom slept on a pallet bed beside the fire in the kitchen. He started to grow pot herbs in the small back yard, and whenever there was sugar available, he would make wonderful sweetmeats for the household.

For Will and I, it was our first chance to live a settled, married life together. His work grew, taking on cases from city merchants and tradesmen. It pleased me greatly to oversee his household, to make sure that his linen was always fresh, that his favourite dishes were cooked in the kitchen, and that his evenings with me were full of love. I saw for the first time the pleasure it can bring to look after a man. Did I miss court? Not really. Here, for the first time in my life, I felt safe, with my family all around me. I didn't give up music. I spent much of my time writing music and singing with you, my darling girl. As for the new ideas, and the fight over how the English should worship, the four of us adults discussed them at length and without fear.

Lady Maria Willoughby wrote and asked me to visit her at Grimsthorpe Castle with you. That summer we hired an old wagon, and Tom drove the two of us up the Great North

Road to Lincolnshire. You were very chatty then and kept us amused through the journey. It took us about a week, going slowly from village to village, staying in local inns.

When we arrived at Grimesthorpe Tom went to stable the horses, while the two of us were shown in immediately. Lady Maria was sitting in an ornately carved chair, but as soon as she heard us announced, she got up and walked stiffly towards us. I was shocked to see that she had aged so much. But her heart was still young. When she saw you, she swept you into her arms and showered you with kisses.

"Come here, sweeting, my little princess! You have your grandmother's eyes, I remember them so well!" Clucking over you, she immediately said she would take you to see the horses in the stables, and the cat, who'd had a litter of kittens.

We spent a happy two weeks with her. I would play with you in the morning, and in the afternoon we would all sing together. When you were asleep, Maria and I would sit together by the fire and share memories of my mother. Sometimes, I would smile, and she would cry out,

"You look just like your mother, God bless her. She had that smile that lit up her face, just as you do."

As for you, my darling girl, you blossomed in Maria's company. You became more ladylike, and you learnt a little Spanish, which you would show off later when we were back home. I promised Maria that we would visit again. But she smiled sadly and said,

"God willing, my dear. I may not be long for this world, you know. I am not afraid, for I will see my dearest Queen again. But oh, I shall miss my daughter and you!" I told her she was very fit, and that I was sure we would see her the following summer. She said nothing and embraced me as if she couldn't let me go. Under her breath, she muttered a Spanish blessing before finally releasing me.

Lady Maria and I continued to write to each other. Short, affectionate letters with stories of how you were getting on. With each new achievement, she praised you as if you were her own grandchild. Truly she loved you. But as the year went on the letters grew fewer, and I heard some weeks later that she had died. I knew she wouldn't mention me in her will. All her goods went to her daughter, and she did not want to call attention to me. Later, I received a small package from her daughter with a miniature portrait of her, which she had wanted me to have. She had given me so much.. Of course, she had given us our house, which had been so important to us. And she had given me you, at the moment of your birth. I grieved for her greatly, as my last link with my mother and as a dear friend. But every day, I thanked her for her generosity.

By that time, I was with child again, with your brother, Roger. Will was exultant. He had taken you, my girl, and loved you as his own. But it meant a lot to him that he could have a child with me. It was our way of pledging that we wouldn't ever part again.

Every summer we visited Mistress Mead at Wolf Hall. She would sit up with me, talking sadly about her earlier charge, Jane Seymour. She wept many tears at the loss of her dearest Jane. But you would always manage to cheer her up – she was enchanted with you. She delighted in your progress and always sent us away with a good supply of mead. We heard from the court that Prince Edward was growing well. The King was terrified in case he became ill, and we heard he had given instructions for the boy's apartments to be scrubbed twice a day to avoid the risk of infection. Lady Elizabeth was also developing her own character, one which she would carry into adulthood. She was becoming a very self-willed little girl, whose tantrums caused her governess nightmares.

King Henry was thinking of marrying again. Of course, he had his son, but he needed another. Also, as he recovered from Jane's loss, he wanted to be in love again. Bizarrely, the King was a great romantic. Although he was getting old and ill, he still saw himself as a gallant young gentleman who needed a damsel to rescue.

So, Thomas Cromwell continued busy, although Will saw him infrequently. What a puzzle of a man he was. I had seen both sides of him. I would never forget his great kindness to the two of us. After all, Will owed him his career. But I couldn't forget his cruelty. Where necessary he could destroy people with brutal efficiency. I think he took no pleasure in it, but equally he felt no remorse. I remembered my days at court sometimes and wondered how I had survived them. So many of the people I had loved were now dead. I prayed for them all: Joan, Maria, Katherine, Anne and poor little Jane.

I saw the queens less and less in my mind as my thoughts were taken up with you, dear daughter, and your father, Will. Although we had parted temporarily, I knew now we were always meant to be together. Had this been my destiny all along? If so, it was so much better than those doomed queens, who all died because of the King, my father. I realised at last that my happiness was because I had been denied my royal birthright, and thanked God for what I had been granted instead. A hard-working life, full of incident and interest, my dearest man to love, and of course you, my darling daughter Alice.

About Atmosphere Press

Founded in 2015, Atmosphere Press was built on the principles of Honesty, Transparency, Professionalism, Kindness, and Making Your Book Awesome. As an ethical and author-friendly hybrid press, we stay true to that founding mission today.

If you're a reader, enter our giveaway for a free book here:

SCAN TO ENTER
BOOK GIVEAWAY

If you're a writer, submit your manuscript for consideration here:

SCAN TO SUBMIT
MANUSCRIPT

And always feel free to visit Atmosphere Press and our authors online at atmospherepress.com. See you there soon!

ABOUT THE AUTHOR

CAROLINE WILLCOCKS has worked in the theatre, freelance journalism and charities. Now she combines being a solution focused therapist with writing about the Tudors and Stuarts. This book is the second in her Tudor Queens series, and a sequel to *Of Aragon*. She also has a successful podcast called *Tudor and Stuart Fairytales*.

She lives in rural Herefordshire with her beloved husband, dog and two cats. Her two children are happily married, and she hopes she doesn't embarrass them too much. Recently she discovered, in common with most of England, that she is a direct descendant of Edward III (he was a most prolific monarch).

Author's Note

I am really grateful to you for reading my first book. I know it is a very short book but I am new to this field and I could genuinely summarise to these many points and i swear i have almost mentioned everything i had in my mind. (*sobs in a corner, cause i dont have ideas for my next publish*). Still, I could add more i know :(

Looking forward for more readers when i write next time, though it is a long time from now because i have my boards examination around the corner. I hope you guys have a clear vision for your life after reading this, and if still not, you can write to me:

Email: koushikagarwalla0310@gmail.com

Instagram : nglkxushik

"'It is a far, far better thing that I do, than I have ever done. It is a far, far better rest that I go to, than I have ever known.' - A tale of two cities"

www.ingramcontent.com/pod-product-compliance
Lightning Source LLC
Chambersburg PA
CBHW031800150726
47989CB00006B/2811